*I am a woman freeborn.
My heart and soul are equal to that of any man's.
I am a healer.
I will not remain here to be sold to the highest bidder.*

Published by Jerry Skell
Version 2

Copyright © 2013 by Jerry Skell

All rights reserved. This book or any portion thereof may not be reproduced or used in any manner whatsoever without the express written permission of the publisher except for the use of brief quotations in a book review.

This is a work of fiction. The locations, events and characters described herein are imaginary and are not intended to refer to specific places or persons.

Printed in the United States of America

ISBN-13:
978-1493655540

ISBN-10:
149365554X

FOR TIME AND ETERNITY

JERRY SKELL

Acknowledgements

I would like to thank my family for the support of my book. Your love and support means a lot.
I'd also like to thank {Life in Print} Photography by Kim for the amazing experience of bringing Jamie to life. Kim, working with you was fun and I look forward to working with you again on my next book. I'd also like to thank my cover model, Brittany E. Brandenburg. You were a delight and thank you for the effort you gave researching and bringing Jamie to life.
Editing services was provided by Simply Polished2.
Special thanks to Mary-Nancy from Mary-Nancy's Eagle Eye Editing for the text formatting.
It can be said that while it only takes one person to write a story, it takes a village to get that story ready and out there.
And thank you to my readers – I hope you enjoy visiting Draco, and the adventures of those that live there.

Table of Contents

Acknowledgements
Prologue
Chapter 1 Outlawed
Chapter 2 Capture
Chapter 3 Mutiny
Chapter 4 Desertion
Chapter 5 RESCUE
Chapter 6 Rosalind
Chapter 7 Camp Life
Chapter 8 Sophie
Chapter 9 Winter Camp
Chapter 10 The Ice Road
Chapter 11 Three Sisters
Chapter 12 Port Hope
Chapter 13 The Long Voyage
Chapter 14 Landings
Chapter 15 The Hunt
Chapter 16 Harvest Festival
Chapter 17 Jayne's Girls
Chapter 18 Edward
Chapter 19 The Militia
Chapter 20 Alone
Chapter 21 The First Encounter
Chapter 22 Clouds of War
Chapter 23 Pink Fish, Brown Bears and Bees
Chapter 24 Summer
Chapter 25 A Second Harvest
Chapter 26 Beth and Sue
Chapter 27 Blossoms of Spring
Chapter 28 Return of the Fleet
Chapter 29 A Furious Garrison of Women
Chapter 30 Peace
Chapter 31 A Covenant People
Chapter 32 Of Kitchens and Horses
Chapter 33 Fiona and Lisa

Epilogue

Suddenly, alone and bereft of family, Jamie, a young gifted apprentice healer, has been declared forfeit and is to be sold into slavery. Facing such grim prospects Jamie runs for her life and in her journey she will cross continent and ocean, traveling to the new world, where she hopes to find an enduring love and her unique place in a free society.

Prologue

Planet Draco date 1076 PL (post landings)

Six hundred years had passed since the last contact from earth. The Firsters had evolved into a stable society. They prided themselves in the great stability they had achieved. The social order was maintained by the heredity civil service named the Magisterium. All later colonists to the planet were organized into semi-autonomous guilds organized around specific skills. The guilds were barred from participation in the Magisterium until the last decade and then only reluctantly because of dwindling numbers of the Firsters. The society had survived a one hundred year civil war that had ended four hundred years ago. Now war and crime was nearly abolished. Everyone knew their place. No deviation from the norm was tolerated. Only a very few dissented.

They would be dealt with.

Chapter 1 Outlawed

The funeral procession walked silently from the grave. The entire village had turned out for the old healer's funeral. Jamie stood silent as the rain soaked both hat and heavy coat. The mood set by the heavy rain mirrored Jamie's mood. Many of the villagers touched Jamie's shoulder in sympathy as they left. Jamie heard whispers. "Poor Jamie boy we buried his mother eight months ago." Another voice, "Who will take the boy in now? Orphaned twice! Isn't he a Roamy? Will they take him?"

Jamie returned to his parent's cottage. It had two sitting rooms. One used to store remedies and as his father's clinic, the other his mother had used for her midwife practice. Both parents had been well respected in the village as demonstrated by the turn out at both funerals and wake meal provided by the village. While Jamie never felt accepted except by a few families, the village had been tolerant. Jamie had been a lonely child with no real friends in the village. The village was poor and times were hard yet the outpouring of support was noted and appreciated by Jamie. The cottage would need to be sold to pay the death tax and little would be left. Jamie was skilled in healing skills thanks to instructions by both parents, but Jamie was Roamy blood and would not be accepted by Healer or Midwife guild. Jamie had often wondered why they were so persistent in his training. They often alluded to a higher calling he would have as a full adult. Climbing the twisting stairs to a small comfortable room with a large mirror Jamie stripped off the soaking oversized coat and hat. Uncurling and unpinning a long thick braid of auburn hair Jamie unbraided and combed out her wet hair. The family's secret was revealed in the mirror. Jamie boy was a girl.

Jamie had loved her adoptive parents and they had loved her. The decision to deceive the world about her gender was made when she was discovered nearly dead from exposure in the ruins of her parent's wagon. Rogue elements of the Imperial Guard had murdered her parents and left the infant to die. It was believed that turning up with an infant girl who was so obviously Roamy would endanger the infant and the village. Roamy were hated but a single Roamy infant boy would be seen as free future labor. The disguise had worked and the family was left alone to raise Jamie with both parents passing on their skills in the hope she would find a happy and prosperous life when they were gone. Jamie put on her secret girl clothes and looked in the mirror. Looking back was a petite young woman with long auburn hair and gray eyes. She wore a full length gray skirt of the midwife guild and emerald blouse of the healer guild. The dress had been a gift from her mother on her sixteenth birthday. "It's time you feel like the woman you are becoming, a healer and midwife in spite of imperial nonsense and you are beautiful to boot," she said then kissing her as both wept. Her mother was ill and both new she did not have long; she passed in less than two months. As she examined her image she saw that the curves of the young woman in the mirror were those of a girl but not as round as the village girls. Jamie could not tell if the girl in the mirror was pretty or not. Then she began to weep for lost parents and for a lost life. She knew she had to leave. Perhaps the sparsely settled western continent far from the guilds, the Imperial Guard and there Jamie could finally be a healer midwife free from guild and Imperial Magistrates. For the present she would remain the orphaned Roamy boy, Jamie. It keeps things simple for now.

*****

Derek sat at the desk at the Imperial Testing Center. It was day five for the testing for admittance to Magisterium training. Derek had prepared for this all his academic life. As the son of a member of the black metal smiths guild his acceptance into the Magisterium and then later as a magistrate in the Imperial Civil Service he would be in an excellent position to help the metal guilds overcome the oppressive Imperial Regulations and taxes. It only had been in the last decade that admittance had been opened to lower guild males when they reached their nineteenth year. That change had happened only because the families of the Firsters were not producing enough males. Each morning the results of the previous days testing were posted. Derek had scored consistently in the ninety-sixth percentile in literature, natural science, art history and law. Today was math, and Derek excelled at math. Day six was rest day and day seven oral evaluation. Derek would get little rest on rest day as the metal guilds were serving. He would be busy serving, busing and cleaning up after meals. He had many friends and cousins in the black metal guild and the white metal guild also. (His mother's father was Master Silver Smith). This would make the work fun. Hard work was always fun with friends.

The posting of results had been especially important to Derek. The other guild boys were joyful in their congratulations and support. He was the first of the metal guild members to test so well. Sid and Biff, nephews to the local Magistrate were scoring in the thirtieth percentile. They ate slowly, their visceral hatred of Derek apparent as they watched him eat during meals. Derek recalled his father's words as he prepared to leave for the testing center.

"Derek just do your honest best. You have already come farther than anyone in our family. Your birth mother would be so very proud. Even if you are not accepted, your place in mine or your mother's guild is secure. I will love you the same as Journeyman or Magistrate," they had embraced and Derek had taken his leave. Derek's father had always been supportive but could not understand how important Derek's dream was as he loved being Master Black Metal Smith, but he always encouraged his son and paid for his education; for that Derek was grateful. With scores as high as he had his acceptance was assured.

Day seven and Derek stood before the Magisterium. He was dressed in the formal black pants and tunic of the black metal guild. The silver braiding on his left sleeve indicated that he had achieved the rank of Journeyman in his guild. Gold braid on right meant equal rank in white metal guild. He breathed a sigh of relief as his test scores were reported. His math score - ninety-eighth percentile. The Chief Imperial Magistrate looked at the assembly and then to Derek. Dressed in imperial purple robes and powdered long white wig he appeared arrogant and bored. At three hundred pounds he was very intimidating." Derek, son of Master Black Metal Smith Olaf, we have reviewed your scores and genealogy and found you insufficient for admittance. Since the time of the first landing the Firsters (initial colonists) have strived to make room for subsequent colonists, thus our long history of guild autonomy and tolerance. We will never permit admittance to a Roamy!"

Derek was shocked. Blood drained from his face and deep pain seared his soul, "Your Honor, I am not Roamy I'm...."

"Silence... your mother's line one generation back were Roamy. Please remove your journeymen braids. Return home and await contact from local authorities. You have a fortnight to arrange your affairs." The entire Magisterium then rose and filed out. Derek stood frozen in place. He could hear his heart beating. Nothing would ever be the same.

*****

A week had past and Jamie decided what she would carry with her on the journey to the western continent. She had packed tiny vials of two hundred of the common remedies thinking she could possibly earn some food practicing her healing skills while traveling and to aide her in establishing her practice. She also packed two blankets, extra traveling boy clothes, a folding knife, some dried food, personal hygiene items, her father's surgical kit and her prized girl clothes. Total backpack weight was forty-five pounds, at least it would get lighter as she walked and if she ate once every other day she could make it. Sitting on her bed she heard a heavy knock on the door.

"Elder James and Elder Casey to what do I owe your visit?"

"May we please come in Jamie?"

"Sorry, please do and welcome."

Jamie settled her guests in her father's sitting room and served cold ginger beer. Elder James looked at Jamie, concern visible on his face. "Your foster parents were held in great esteem by the village and you also Jamie. We had a meeting last night and tried to raise enough money to purchase your property at an honest fair price to pay the death tax. But since then we have learned the Magistrate has declared it forfeit and you are to be sold. It seems our illustrious magistrate has just discovered you are Roamy and not allowed to own property."

Jamie sat dumbfounded. "Sold?" she uttered in a squeak. Her head spun. No other words would come as she stared in wide eyed terror at the Elders.

Elder James put a gentle hand on her shoulder, "Jamie girl... yes, Jamie we knew...did you ever wonder why a boy would be allowed to attend births as an apprentice midwife? A few of the families knew and were eager that you be trained well for your future calling. You are destined for great things." Jamie looked puzzled. "We want you to take the money we raised and run. It's not much, barley equal to what was owed to your parents. Find the Roamy encampment to the south. They will help you. We will all swear you traveled north a week ago. Do you understand?"

"Yes, does the whole village know?"

"No, only the council of Elders and some of the village mothers. You were far to pretty to be a boy. We let your father believe we didn't know so as not to cause him extra anxiety. Your mother knew that we were aware. It was our way to help protect you. Now you must leave tonight. When the Roamy find you ask for counsel. They will be bound to at least listen." The Elders stood and Elder Casey said "May the gods protect you Jamie and guide your travels, May you find happiness." Then they left. Jamie sat paralyzed by cold fear. She fought back tears; she walked through the little cottage touching things she wanted to remember. The little cottage was made of stone and had a shale roof. Moss and flowering sedums inhabited the areas between the shingles giving the roof the appearance of being ancient. Clemencies vines were planted and well established. The herb and vegetable gardens were in raised beds. There were planted window boxes on the windows facing the road. The little kitchen was cozy and bright with a large hearth with a built in oven. Her father's rocking chair was near the hearth and she remembered sitting in it with him for stories when she was very young. The kitchen held many memories of shared meals and prayers. Her mother's prize tea setting, with which she and her mother had enjoyed long conversations. Her father's story books from which he read to her were there. Her parent's room was made up and cleaned just as it was when they lived. She climbed one last time to see her room. The windows softened by lavender flowers from the Clemencies vine, her bed made and the foot locker empty. She took a final look at herself in the mirror. She wore an oversized short coat of a brown and tan herringbone weave. Her floppy hat made of the same cloth was constructed of eight panels and pie shaped. There was a button on top and hard visor which she wore backwards. Her pants a coarse weave tan material. Her boots seemed oversized so she wore two pairs of very thick socks. She referred to her boots as her waffle stompers. Descending the stairs she then tied the money pouch to her belt, shouldered her pack and walked out the door. She did not look back.

Derek's journey home took four days. He slept in the open in farm fields and ate little. He could not really face food but forced himself to eat. His despair was total. All the sacrificing by his family was for naught. Neither civil servant nor journey man was open to him now. He could not marry or own property. He could be sold or killed without recourse. As he approached Irontown Village he was met by the nephews of the Magistrate and four of their thuggish friends.

"Well look here Sid, if it isn't a stinking Roamy." The group of thugs snickered, "We've come to give you a proper welcome Roamy. Don't worry though, our uncle has real plans for your future we just want to teach you your place smart ass. We got admitted to the school you failed." At that all six descended on Derek beating and kicking him to the ground one stood on his arm while another stood on his hand forcing it open palm up while Sid put a hot branding iron to his palm marking him with an "R"." Now Roamy, get on your knees and thank us." When Derek refused they continued to kick him. Just as Derek expected to die from the beating the thugs ran off. Derek, only partially conscious, thought he saw three very large and muscled men, his father and uncles? Derek blacked out.

Derek drifted in and out of consciousness over the next two and a half days. He recognized his father and stepmothers voices and Uncle Ben and Don. There was hushed talk about a funeral pyre, his funeral, the Imperial Guard and western continent. When Derek finally awoke he was aware of a severe headache, very sore ribs and his burned right hand. Sitting at his bed he saw his exhausted step mother. She has apparently dozed off. Aroused by Derek's stirring she quickly called "Olaf, Ben, Don, come he's awake." Within seconds three large men crowded into the small dark room Derek closed his eyes and turned his face away in shame.

"I have ruined you father. I have been cast from the guild I don't know..."

"Derek," Olaf interrupted, "You did nothing wrong, it's the Magisterium that is wrong. We all know what happened and have a plan to save you, so listen carefully. Everyone believes Biff and Sid killed you. They will suffer no consequences because you have been declared forfeit. As soon as you can you must go south to

Lands End and there go to the western continent. You can start over. We have no idea what you will find there but go you must."

Looking at his family Derek asked "Am I Roamy? I don't understand..."

"No Derek you are Guild. My first wife, your mother had some tenuous connection. She was beautiful with auburn hair and gray eyes and was guild at least five generations back. She died birthing your sister Rosie, you were only three. I know you don't remember her."

"I remember and I remember Rosie too!"

Carole brushed her hand on Derek's forehead, "It's very important you do not get caught. All of us including you younger sisters, Fiona and Lisa could be declared forfeit. Only we four know you are alive. We told none of them, all must believe you are dead for this to work. Do you have any questions son?"

"Where am I now?"

Derek's uncle Don spoke "The abandoned coke shed just south of Irontown Village. Everything you need is packed for you in the shed. We have very little money but included are some small game snares and cooking pots. We will leave and be conspicuous among Imperials you must leave tonight. Do not use the roads. Imperial Guard is about looking for a runaway Roamy slave. They are mostly scouring the north but some are here." With that, each hugged Derek, Carol wept openly as Olaf and his brothers led her out leaving a small miner's lamp and overstuffed back frame.

Derek lay on the small cot for several more hours. His appetite ravenous he looked about and found bread, cheese and cider had been left for him. Initially sitting up caused some dizziness and a lightning bolt of pain in his ribs but it passed. His right hand was wrapped and hurt too much to be of much use, but Derek was left handed, so eating was no problem. Derek forced himself to eat slow as he wanted to keep the food down and leave when darkness fell. With the large back frame on, Derek needed a stout walking stick but could manage the weight well.

Eating every other day just had not worked out well for Jamie. Walking south only four days she had gone through much or her food and rodents the rest. On day six she was dirty, exhausted and very hungry. She spotted a small campfire on a sandbank just a hundred yards along the small river she had been more or less following south. She approached very slowly. She could smell food, blessed food. She noted a very tall blond haired man lying on a blanket apparently asleep. She approached with caution. "Would you share food with a fellow traveler?" she inquired. He muttered something which she took as a yes and descended on the cooking pot. As her companion had not spoken or moved while she ate she looked closer. He was beautiful she thought but too tall. He was well muscled but not heavily so, like a metal smith. His face intelligent, heavy sweat on his brow. She noted the bandaged right hand and could smell the infection. Kneeling at his side she saw the wrapping on his hand was loose, flies everywhere and maggots moving on and in his hand. After a gasp she moved into healer mode. Shaking him gently she said "I'm a healer, my name is Jamie can you hear me?" He nodded and she continued. "I will give you a remedy to stabilize you then I will get help and move you, okay?" No response. Looking at his face it was flushed. His eyes dilated. She would start to treat the infection and also use a flower remedy to prevent shock. Jamie then went to an inn in the nearby village and arranged to have her "elder brother" carried to a small room in the back of the inn.

"Will you require a healer?" the innkeeper inquired.

"My brother and I are apprenticed to the healer guild. I will need clean cloths, honey and any strong spirits you have. Otherwise, we will manage."

The Innkeeper looked relieved and inquiring about payment settled with Jamie for the room for a week, meals for two and the supplies she ordered. It took most of her traveling money but she was a healer. Jamie unwrapped the damaged hand carefully and washed the wound removing any maggots large enough to see. She did a nerve block touching him on the shoulder and forearm. Then, cleaning her surgical tools with the whiskey she had been brought she gently cut away any necrotic tissue. The maggots had already disposed of most of the dead tissue. Pouring a generous amount of honey on the wound she waited for additional maggots to wiggle out then cleared the wound, reapplied the honey and wrapped the hand with the clean cloths. Now for the more difficult part. The room was already very warm so Jamie removed her heavy boots and socks. Then she removed the baggy hat, coat and pants. Her heavy shirt was so long it nearly covered her knees and she felt free to work and still be decent. She began with a scan. Holding her hands palms down about four inches from her "brother's" body and starting at his navel she moved her hands over him. Jamie kept her eyes closed and concentrated deeply. In her mind's eye she could see his aura. Not the white light of a healthy aura but gray with red areas caused by the infection. She noted several broken ribs healing well enough for her to ignore. He had recently suffered a concussion too. The infection in his hand had spread into his blood and he was dying. He was beyond any remedy but there was some hope. The next step was fraught with danger; Jamie would link her life force with his and attempt a cure. If he were too far gone it could take both of their lives. She had never done a laying of hands without at least one other healer, more often two. She would break the link if she could not cure and use a pain block to maintain comfort. Jamie started with a prayer to the mother god for healing. Then Jamie began by taking a deep breath then releasing it slowly as she relaxed. She felt rather than saw her aura pure white slowly take on the colors yellow then the green of a healer as she placed her hands on his solar plexus. Thick bands of white light circled from her hands and were met by similar bands rising from him. Then visualizing the infection as a dragon they began to battle it linked together by their shared life force. The battle lasted for hours. Jamie was frightened and nearly overcome by the dragon more than once. Then his life force began to rally and his aura now white joined the battle, his aura had blues, pinks and gold. Together they prevailed both wet with sweat. Satisfied and exhausted, her energy drained she lay next to her patient and fell hard asleep. Derek slept heavily; he felt better than he had in days. In his dream state he was aware of a small woman curled up next to him her arm loosely around his waist, her head on his chest. She had soft curves in all the right places and fit well against him. Her leg was slightly flexed lying on top of his. He could feel the warm smoothness of her thigh. He could smell the scent of her hair and stroked her soft silky hair and thigh with his left hand. She had a thick braid that curled behind her ear and disappeared under her. Derek liked his dream and slept on. Jamie awoke early seeing her patient sleeping easily and without a fever. She went to the innkeeper to inquire about a bath and breakfast. The danger now she thought was that he would mistake gratitude for love. This was common after such a hard won cure. She did not feel very lovable and had no desire for any ones affections. I will just be a shrew she decided. That way my dear "brother" will seek to avoid me she thought. She sighed but what about his aura, he has power, passion and beauty. He was a creature of fire, forceful and dangerous. "Best I guard my heart too," she whispered.

Returning to the room Jamie let down her hair and began to comb it out. Derek groaned and opened his eyes and saw Jamie's gray eyes and long auburn hair, "Dear Rosie, you've come for me. I can't believe..."

"You're just dreaming close your eyes. You will be ok," she whispered in his ear. And he did. When Derek finally awoke he found a small young man (a boy actually he thought) sitting next to him. He was dressed in the dirtiest baggy clothes and floppy cap. He looked like a foundling. "I'm Jamie. I'm a healer. I found you and brought you here. I need to redress your hand."

"You're a healer? Am I dreaming? What about the young woman in my bed? No you can't touch my hand. Go away."

"Listen meathead, I'm a healer. I saved your useless hide. I will treat your hand so you survive and pay me back for my expenses. Do you follow or do you need a repeat!" Jamie was furious. Her patient may be beautiful but he was a blockhead. A shocked look on his face Derek held out his hand as Jamie examined the wound. "Damn, I do good work!" she said then poured more honey on the wound and redressed it. "Why was an "R" burned on your hand, you're not Roamy? You got bruises all over you and recently suffered a minor concussion tell me what happened?"

"How did you know that?" Derek stared amazed.

"Are you not listening or are you just a dumb blockhead. I'm a healer and a damn good one!"

"You look like a runaway orphan, but you sure are arrogant."

"Looks can be deceiving. You look fairly intelligent... in an oversized muscle way. You a metal smith? If so, you have a trade and can pay me back."

"To be honest I have little money. You are welcome to it. I must warn you though I'm on the run. I could be trouble for you if I'm found. Imperial trouble."

"I too am on the run. We are listed here as traveling healer guild apprentices. Let's make a bargain. We can stay here until Saturday you should be able travel. Then we go together. You help me get to Lands End then we go our separate ways. By the way, you're my elder brother. Can you remember that?"

"Why are you so angry?"

"I'm not, you are just so frustrating to talk to."

"Okay deal. Little brother Jamie call me Derek." The remaining days at the inn were uneventful. Derek healed well. He slept in the bed and Jamie on the floor. He suggested sharing the bed which really seemed to rile Jamie, she also refused to trade bed for floor. Derek would be glad to be free of his angry caustic companion, but he also found Jamie intriguing. He could not put his finger on it but there was something special about Jamie. He felt something between them, a tingling sort of; he was unable to sort it out. Who was that young woman in his bed? She was real. He was sure.

The fourth night after the deal Jamie and Derek took the evening meal in the inn's private dining room. She had been avoiding him as much as possible but he had said they needed to talk. Derek started "So tell me are you the runaway Roamy they are searching for up north? No you don't have to answer. It would be best not to know. You were right though I was a journeyman metal smith and a scholar. Now I'm just outlawed. The beating and branding were my welcome home after being forfeit and named a Roamy." Pausing he continued "I'm truly grateful to you for saving me and putting yourself in jeopardy. You are a gifted healer I'm sorry for my earlier doubt"

Jamie's smile was radiant. "I'm sorry to for being so caustic. Normally I'm very pleasant. To be honest, I was scared, you were my first unsupervised patient and for some reason you seem to elicit the worst in me." They laughed enjoying the warm bread and thick stew and each other's company. They then quietly shared shortened stories of their forfeiture and outlaw status. "I always wanted an older brother. You will do nicely" Jamie said with a warm smile. The disclosure caused warmth as well as mixed feelings in Derek's heart.

"I've always wanted a little brother," he replied.

Two weeks had passed since they left the inn and they continued south. The Great Imperial South Road would have been markedly faster and comfortable but not worth the risk as Imperial Guard were everywhere. Their routine was well worked out. They would stop mid-afternoon. Derek would fish or set traps. Jamie would collect wild tubers or liberate corn from fields they passed through. Once she had gotten a large melon. Squashes were abundant they frequently ate well. Game was hard to find but fishing was good when near deeper rivers. Derek made fire and both cooked. Because Derek's pack was nearly eighty pounds the cooking pots had made their way into Jamie's backpack. The heat and the strain of travel continued to take its toll. Both felt exhausted and filthy when they stopped early at a small clear pond. They planned to rest at the site for two or three days. They were now so far south they could see the Southwestern Mountains in the distance. They needed a break. The pond looked cool and Derek, removing his pack and shirt, said "I'm hot. I smell bad. Let's take a swim!"

Jamie looked horrified "No way!"

"Suit yourself." Derek splashed loudly being especially loud about how refreshed he felt. He watched as Jamie sat tailor style back to him in the shade. After drying and dressing he returned and sat with Jamie in the shade.

Her face stony she said, "I hope you enjoyed yourself."

"I did, immensely," he looked at Jamie's rather sullen face. "You know Jamie, my lad, I think you're a prude."

"Don't like swimming."

"Jamie you stink" he chuckled holding his nose and fanning the air.

"You Derek smell like a fish."

"Time for swimming lessons little brother!" Derek made a grab for Jamie but she was faster. Derek got a handful of the floppy hat. It came off and dark auburn braids fell to Jamie's waist. Derek stood dumbfounded. "You're a girl. I mean the young woman in my bed.... no didn't mean that...You're ..." before he finished Jamie's face went from hot anger to tragic loss in an instant. Tears followed. Derek was at a total loss. He stood holding Jamie as she wept on his shoulder.

"I only ever wanted to be a girl. I'm so tired of being a boy. I can't even be a proper girl when I try. My curves are all wrong, my feet are to big..." Derek knew a little about her curves as he was very aware of them when she had curled in his bed, but he was smart enough to just listen. She continued "You're beautiful Derek, and I am an ugly mouse..." Derek nearly gasped. She thinks I'm beautiful. His heart skipped and he felt warm. She continued, "And my eyes, look at them Derek, they're too big!" Holding her closer he looked into her large gray tear filled eyes.

"I really like those eyes Jamie, and I like you."

"See I find somebody I like and he's an idiot..." Derek just kept quiet and let her cry it out. Jamie liked him, he was happier than he could ever remember. The embrace lasted a long time. Jamie's tears had ended and they separated. They both remained silent and Derek prepared a simple dinner of baked tubers and corn. "I would like to bathe," she said quietly.

"I'll rig cover for you and guard from prying eyes"

"No peeking Derek."

"Jamie I would never."

"Well I did," she said with impish grin.

"I will never do anything to hurt you." Derek used saplings and their blankets to rig a screen and Jamie bathed. Jamie returned from her bath in her girl clothes. She was bare foot and her hair brushed out in long gentle waves. She was smiling. She looked so beautiful Derek was speechless for a long time. Finally he started "I need to re-evaluate what I call you. How about little sister? Obviously you're female."

"Okay, then I will call you "D" brother"

"What's the "D" for? Derek?"

"No Dumb," Derek felt a little hurt at first but then he saw the twinkle in her eye and a twisted little smile. "Gotcha didn't I?" She laughed. "Derek who is Rosie? Is she your girlfriend or lover maybe?"

"How did you hear of my Rosie? I loved her very much. She was my little sister she was eight when she died. I was eleven. She promised she would come back when the troops came for her. She never did. We were very close. She had auburn hair and gray eyes like you. You do remind me of her a lot, but you're a grown woman, I must have been really confused."

"What happened to her?"

"We don't know. She got sick. A healer came but so did Imperial Troops. They said she could be contagious and took her to the hospital to the north. We never saw or heard from anyone."

"Derek I'm so sorry!"

"It was a long time ago little sister. As for girlfriends I never had time between achieving journeyman status in two guilds and studying for entry into the Imperial Academy"

"What ever for Derek?"

"I thought I could change the world, make the terrible restrictions and taxes imposed on our guild become fair and encourage growth, but instead I caused nothing but pain and sorrow."

"I think you, big brother, are a secret romantic at your core. Let's just stay here for a few days. I feel safe and would like to stay a girl for a little longer."

"I would like that too," Derek replied.

"Staying here... or me as a girl?" Jamie asked biting her lip and looking pensive.

"Both!" Derek took her hand.

Chapter 2 Capture

A few days passed then seven, then fourteen. They remained at the pond. Both felt happy and free of the stress from running. The setting idyllic, fresh water, fish to eat, rabbits abundant for Derek's snares. There was plentiful corn, tubers, and squash in laxly guarded fields. Mornings were spent swimming. Swimming fully clothed allowed them to swim together and do laundry. Derek liked the way her wet clothes clung to her body, but he respectfully looked into her eyes when addressing her. Jamie changed in the improvised shelter Derek made in the bushes. Much of their time was spent in food gathering and meal preparation, but there was time for long walks holding hands, lying in the grass talking. The more time Derek was with Jamie, the more he wanted. He watched her blossom from petulant boy to a happy young woman barefoot most of the time who was intelligent and funny.

The night was warm and the sky clear as they lay out watching the heavens holding hands. The smaller blue moon was full and very bright nearly obscuring the larger green moon in its final phase. "Derek could we just stay here forever. We could build a cabin. I'm happy here. I don't ever remember being happy. I wasn't sad, but happy is different. "

"I would love to be here forever with you little sister, but the season will soon change and food harder to find. Didn't you have friends in your village?"

"I was Roamy. I was sent to the village school at six. I really didn't understand what Roamy meant and had difficulty staying in boy mode." Jamie rolled onto her stomach feet in the air looking at Derek, there was a sad note to her voice, and "I think I thought I was in love with an eight year old boy named Jason. He had dark curly hair and brown eyes. He was the copper smith's son and very popular. I asked if we could be friends."

Derek sensing her coming grief rolled on to his stomach facing her and took her hands, "What happened little sister?" he whispered.

"He spat in my face and called me a dirty stinky Roamy. I was enraged. I screamed and started flailing at him with fist and pulled his hair and biting. I terrified everyone in the school with my rage. My father was there and pulled me off and held me while I sobbed and screamed and tried to bite and hit him."

"You did that?" a little shocked Derek kept his voice calm and continued. "What did your father do?"

Blushing Jamie continued "He just held me until the rage passed then he continued to hold me, he told me he loved me more than anything in the world and I didn't have to go back to school." Jamie's eyes were wet with tears. "After that I stayed home. My parents taught me. I learned well and was allowed to help with prescribing, surgeries and did several deliveries with my mother. I was too busy to be bored. It was lonely."

Derek was moved by her story and its mater-of-fact delivery. From the tears in her eyes and his own experience he understood loneliness well. "Little sister you never need to be lonely again," and he kissed her forehead.

"Big brother, you are such a goof!"

Another two weeks passed and Derek began repacking his back frame as they needed to travel soon. He would like to continue to postpone the trek and just spend time with Jamie. At the bottom of his bag he found his guild clothes. Not the richly black formals but charcoal black work clothes. As he held them a wave of sorrow engulfed him. He then noted slight bulging along the bottom seam of the tunic and extra thickness to the collar. Taking his knife he opened the seams and removed more than a dozen imperial notes. It was the money his family had mentioned. "Little sister I found something you need to see!" Jamie came to him barefoot, flowers woven into her braids, the red highlights of her hair blazing in the bright sun, and sprawled on the short grass facing him. "Look little sister, imperial notes. The equivalent of forty imperial sterling, but as its paper currency merchants will discount some of its value. It's a two years salary for a journeyman. I can pay you back. I can book passage to the western continent for us both."

"You would buy my passage too!" Jamie's smile looked radiant as the sun to Derek; she leaned forward and kissed him on the cheek. Derek shocked sat open mouthed, his hand covering his cheek. "We can go together big brother. I love you Derek!" All reluctance to leave the camp site gone they packed in haste." It's time for me to be Jamie boy again. Can you remember not to call me little sister?" Looking at her feet as she started to put on stockings, "Derek do you think my feet are too big?"

"You always wear those heavy socks and boys' boots," he

answered slowly. "I think you have cute feet little sister. Tell you what let me take a tracing of your foot and just maybe we can find you girl shoes." Tracing her foot Derek was surprised touching her sent electric sparks through his hands. He wanted to touch her more but did not. "I got a great idea. You stay Jamie girl. We use the imperial road traveling as brother and sister. No one is looking for traveling siblings."

"Derek you are a goof, I'm a little brown mouse your ten foot tall and blonde. No one would believe we are brother and sister. Little brother worked because I could stay covered in bulky clothes and floppy hat."

"I'm only six foot... Suppose your right... I got it we could pose as an eloping couple. We are only two days from Lands End by imperial highway we can stay at an inn in Milford tonight and Fenton tomorrow. Besides tomorrow starts the fall festival. There will be food and dancing. No, better yet we can spend the whole day in Milford, would you like to go to the fair with me little sister?" Derek went down on one knee hands folded in a mock plea with the best pouty look he could muster.

Jamie looked at him and laughed, "Poor little puppy dog. Oh, Derek, you're so funny! Yes I will go, it will be two firsts. First fair and first date ever!"

Holding hands they walked into Milford. The village square was all decked out with bright ribbons and streaming banners. A platform was being assembled for the band. Imperial Guard were present but not more than expected. Bright paper lanterns were being strung everywhere. These would be lit after twilight. Venders were setting up in every available spot, many of them in brightly colored booths with banners bearing the various guild colors. They stopped at a shoe maker's stall and Jamie longingly held a red-brown colored half boot. It was edged in soft fur of the same color. The leather was soft and the boot well made. It was lined with a fleece like material on the inside so ladies could where it without stockings. As it was five imperials she reluctantly handed it back to the vender. At the inn Derek requested a room for two days.

"That will be a tenth imperial per day. Don't expect you to take meals here with all the food vendors." The inn keeper looked at Jamie with mild interest. "You traveling together?"

"Newlyweds. It's our elopement. We'll need to return to guild hall but we came to the fair." Derek handed the man an imperial silver certificate.

"You got paper currency. I see its good but it will cost an extra tenth and for an additional three tenths I will give you the bridal room with a hip bath."

"A bath!" Jamie whispered.

"We have a deal," Derek said shaking hands and collected his change."

The hip bath was brought to their room as Jamie sat on the large soft bed. Scented soap and clean towels were already in the room and a decanter of wine and two glasses were on the table. "Jamie, go ahead and take a long bath and relax. I will lock you in and return shortly." Jamie nodded then undressed and slipped into the tub. She loved the feel of the warm water and the smell of lavender soap. She felt exquisitely female. She looked at her feet and examined her soft curves. Derek liked her so she must be at least passable. As she lathered herself she wondered what it would feel like to have Derek's hands touching her. Her face flushed and she shook her head to clear her mind. Finding the shampoo, she let her hair down and washed it. As the water became cooled she left the tub and combed out her hair leaving it unbraided, it cascading below her waist with gentle waves. Finishing Jamie realized that Derek had been gone half the afternoon. She began to worry and started pacing. All kinds of thoughts assailed her, was he hurt, could he be caught. Then a faint knock at the door and Derek entered. Jamie flew into his arms, "I was so worried Derek!" then her mood changing "I WAS SO WORRIED..." and she kicked him in the shin. It hurt. She had forgotten she was barefoot. She fell back on the bed rubbing her foot glaring while he looked at her with a pleased smile.

"Got you a present little sister," he handed her the little half boots she had admired earlier. For the first time Jamie was at a loss for words. She took the boots caressing them then putting them on. She wiggled her toes in the soft leather. Rising quickly from the bed she planted a kiss on Derek's lips. Their first.

"Big brother... my first real girl shoes... I love you Derek. You're so thoughtful." Her smile was radiant and Derek was breathless from the kiss.

"There's dancing and food for tonight little sister, are you ready?"

The lanterns were all lit now transforming the village square to a dazzling world of bright lights. There were acrobats and fire eaters. They visited food vendors and sampled fried dumplings stuffed with fruits, tubers and cheese or spicy meats. Jamie tried the fried pastries and Derek laughed as she made funny faces after trying the "stinky" cheese. Small bubbly fruit pies were hot but very sweet. Small sausages on sticks were also tried. Derek won a gold necklace with a heart shaped pendant for Jamie in the hammer throw; she wore it clutching its pendant to her breast. Derek's win was easy as he was a metal smith and had excellent arm strength. A large party of on lookers watched as Derek slammed the hammer against the target multiple times as his score rose higher until the pendant was won. The onlookers cheered and many cued up to play. An early win was good for the game tables business but Derek knew vendors would no longer welcome his business at games. Most of all Derek enjoyed watching Jamie. Her enthusiasm unbridled. Her happiness was contagious.

"Little sister it's time for dancing!" He gathered her to the dance area and whispered, "Can you dance?"

"Yes big brother but until now only with my father." Derek then nodded to the band leader and the music stopped.

The band leader raised his voice "The next dance is dedicated to the newlyweds Derek and Jamie." The music started as the dancers paused and allowed Derek and Jamie to start the dance.

Jamie blushed bright red. "They're staring at us big brother. The girls are all swooning at my beautiful partner asking how such a drab little mouse got her hooks on you."

"More likely little sister they are looking and thinking boy is he lucky to have the most beautiful girl at the fair." Jamie looked up and smiled holding Derek a little too tight to make dancing easy. They danced every dance together until the music ended and the vendor stalls closed. They returned to their room exhausted and happy. Feeling thirsty Jamie poured a very large glass of wine and downed it quickly. She hiccuped then giggled. "Little sister that was wine. Did you ever have wine before?"

"No, another first. Really don't like the taste!" she hiccuped again. "I'm so tired." Jamie lay on the bed in rather dramatic fashion. "Derek, did you like my kiss!" her voice sultry, then another hiccup.

"Very much so."

"Would you like another?"

"Yes only one. You're not yourself right now." Derek gently removed her boots then covered her with the blanket. She unfastened her skirt and Derek pulled it off while she was covered by the blanket. Jamie then wiggled out of her shirt and handed it with dramatic flair to Derek. Then he gently touched her, cupping her face in his hands and tenderly kissed her lips.

"Derek you don't have to sleep on the floor, it's a big bed." Her eyes were very dark and half shuttered by her thick lashes. Her face flushed. She looked so young, so vulnerable and beautiful Derek had real difficulty with his decision.

"Yes I do little sister. Sleep now my love."

"But you did before..." she was asleep before she finished her sentence.

Derek lay with blanket on the floor next to her bed. He could hear Jamie's soft breathing. His mind raced. He could not sleep. In two days they would be in Lands End and soon after the western continent. Jamie loved him. She was such a remarkable woman. She was so innocent, so trusting. She could be so tantalizingly seductive. He wanted her to be his real wife. He badly wanted to sleep with her. As he dreamed of the possibilities of their life together he slept.

*****

Jamie woke hearing a drumming in her head. At first she thought it was part of her headache but suddenly recognized the sound. She sprang from the bed and began shaking Derek, "Derek wake up now!"

"Mmm"

"Derek, Imperial Guard is entering the village we've been discovered!" Derek shot up.

"We must run, leave everything and run!"

"But my remedies, my new boots..." Derek opened the sash on the window facing the alley as Jamie put on thick socks and her heavy boots. Derek assisted Jamie out the window. Hesitating he returned to the room then joined her in the alley. They ran south down the alley and joined the highway to Fenton while the village slept. "Can they catch us? No one could have recognized us... What will we do without our stuff?"

"Not sure we were recognized, but we can't risk that it's not us they are after. Pace yourself little sister they will search the village, that will give us at least an hour lead. We have money. If we can keep going all night we can make Lands End tomorrow morning." They continued their brisk pace all morning when Jamie caught her foot in a loose tree root in the road and fell hard tearing the soul from her boot. "Are you hurt little sister?" Derek rushed to her side gently removing the torn boot and heavy sock as she winced.

"Oh no! My boot, I can't run." Derek smiled and pulled out Jamie's new boots from an inner pocket.

"Look what I found," and slipped the boots on her feet.

"That's what I love about you big brother, always thoughtful," Then trying to stand she felt a stabbing pain in her ankle. "Derek I can't walk ... I CAN'T WALK!"

"Not to worry I can carry you. My back pack weighed more then you my little shrimp. I will take care of you." Derek helped Jamie on to his back and they continued at a slower pace. She liked the idea of Derek taking care of her. She liked it a lot the more she pondered it. She felt guilty about being carried but liked the press of his hard body against her. He was her giant protector. Feeling safe and happy, she bent to nibble his ear. It felt like lightning zapping across Derek's body.

Almost dropping her Derek exclaimed "Jamie! You've got lousy timing."

"You didn't like that?" she said sounding a little hurt, "I just wanted to distract you from your worries."

"No I did like it, I liked it a lot, and it was truly distracting. Hope to return the distraction when we're safe." She smiled. She loved her giant protector. The day wore to late afternoon and Derek refused to stop or rest. She knew how sore he was getting and began to be concerned for him. Derek was sore especially his back and shoulders. He was soaked with sweat, he could hear his heart drumming in his ears.

Jamie also heard a distant drumming. "DEREK IMPERIALS! We must get off the road!" Sprinting off into a thick cover of bushes they hid and watched. A squad of fifty men passed them in a fast lope. They wore tunics that were imperial purple on the right and had a black and white checkered pattern on the left. Their pants were bright red and they wore shining bronze helmets. Each carried a fifteen foot spear topped with a long streaming banner of purple ending in a checkered pattern. The drumming was made by them as they struck their spear shafts against leather covered shields in cadence to the march. They inspired awe and fear as they moved on the road. Derek carried Jamie farther into the woods to a small clearing with a large upright rock. Sitting back, braced by the rock, he cradled her across his lap. She pushed into him, arms around his chest, head on his shoulder. He held her waist in his arms. Derek what are they doing?" she whispered.

"They are flanking us. They will cut us off from the south."

"Will they catch us?"

"Unless we sprout wings and fly, yes." He could feel her start to tremble as if chilled. He knew she was weeping quietly against his shoulder. He wanted to scream and rail against the gods but his little sister need him to be strong.

"Are you afraid of death?" she whispered.

"Yes, I was planning to grow old with you. This is not how I want us to end."

"Do you love me Derek?"

"With all my heart little sister!"

"Then you must promise me something."

"Anything my love."

"When they come you must take my life."

"No, my darling little sis..." reaching up she put a gentle hand to his mouth and looking into his now tear filled eyes continued.

"About two years ago a young woman who had been caught by the guard was brought to my father. They had raped her, beat her and tore her body. She died within hours. Her sole broken in shame, her body broken in ways I cannot describe. I'm so afraid. I can't find it in me to take my own life. I don't want to die like that poor woman. I can face death with less fear if I can be in your arms my love. I can die with dignity." Derek's heart felt like it had stopped and it hurt in his chest. It felt like he had no air in his lungs and his throat was almost too tight to speak now. He was shaking. Cupping her face gently in his hands and looking into her wide terrified eyes he gently kissed her lips.

"Yes, my dear little sister, I promise." They stayed wrapped together for what seemed forever and Jamie's tears ended and Derek no longer shook. He would take her life then fall upon the guard until he joined her in death. They waited. Then a voice.

"Well look what I found!"

Derek rose quickly facing the arriving men putting Jamie behind him. He drew his dagger and held it behind his back in his left hand. Jamie, kneeling behind and to his left, took his dagger hand in her right hand placed her left hand on her breast to help guide the blade. She whispered, "I love you dear brother!" She glared with anger at her enemies and raised her chin in defiant pride then steeled herself for death.

Chapter 3 Mutiny

Fleet Admiral Casmir strolled along the deck of his ship and watched as the rest or the fleet sailed out of Rok Harbor and the adjoining city harbor of Lands End. This would be his last voyage. As usual, his wife, Ruth, was aboard, as well as the captain's and first officers' wives. He was excited to be at sea. He had spent his life at sea coming over the bow as former cabin boy rather than paying for his commission as in the northern fleet. He suffered from alopecia as a child and had not a single strand of hair on his body. This condition had helped hide his Roamy parentage and his skill and intelligence allowed him to advance quickly. At forty he had been the youngest junior admiral in the history of the Imperial Navy. Now he was seventy-eight. His only regret was he and Ruth had never had a child that survived infancy. Ruth had contended herself mothering the boys and young midshipmen who had been with them. She was well loved by multiple generations of sailors, many now serving as officers on the decks of many ships. She had cookies and tea with homesick young men, mended socks and acted as counselor. She tended the wounded and had held many young mortally wounded youth calling for his mother. Wives were not the usual fare on the northern fleet but whores were. Wives were essential for ship life and curbing male bad behavior, the admiral believed.

The ship was the first and newest of the First-raters. Her class was designated Maxi. She has five unstayed masts setting heavily battened lug sails. Each also had top sails on three of the masts. She carried forty massive crossbows that could fire heavy fire bolts as well as forty pound round stones. The crew was two hundred strong and they were quartered on the second deck. The forecastle contained the crew's toilet, and the animal livestock. The second, third, fourth and fifth decks carried at times a platoon of Imperial Marines, food, kegs of beer, kegs of ale and ammunition for the crossbows. This trip they carried only food stores. The officers lived in the huge castle in the stern. The ship was square and looked slow and clumsy but her lines were sweet, and she was fast with a gentle motion. The admiral had successfully driven all pirates from the Western Sea. At one time pirates from the southern islands wreaked havoc on the coastal cities, no longer. The navy's success over the last three decades had permitted it to develop a great degree of autonomy. The northern fleet rarely left home waters. Much of their energy and resources was spent guarding the estuary and harbor of the Imperial City. Given this autonomy in the southern fleet the admiral had achieved his greatest plan. The southern fleet was all Roamy.

"Captain Ron, signal the fleet all captains and their wives to dine with me tonight." The signal flags hoisted, the various ships sent long boats bearing the captains and wives to the admiral's diner. All knew this voyage would be unique but little else. There had been much excitement and speculation among the crew.

The admiral's dinner finished and wine was served. Caption Ron stood. I have the privilege of the first round of toasts. "To Mother Ruth, our ships mother!" Ruth blushed scarlet and beamed at all "her boys". After all the toasting the dinner concluded and the men met in the admiral's quarters.

"Gentlemen its time. We have worked for this moment for three generations. I have been blessed to have played the role I have. It's time for phase two. Our destination is a secret harbor on the east coast. We will then sail east, the long way around to the eastern continent after picking up cargo in the secret harbor. The harbor now named Hope Harbor will be the new fleet headquarters. Three luggers will proceed to the eastern continent by sailing west. You will proceed to the designated isthmus and build fortifications and secure a harbor on the west coast of the isthmus. You will then return to Hope Harbor. You will need to cross the isthmus by land and sail west to Hope Harbor. The isthmus is less than a mile wide and you will need to build a log rail road. By the time you arrive we will have left with the first load of colonist for the eastern continent. We have stolen the navy! Gentlemen lets raise our glasses to mutiny!"

Chapter 4 Desertion

David stood proudly at the Imperial Guard officer induction. All his life he had listened to stories of great service and sacrifice of the chivalrous officer corp. He had been an Imperial Scout and excelled in wilderness survival and first aid. He had honed his body and could run like the wind for hours. He was lean and lightly muscled. His height was average. His hair was black and curly. His eyes were brown. His skin was bronze. He had been orphaned early but had fared well in multiple foster homes. The guard would be his home for the next thirty years. Then he would retire and marry. If lucky he could retire wealthy. But most of all he wanted to serve his country. To be part of something grand.

The ceremony did look grand. Torches lit the great hall and the colored banners of regiments hung from the walls. Black checks for the southern regiment, red checks for the north, and orange checks for the east, blue for the west. The most elite of all the praetorian had gold with thin purple stripes. The communion meal finished they stood for the oath. They swore to protect the weak and widowed, to reverence the elderly, to guard the children, to love the nation. The drums and brass sounded and each candidate was called to the raised platform of the Magisterium and presented with the colors of his regiment. The chief magistrate (the Pontiff or Dictator) sat flanked on each side by his first and second assistant. They all wore the purple robes of office and long white powdered wigs. Great speeches were made attesting to the guard's long history of valor and sacrifice. How they alone stood as a lone thin line that protected the land, the guilds and the lives and property of the people. David's heart swelled with pride as his name was called and he approached the podium. David was shocked and delighted to receive the colors of the vaunted praetorian. Sub lieutenant David marched off with his regiment.

Over the next several months David was surprised to learn how utterly boring and predictable life in the guard was. The ranks were filled with the coarsest of individuals, many recruited from the prisons. Drunkenness was common as well as gambling and fighting. The regiment had its own brothel which he avoided. The girls were so young and so badly treated that many died from the brutal handling they received. No one in the officer core seemed to care about these women or attempt in any way to intervene. This disturbed David greatly but he did not know what he alone could do and he was afraid to attempt any intervention. David hoped for action, something to give meaning to his lofty oath. Eventually he was told a village in the east near the desert had rebelled. The village named Holly consisted of five hundred families held hostage by the rebels. Both regiments of the elite praetorian were sent because of the seriousness of the rebellion. Eight hundred and fifty men at arms with baggage and camp followers marched out. The train was a mile long as they marched at a fast lope. There were baggage carts filled with hundreds of spiked poles. Fortifications David thought.

They reached the village of Holly late in the evening after several weeks march. They set camp a quarter mile from the village then secretly surrounded it. In the early morning a contingent of guard marched into the village demanding tax money or surrender. The village, not having the money, surrendered and were marched to a field outside the village to an area of shortly mowed lawns about an acre in size. David stood with the officers, ordered to watch and learn how imperial justice was delivered. The method to train new officers was termed Shadowing and today he was attached to the commander and was responsible to run messages. The officers shouted, "Sound the no quarter," and the brass and drums sounded the signal. The guard fell upon the town.

The carnage was unbelievable. An unarmed populace against trained shoulders were no match. Many were simply seized and impaled on the spiked poles set along the road at forty-five degree angles. The treatment of the women and children vicious beyond anything. David could not believe the carnage. He fell to the ground vomiting and weeping. His head and heart ached and he was racked with shame and anger. On the march back he overheard the evil banter of the men.

"Did you see that little blonde cutie I stuck, she squealed like a pig." Much laughter.

"You ways like the young ones don't you?"

"She could fight. Took three of us to hold her down for a little fun. She really kicked and bit me, look what she did to my pretty face." More laughter. "Going to request a medal for being wounded?" more laughter

"Might of kept her for a bit but she spit on my face."

"Dumb ass we aren't allowed pets," more laughter.

David was shaking so bad he retired to his tent. As he left the first lieutenant said "First time is hardest, next time we let you get blooded!" David collapsed on the floor vomiting again but only bile came up. He wept bitterly. He had said or done nothing. His vows had meant nothing. His shame was total. He contemplated taking his own life. He wept again for the little blonde girl. Outside the tent he heard sounds of drinking and partying. David could not abide another minute with these vile men. Deserters were crucified then skinned alive when caught but to stay was even more cowardly. He had been a coward standing mute before that awful carnage. Late at night David ran. He took nothing except his civilian clothes and money. The regimental tattoo on his right shoulder marked his awful shame. He ran through the night and most of the day. He purchased a small tarp, a knife, a small ax and survival gear and walked into the desert. If he died no one, not even he would care. He hoped for redemption but in his heart he knew he was beyond redemption, beyond hope.

The desert was harsh and in spite of his skills David was always too hot, too cold, hungry, thirsty or some combination of the three. The desert was also lonely. David was used to loneliness and he felt that he could manage that feeling. He recalled the awful loneliness of being orphaned that followed by loneliness he felt as he was passed from foster home to foster home. He had always been well treated and was well educated, but he still felt lonely and isolated despite valiant efforts of numerous foster parents. David had taken several lovers, but in those relationships he had still felt an enormous emptiness. David sorely wished he had come to terms with his feelings of complete emptiness before he had made decisions that so dramatically impacted his life. David knew he would die in the desert, he loathed that he would die with his empty loneliness unresolved. David, never a man of faith began to pray to the gods. He did not ask that his life be saved, he wanted to die. David asked for forgiveness.

Chapter 5 RESCUE

Six men stood in the clearing; they were wearing shades of green-brown long tunics and pants. Each had a large dagger in his belt. Their hair ranged auburn to bright red. They all had gray eyes. Their expressions were tired and grim. "You're not Imperial Guard?" Derek asked his voice raspy.

"Roamy."

"Do what you will to me, please spare the girl she's Roamy."

The red haired man smiled "We mean you no harm. We're an extraction team. Hello Jamie, you don't know me but I'm your cousin Roland. We plan to rescue you!"

Derek's legs were now shaking so bad he was unable to stand. "Can you fly?" he asked grimly.

"In a way, yes," Roland said with a broad smile. He handed them cheese and coarse bread and a light ale to drink. Jamie and Derek fell on food without thought both badly shaken, tired and hungry. "We have a little time. The imperials will not start to move on you until they complete the flanking. They will most likely try to strike you at first dawn we will be long gone."

"Jamie has a badly sprained ankle. I will carry her until you fly."

The Roamy looked at each other smiling at some unknown humor "We have camelids posted close by. We will ride out when it's a little darker. Now rest we will be moving all night." Derek and Jamie continued hold each other in a tight embrace but neither could rest. Jamie's very slight shaking had returned and she said very little. She had come from seconds to death to what, was this rescue real. And Roland, was he really her cousin? Did she have family?

"Derek, my dear brother what will happen to you when they take me... I don't want to leave without you..."

Overhearing Roland assured Jamie "We are taking you and your husband." My husband she thought. He's only my big brother, my best friend, how could they think we were married? Derek deep in thought had missed the conversation. He was so relieved his little sister would live. He would carry her until they could put her on the camillid but his heart ached with the prospect of losing her. She had become a part of him. He loved her.

As the sky darkened they approached the hollow where the camelids were tethered. Derek had seen camelids in the Imperial

City pulling carts and fancy carriages; they were all smaller animals not more than a ton in weight, these were huge. Some were already standing; their legs alone were taller than Derek could reach. Their thick curly hair was a patchy mix of greens, browns and gray. They had long muzzles, erect ears and intelligent eyes. Their mouth had thick broad yellowish teeth and they all were chewing. Ten of the animals were carrying packs. These were standing. Roland directed Jamie and Derek to a camillid "You will be riding double. We will travel through the night; just hang on. We should make over fifty miles by dawn. We will just fly away right under their imperial noses. Stay awake. If you fall asleep, you will fall off. We may not be able to find you. Derek you ride up front Jamie behind and hold tight to him."

As they mounted, the animals growled loudly. The animals stood back legs first then front almost dismounting its riders. They sat on padded leather A-frame that had stirrups for two. The animals were tethered together in a long line led by Roland then Derek and Jamie with the pack of animals in the rear. The camelids do not run but traveled with a long gait on large padded feet. They do not leave a trail and could cover great distances.

"Dear brother, could you take off my shoes. My foot is so swollen and I don't want to lose them," Derek gently removed her shoes and stuffed them into the inner pocket of his coat. The animals walked in a rocking gait no bumping or jarring which seemed odd as the speed was very fast. Jamie pressed into Derek's back one arm around his waist, the other his chest. Several hours passed and the exertion, ale and stress had taken a greater toll on Jamie than she had realized "I'm so tired, my love, that I can't stay awake," she whispered.

"Roland could we please stop I'm afraid Jamie can't stay awake!"

"Can you lift her and place her in front of you or do we need to stop?"

Derek twisted around in his seat. "Yes but she will be facing the wrong way."

"Exactly, it's how mothers carry small children. It looks a little lewd but she's your wife so it's ok. Put her straddling your lap and she can wrap her legs around you then hang on to her so she can sleep safely." The maneuver went smoothly in spite of the movement of the camillid. Sitting astraddle Derek's lap brought Jamie's skirt well above her knees. Derek took a deep breath when he saw her pale legs and thighs and tried to think distracting thoughts. She put her arms around Derek and her head on his shoulder. She then wrapped her legs around his waist.

"Didn't you know we were married my love?" She whispered. Then kissing his rough fuzzy cheek she fell asleep. Derek continued to hold her with his left arm while grasping the saddle horn with his right hand. Between her closeness and the rocking of the camillid he had no trouble staying awake trying hard to think even more distracting thoughts.

They stopped at a small pond at dawn and unpacked the pack animals. They got water from the pond for their use then let the animals drink as they hobbled then. Camp was set up with great efficiency. A fire was set and cooking started. Derek carried Jamie and put her on a blanket. He then brought her water to drink and wash up. "Shall I wrap your ankle little sister?"

"I really wish I had my back pack it's got all my remedies." Just as she finished speaking Roland walked over carrying both packs.

"We picked these up for you Jamie."

Jamie gave Roland one of her dazzling full bore smiles and eagerly dove into the bag. As the day heated up the party slept. After sleep they ate more food. Derek continued to carry Jamie everywhere. Sometime in the mid-afternoon Roland presented her with a crutch he had made, "Thank you, Roland, for your thoughtfulness," then in a whisper mostly to herself, "I wonder why Derek didn't think of this?"

"That's easy Jamie, he likes carrying you!" he said with a wry grin.

When darkness fell they we off riding again. "Roland how long will we be on the road?"Jamie asked.

"Twenty days, Jamie. We need to reach summer camp."

Jamie unobserved nibbled Derek's ear and whispered, "Do you think they would buy that I'm falling asleep again?" The effect was electric, Derek shuttered.

"It's worth a try!" he replied, his voice raspy.

As they traveled a pattern developed. Travel two days then rest the third then the pattern repeated. Jamie's ankle healed and in two weeks she was walking well. Derek missed carrying her. They were well into the eastern desert. Days were very hot and nights very cold. The troop carried three tents a large tent that could hold a dozen men and the cook kit. They had a smaller tent which Roland decided to set as the wash area and latrine as they were traveling with a woman. The third tent was very small a two man tent which they offered to Derek and Jamie. They accepted the tent dividing it with a canvas tarp to his and her sleeping areas. In spite the rest patterns the travel was very difficult as traveling always was at night. Several times in their travel Jamie's healing skills were called upon to remove deeply imbedded thorns, stitch deep cuts, lance a boil, and once to treat an accidental amputation of a toe.

Traveling together they got to know the men in the rescue group. One was Roland's older brother Robert. He was a grim, quiet man, later they learned he had very recently lost his wife and twin daughters while she gave birth. It seemed that no midwife was available in their community. Jamie grieved for the man's loss but was grateful she would find a place for her skills. All the men were kin or married men. Roland was betrothed and kin. All were very friendly and courteous to Jamie. They learned that they had been tracking them for some time. They had learned they were in Milford, some having seen them at the fair, the bulk of the group arriving moments after they ran. Roland had taken the packs to cover their identity. Derek made himself helpful when iron tools needed repairs or blades sharpened. In his spare time he made Jamie a bracelet with small gold coins. She loved wearing it along with the gold necklace he had won for her at the fair.

One morning after setting up camp they were treated to a thunderstorm. Derek and Jamie took refuge from the storm in their tent. The storm brought a downpour of rain and a cold wind. The thunder loud and very frequent with lightening striking close by. Jamie slipped under the dividing tarp and under Derek's blanket. Cuddling close together in spoon style she said, "I hate lightning!"

Holding Jamie close Derek said, "I've always liked thunderstorms, but right now I like them even more." Then turning her slightly so he could see her face he kissed her. Derek knew immediately what a bad idea that was. As Jamie turned into him pressing and kissing him back and they were rapidly becoming breathless. Derek felt Jamie as she melted into him. He could feel her heart beating next to his. Her kiss was intoxicating and he wanted her. She was wearing only a thin well-worn cotton chemisette and he could feel her soft skin with just a thin piece of cloth between them. She wound her arms around his neck and moved her hand through his hair, their bodies touching at the most intimate places. He gently stroked her with his left hand running it down from her arm over her ribs, hips and buttocks until he contacted the hem of the chemisette. Starting to pull it up he stopped. He wanted to touch her all over and feel the softness of her skin. He felt like he was on fire. He wanted her now! But he also knew if he did it could alienate her from him as he knew how innocent and trusting she was. With all the resolve he could muster he pulled away and said. "Let's just cuddle for now and listen to the storm."

Jamie settled next to him. "I love cuddling, but kissing was fun too, why did you stop? I could tell you liked it too!" she asked.

"Because I love you! I would like to wait until we are truly married before we make love."

"We were only kissing. I'm not ready to go that far!" Jamie replied.

"That's why I stopped before it got to hard..." Before he could finish Jamie laughed and said with a bright smile.

"It already got too hard!" and ground herself against him harder and rocking her hips seductively against him with a devilish twinkle in her eyes. Derek gasped fearing that he would burst into flame and waited for the fire inside him to cool. They stayed holding each other as the rain fell and Derek noted that Jamie flinched when the lightning seemed close. He kept his hands on her hands as he feared he could not keep his from wondering. Eventually Jamie slept. She too felt the fire between them and it scared her. She realized she wanted him as much as he wanted her. She was not sure she could give herself, she could not understand why he wanted her. She was happy just being held, at least for now.

Finally the day arrived when they approached the encampment. Riders had come out to greet them long before the camp was visible. There was much excitement with return of the men. A slight build red head girl with emerald eyes ran out, very animated in her happiness and was lifted up to ride with Roland. Hugging she ruffled his hair, "I've missed you angel girl," he said. She chatted continuously to Roland. Then she turned her attentions to Roland's brother. He also addressed her as angel girl and the lift in his spirits she brought was clearly visible. The camp was huge. Derek saw that it was slightly smaller than Irontown. It was organized in straight rows with a large open area in the center, unlike the higgledy- pigilty pattern of villages. It had large eating tents and cook area along the edges and in the center a large amphitheater with squared stones for seats. The amphitheater seemed very old. Everyone lived in a trailer. Derek could see that they were all of a similar hinged design that would fold down flat. They were twenty feet long by eight foot wide. Unhinged and open twenty feet by twenty-four feet, some larger some smaller. All were brightly painted and had glass windows. They obviously did not pay the yearly imperial window tax which had caused so many windows in the towns to be boarded up. The roofs were peeked and made of thick leather and had a single chimney. The Roamy seemed pleased to see one of their own return. They eyed Derek with caution and suspicion. The "R" burned on his right palm also brought comments. Jamie tried her best to explain they were not married just close friends, very close, very platonic friends. Jamie, who never before knew she had living relatives, now was overwhelmed with at least a hundred well-wishers.

"I've suddenly gone from being bereft of all friends and family except you dearest brother to now this. I'm feeling dizzy and a little scared." Jamie whispered as she clung closely to Derek.

Chapter 6 Rosalind

Roland took Derek and Jamie aside to explain what was to happen next after the evening meal. "You will stand before the counsel of clan chiefs. You need to address the clan leader as Lord Grandfather. The others as Grandfather or Grandmother. Don't worry, Jamie you're blood, and Derek you protected her. Even though you both deceived us regarding marriage you will be fairly treated." The evening meal was taken in the dinner tents. Most of the community was there but some did choose to eat in their wagons. An even larger number greeted the couple with warm smiles and hugs for Jamie and handshakes for Derek. It seems that most of the older Roamy remembered her parents and were full of anecdotal information about them. Jamie felt at home for the first time and Derek felt the warm accepting spirit in spite of all earlier misgivings. The meal was started with an invocation to the father god and closed with thanks to the mother god. Then the entire community assembled in the amphitheater. The counsel sat as Derek and Jamie approached holding hands and feeling very intimidated. Roland stood beside Jamie.

Lord Grandfather stood and addressed Jamie, "Welcome home dearest child. You have never been far from our hearts and our sight. Roamy are numerous and present in every village, guild and inn. We watch out for our own. We had expected you much earlier but you proved hard to locate in your travels."

"Lord Grandfather," Jamie started "We were so careful. How did the guard discover us?"

"They didn't. Someone at the fair reported that a newlywed couple, one runaway slave Roamy, you Derek, and a possible Roamy girl were in the village. They planned to capture you and sort it out. I believe they are still searching for you, Jamie, in the north." Then shifting his gaze to Derek, " Account to us your story and why do you bear the mark of a Roamy slave?" Derek then related his story with Jamie filling in more details. "Are you Roamy son?" he asked.

"No, Lord Grandfather, I am not!"

Then looking across the gathered crowd, "Is there anyone who can speak for this young man?"

"I will Lord Grandfather." It was the voice of a young woman. Derek looked as she approached thinking at first she looked so much like Jamie just slightly taller, then he thought his mother, but that was not possible.

Then recognition, "ROSIE!" he gasped no other words possible. Jamie stepped aside as they embraced, both in tears of joy. Derek smoothed back her hair and kissed the crown of her head.

"Lord Grandfather, this is my birth brother, son of Rachel and Olaf."

"Then you are Roamy. Will you join with us and accept our laws and covenants?"

"Gladly Grandfather." the crowd murmured approval.

"Now one last item. In our current law a couple only need to declare that they are married before two witnesses that they are married for it to be a binding marriage. You have done that twice. Once before the innkeeper and his wife and again before the entire village of Milford. But this clan prefers the old way. So Derek take Jamie's hands in yours." They held hands facing each other. "Roland will you stand as witness for Jamie and Rosalind will you stand as witness for Derek?" Both nodded and affirmed they would. "Now Derek and Jamie I now wrap your hands with this black scarf to represent the father god and a white scarf to represent the mother god, together the signs of law and creation. I pronounce you betrothed man and wife. You may now kiss the bride."

Derek had not expected this he was literally trembling with joy. Jamie looked puzzled. He bent and placed a long gentle kiss on her lips. She held him very tight melting into the kiss for a long time. Then he felt her stiffen. Her eyes opening and blazing in hot anger. She kicked his shin, "Big brother it's all your fault I liked it the way we were I hate you!" She then stormed off Rosalind trailing, looking confused and embarrassed. Some of the crowd were chuckling others touched Derek's shoulder as they passed. Derek just stood totally at loss to what happened moments before he had been so happy now he did not know what to feel. He then felt Lord Grandfather's hand on his shoulder.

"You love her deeply do you not?"

"Yes Lord Grandfather, but how do you know?"

"I am Lord Grandfather and the father god has given me his power of discernment so that I know the hearts of all men. She loves you too Derek. She trusted you with her life, hasn't she?"

"Yes but I don't understand, how did you know? ... She hates me!"

"Women are very complicated. I have been married fifty-two years; have five daughters and eight granddaughters numerous great granddaughters and I still find women incomprehensible. You must learn to listen to what they say."

"I do intensely, Lord Grandfather."

"And most important you must listen to what they don't say."

"How can I? I've got no idea what she didn't say!"

"She didn't say no, Derek. She could have. Be patient she is well worth the wait." Touching Derek's back Lord Grandfather moved away and Roland approached.

"Follow me Derek you will be staying with me. Sleep now. We have tomorrow to talk."

Rosalind caught up with Jamie and found her weeping. "Jamie you are staying with me so let me take you home." Rosalind took her hand and led her to her trailer. "This wagon is reserved for betrothed women. That's you and me now. We are now sisters could we also please be friends?"

Jamie smiled gratefully, "I've never had a sister or girlfriend ... oh, yes, I would love to be your friend."

"Well its settled then girlfriend!"

"Why did every one think we were married? We always address each other as brother and sister?"

"You didn't know?" Rosalind asked surprised. "Well in the old days we all called each other brother and sister but that custom passed as people began using the less formal first name. Rarely betrothed lovers will use brother and sister. It's a very tender and very formal way to address each other and very old fashioned. We all thought you both were so cute speaking as you do. Don't you love my brother?"

"Oh, I do, with all my heart, Rosalind!"

"Call me Roz."

"But Roz, I think he's crazy"

"Why crazy?"

"Because he loves *me*..." she sobbed. Rosalind now understood Jamie's behavior at the ceremony.

"You aren't worth being loved? Listen sister-girlfriend if Derek loves you then you are definitely worthy of his love. Do you hear me Jamie? Derek was the gentlest loving brother a little sister can have."

"I know and I love him. He's been a wonderful big brother. Sometimes I really want much, much more. Like when I tried to get him to kiss me and sleep with me..." she sobbed.

"You did that?"

"And I peeked when he bathed and nibbled his ear..." she continued to sob.

"I heard your story from Derek, now let me hear it from you." They spent the night talking, laughing and crying as Jamie told her story.

"Now, you tell me yours Roz." "Well, I loved him too. He would carry me around on his back. He read me stories and defended me from bullies."

"That sounds like my Derek."

"I was afraid of the dark, loud noises and especially being alone. I would sneak into his bed at night and he was so kind. He never put me out or gave me away to our parents. I would tip toe back to my room in the morning. Our mom died when I was born so I know Derek was very sad and lonely. He really missed her and threw himself into studies and the guild. He had few friends and as far as I know no girlfriends he was so serious except with me."

"What happened to you Roz?"

"I remember getting ill, Derek was sick with worry and would not leave my room. A healer came and I was getting better. But the healer told the magistrate that I was Roamy so I was forfeit and taken to be sold as a slave. They thought to put me in a brothel for the guard."

"You were eight Roz!"

"Some of the guard like them young," she said grimly. "But Roamy were watching over me and I was rescued even before they got me close to the brothel. Now I'm here."

They talked until morning and then a young woman with red hair burst into the room. "Hi Roz, whose our new girlfriend?" she made a lot of large gesturing as she spoke and sat on Roz's bed legs folded under, her skirt bouncing as she talked.

"Our new girlfriend is Jamie. Jamie this is Sophie, Roland's little sister, angel girl."

"Can I move in with you now Roz?" she rolled to her back

feet in the air.

"We have been thru... Sophie where are your shoes?"

"You sound like my mom. Sophie where are your shoes, Sophie that shirt is too tight, Sophie are you wearing underwear. I'm invisible around here. All the good men are taken; the rest are cousins."

"Is she always like this ... so dramatic?" Jamie whispered.

"She's just getting started, just wait!"

Sophie continued, "What if I don't believe in shoes? What if I don't believe in underwear, who'd know anyway? I might as well go about naked!"

"You would get a lot of male attention if you did that!" Roz said laughing.

"Ewwww, don't want that from my cousins, but from your man, Jamie that'd be fine... Can I have him?"

"Okay, he's yours."

"Hold on Sophie, Jamie's just joking." she looked at Jamie worried.

"Just joking Sophie."

"As for moving in I've already told you that you're too young."

"I'm sixteen."

"Since when Sophie?"

"Two months," she replied pouting.

Roz continued, "And more importantly, you are not betrothed."

"I'm so tired of being single, when will I get my man?" Sophie wailed. Then they all laughed and began throwing pillows at each other.

Chapter 7 Camp Life

Two weeks passed and Derek and Jamie had found their place in the community. As healer and midwife Jamie was busy. She had two pregnant women in her care, one due in a few days. Derek's skills were also needed. The clan did have men who worked black metal but their skill and proficiency was marginal. Derek found he was spending more time teaching than doing but his students were intelligent and motivated. He was a journeyman after all and journeymen traveled and taught. They both missed the constant companionship they had when they were on the run but here they were safe and happy. Both had been able to draw clothing from the clan warehouse and Jamie now had three sets of woman's clothing and one very pretty dress for more formal ware. Derek was sitting with Rosalind for the noon meal. Jamie was busy with a pregnant woman, early labor she had mentioned. He was already missing her and a little ashamed of the jealousy he felt toward her pregnant clients. He needed to learn to share Jamie's time a little less grudgingly.

He watched as Sophie twirled about the dinner tent barefoot. He thought she was an awful flirt as she went from table to table ruffling hairs, talking with large arm movements and sometimes sitting on tables to talk. When Lord Grandfather and his wife entered she skipped over to them hugging them both. Lord Grandfather smiled warmly and said "It's so good to see you my angel girl!"

"Rose help me I don't know how to handle Sophie's flirting and attention. I'm so afraid of hurting Jamie."

"Sophie is always happy and enthusiastic with everyone. She is the youngest in a large family of all boys and has always been their darling little sister. It's mostly brothers and cousins she flirts with. She would be horrified if anyone took her flirting as sexual. She sees you as family and you are getting some of her attention."

"Thanks that is good to know. I feel less anxious, but Lord Grandfather?"

"Lord Grandfather is her great grandfather. They are very close. He truly loves all his daughters and granddaughters. Sophie is just full of love for everyone; someday it will all be directed toward one very lucky man."

"He will indeed have his hands full!" Derek said with humor.

"Oh, Derek, before I forget Roland and I have been asked to

give you the first lessons."

"About what Rosie?"

"No time to talk now, there's my Roland. Oh, Sophie might come too she's very lonely and has attached herself to Jamie and me by the hips."

Derek sat alone at the table for a while when Jamie appeared. "Miss me dearest love?"

"Oh very much little sister. I really miss having you all to myself!"

"I'm so excited, I delivered a baby boy. He was early but mom and baby are fine. I'm so happy my love, we should have a baby! What do you think?"

"Now?" Derek asked smiling.

"No silly, you are such a goof. When we are ready my love. My feet really hurt, been on them for the last eighteen hours."

"My step mom used to give the best foot rubs. She would give each or us one every night before bed. We loved it. I believe she meant it as a bonding ritual. Would you like a ritual bonding foot rub from me my love?"

"Ewww ritual bonding foot rub. Lead on dearest brother." They walked to the amphitheater with Jamie taking a seat and Derek seated on the lower tier. He gently removed her shoes and she hiked up her skirt. "Dear brother is this just one of your elaborate schemes to touch me?"

"You see through me so well my love. Yes, it is my devilish plot to get my hands on your flesh!" He then began to gently knead and massage her feet. She slowly began to relax. Derek's strong hands were adept at the task and she really enjoyed the massage. She liked him touching her.

"Okay beloved brother, its time I reciprocate!"

"I'm not so sure. I'm very ticklish. I'm afraid, you might get kicked."

"Afraid, of little me... my love?" she smiled brightly.

"Yes."

"I promise to be gentle." She gave him her most sultry look with slightly parted lips, her dark eyes partially shuttered with her thick lashes.

"Proceed on my love I surrender to your wiles!" Both laughed and she began to knead and massage Derek's feet. He relaxed and let her continue. Not observing her closely, he missed the beginning of a devilish smile on her face. No longer able to resist she began tickling. Derek jumped and fell off his seat with Jamie falling on top. A wrestling match ensued. She was out classed in strength and weight so Derek held back but was still winning. Then she kicked out in an attempt to wiggle free; her heel accidentally contacting his nose. There was a cracking sound and Derek's nose bled profusely. An alarmed and repentant Jamie stopped the bleeding and reset the nose.

Looking very worried Jamie asked "Did you get hurt anywhere else?" Derek pouting pointed to his forehead so she kissed it. He pointed to his cheek and she kissed that too. Then he pointed to his lip and she laughingly kissed that. They embraced in a long kiss both breathing heavily when Rosalind walked up.

"Derek you're bleeding!"

"Jamie broke my nose!"

"It was all his fault!" Jamie said and both laughed.

Derek and Jamie met Roland and Rosalind; Sophie also came and was delightfully happy at being included in an adult activity. They were just north of the storage barns and they descended a series of terraced stone steps to a beautiful river valley. The valley was green and lush and totally unseen from the high desert. "This is the River Skell. It begins high in the northern ice fields and runs in a serpentine course another two hundred miles south. The valley was about a mile wide and the entire valley was dedicated to agriculture and fishing. We control the salt trade and the fish trade. The Imperial city is fed by salted fish from this river. This is our great secret. We are much more numerous than the Magisterium can even guess. There are permanent and seasonal settlements every ten miles," Rosalind said.

"Does the river flow to the sea?" Derek asked.

"No, it ends in huge salt flats near the eastern ocean. It's our source of salt. We are the hub settlement in the salt trade. That's the reason you see all the stone storage barns," Roland replied. "We are here to teach you our history and explain the covenant. The official history is not true. The Firsters were not the first settlers to land on this planet. We are Roamy, originally part of the Guild of Roaming Terraformers. Our guild for thousands of years, ever since the home planet, Earth, began colonization of the stars was tasked with terraforming planets. We went to water planets and began organizing the planet and making it fit for life. We introduced animal species and plants from Earth. We then would open the planet for colonization, and move on. This was a difficult planet. It took ten generations, not the usual one, to terraform. We had spent so much energy to build and had lost so many of our own in the process that some of us elected to stay. The eastern continent was not completed when settlement began so it was abandoned. We elected to stay and initially lived easily with the Firsters."

"I thought the gods made this planet." Jamie said.

"They did, Jamie, but they also gave us the knowledge to shape it to our need. That was a long time ago and much of the knowledge lost. It's been six hundred years since our last contact with the mother planet." Roland continued his narrative about the conflicts with the very aggressive Firsters. He told of the difficulty introducing larger mammals from Terran like the equine and bovine lines and how that was abandoned early to rely on more vigorous species from arid mountain areas of the home planet, the camelids. There were now over a dozen camillid species from the large ones they use for riding to smaller ones used for milk, meat and wool. He told of the hundred years of war and how they had decided the carnage and destruction was too costly and fled to this hidden river valley in the high desert. For the last four hundred years they had lived under the covenant and followed the ten great laws brought from the home world. Then Rosalind explained the sacred covenant of marriage and the laws of chastity.

"If you live such strict lives why the long betrothal period?" Jamie asked. Rosalind explained that physical intimacy was a gift of the gods it burns very hot and is wonderful but short lived and fickle. The spiritual intimacy for a happy marriage took longer to build and burned slower. The few months of betrothal time is when couples are to concentrate on spiritual intimacy while looking forward for the second. Roamy marriages were very happy and stable with large families and numerous children. Divorce was rare.

Derek said "I have noticed your families have many more girls than boys unlike the Firsters."

"That's true, many girls end up marring outside the clan but their men most often join us. As for the Firsters they kill their infant girls preferring male offspring so their depleting numbers is on their own head." Rosalind continued. "Women have a settling effect on society."

"Settling? When I'm around you dear Roz I feel frisky." Roland quipped.

"Now you sound like Derek." Jamie said.

"Actually I agree with Roland." Derek replied laughing.

"Don't respond Jamie it will only encourage them." Then they all laughed. Rosalind continued to explain how the Firsters have set their society on the bureaucratic stile of governance and how that makes it a very stable society but one that lacks innovation and the ability to grow or temperance. It also makes for tyranny as the bureaucrats always with the best intentions limit choice and freedom until society becomes untenable.

Roland continued, "You have come to us with special skills at our greatest hour of need. This has been foreseen by the Lord Grandfather. We plan to begin to colonize the eastern continent. Jamie and Derek embraced each other and smiling into each other's eyes then looked at Rosalind.

"That was our very plan when we ran away. We hoped to start our lives in the new world!"

They continued their walk with Sophie asking as many questions as Jamie and Derek together. "Every three weeks we have a dance. It will be tomorrow. The following week is a play in the amphitheater. Some very old plays from the home planet and some more current comedies are planned. Men and women have organized sports," Rosalind continued.

"I miss sports but for now I really want to spend as much time possible with Jamie as she is so busy. I'm getting jealous!" Derek said as Jamie smiled and held him tighter. "Will we all be going to the new world?"

Roland answered, "Yes and hopefully you too Sophie."

"Tell me more about the salt trade." Derek asked. Roland told them that salt is moved from the salt flats during the winter over the frozen river and stored. During the rest of the year it is dispensed by way of the hospitality guild. Roamy controlled the hospitality guild and ran all the inns with the Magisterium totally unaware. "That is how you were located. Imperial salt was very expensive because of high taxes and often adulterated with sand by unscrupulous merchants. Most people use our salt." Roamy also controlled the Communications Guild and ran the semaphore signaling stations. "The Magisterium's prized secret code was Roamy and we read imperial message traffic before the government officials do."

"Would it be possible for me to send a message home that I'm okay and married, and I have located Rosie?" Derek asked. Roland promised to arrange the message and to let Derek's parents know how to message him. "Why was I not aware of the large camelids before our rescue?" Roland told of the secret breading program and how the large camelids called walkers were the Roamy's best kept secret. Only rarely were walkers taken out or the high desert region they controlled. They were used to rescue Rosalind and other highly strategic missions.

The dance was held in the village square. Jamie wore her new dress. It was a deep blue with gold piping and very attractive gold lace patterns along the neckline hem and sleeve lines. Derek especially liked the décolletage of the dress sweeping just low enough to hint at her soft curves and cleavage, and show the silky smooth lines of her neck and back. She also wore a vest with intricate beading in a similar pattern to that on the dress. The vest was cut low in the front and back and secured with laces and emphasized her small waist and rounded hips. She had the gold necklace and bracelet on. Her hair was braided with the braiding starting at her temples and crown and flowers braided into her hair. She was barefoot as the night was warm. The dress had an open seam on the right side extending to her knee. Derek could see her elegant feet and a tantalizing flash of ankle and calf when she walked. She had darkened her brows and eyelashes and had large circular dangling gold earrings on and a gold chain anklet which gave her an exotic and innocently alluring look. Derek was totally entranced by her beauty. But unlike their first dance in Milford Village Derek had to share Jamie as Roland and numerous cousins who also demanded her attention. Derek had never seen Jamie so happy and exuberant. Derek danced with Rosalind at least twice. Sophie preferred the more energetic dances and managed to snare several with him. To Derek's surprise Jamie seemed pleased that he allowed Sophie to have so many dances with him without any evidence of jealously. Derek, as for himself, was struggling with very strong feelings of jealously. The dance went late into the night. Food was plentiful. When the dance was over Derek walked Jamie hand in hand to her wagon. They embraced for a long time before Derek was willing to relinquish his hold.

"Did you know my love I'm having real trouble waiting to have you all to myself!" Jamie whispered. She had a shy smile and her dark eyes sparkled, her face flushed. Loose strands of hair had escaped her braids and Derek brushed the gossamer strands from her face. Derek embracing her again kissed her on her exposed neck working from just below her ear to her shoulder; she gave a breathy gasp and clung tighter to him fearing her knees would buckle. She returned the kiss with passion gently biting his lower lip. Breathless they parted.

Back at the wagon Roland was also restless so both decided to talk. Roland told how he had first met Rosalind when she had been brought to the camp at age eight. He was ten and decided then that he would marry her. They had been best friends long before he had dared to talk to her about marriage but she seemed to like the idea. They had been betrothed about two weeks when he had left on the rescue mission. To him Rosalind was the most beautiful desirable woman he had ever met and he was having a very hard time waiting for their marriage. Rosalind had excellent organizing skills and could delegate tasks well without raising anyone's ire or hurting feelings. He was sure she would become Head Women in the clan before long. He shared stories of how Rosalind's life had been when she arrived and how sad she was. "She sort of adopted me as her big brother, and I relished in it." Derek also shared stories of Rosalind when she lived with him, and the deep loss and sorrow he had felt when she was taken. Not knowing what had happened to her made the sorrow even worse. Derek was happy that his Rosie had found love with this good and decent man. They also discussed sports and fishing. Both loved fishing and Roland liked hunting with crossbow. Roland's calling was as wheelwright and also acted as the cooper and carpenter. He had already designed the wagon that was to be their home but now realized that it would never be built as they would be sailing to the new world in early spring. So now he had been tasked with designing homes that could be quickly erected. He had chosen several possible designs based on village cottages, he had no specific information in available materials in the new world and asked Derek, who was now his brother, if he would like to assist in the planning. Derek agreed to assist with the planning. Derek suggested the daub and wattle method as the inside could be white washed and women liked brighter interiors. Roland felt that wood floors on a raised foundation would be best as he did not know how wet winters would be and rammed earth floors could become mud floors making life untenable. They discussed the village layout for the colony and decided they would build their homes next to each other.

Jamie was restless. Rosalind was already asleep, most likely exhausted by the dancing and the elaborate preparations she had participated in. Jamie wanted badly to talk. Derek's kiss had ignited passion in her she had not felt before. She had always enjoyed a stolen kiss. She recalled the thunderstorm in the tent with a blushing smile. But tonight something deep inside her stirred. Her body had responded with urgency and pulsing fire deep in her belly. Was she a wanton? The intensity and urgency she had felt was new and she liked it. She had always been aware of a barrier in her heart which limited the closeness she could feel to Derek. Tonight there was no barrier and she would have given herself without thought if he had continued, right in the middle of camp, no less. Something in her had changed. She felt giddy. Finally, she slept. Her dreams equally unsettling, she dreamed of Derek and her locked in passion. When she finally awoke she was wet from perspiration and felt exhausted and empty.

Derek and Jamie sat with Roland and Rosalind in the amphitheater to watch the play. It was a musical farce written by Roland's older brother Robert, who also plaid the lead character a young knight and Sophie the fairy princess. In the play the knight was captured then held as a slave by the dragon. Robert who to most people appeared quiet and often grim fit the role very well. Jamie was surprised he could sing so well and even dance. The fairy princess would free the knight by tricking the dragon. Sophie was wonderful as the fairy princess. She had a sweet singing voice and tremendous energy. She quite literally bounced and twirled about the stage. Her style of dramatic overacting fit the play well and she had the audience laughing until they cried. The most amazing part was Robert's transformation from grim self to actually seeming happy as Sophie flirted dramatically with him and rescued him from the dragon. "When did they have time to do the rehearsals for the play?" Derek asked Roland.

"No idea. It was great. Angel Girl was wonderful. I have not seen Robert so happy since he lost Abby and the twins. I'm so proud of both of them. It was the best play this season. Angel Girl was magic!"

There was a party after the play and the actors received long energetic applause. Sophie was presented with a bouquet of roses from Lord Grandfather. The dragon was played by four of Roland's cousins and the chorus by family friends. Most remarkable was the change in Robert, he seemed to stay in a happy mood. He was even seen speaking to a young widow and smiling as they held hands. Jamie nudging Rosalind whispered "Sophie really is a fairy princess." Rosalind laughed and agreed.

"He has been so sad for so long we had forgotten what he was like before he lost Abby. Jayne is a distant cousin and they were very close as children. It would be a good match. I would like to see both of them as happy as Roland and me."

After the play and party Derek finally had Jamie to himself for a few minutes. "Little sister if I was entrapped by a dragon would you rescue me?"

Jamie smiling mischievously said, "That depends brave knight in what would be my reward!"

"I would be very happy to show you now but we would need to elude all chaperones."

"You are so bad my love. You are lusting for body again?"

"You are most perceptive. I'm counting down the days."

"As am I!"

The next afternoon Jamie, Sophie and Rosalind were sitting at one of the dinner tables after the noon meal. Jamie was free that afternoon but the men were busy so the three sisters were just relaxing and enjoying each other's company. Then Robert rolled up to them with a small wagon. "Jamie I've got these boxes for you. I think they came from your village. There are four boxes, three kind of heavy one larger marked fragile. Where do you want them?"

"I'll take them here, thank you, Robert, so much. Could I keep the wagon for a bit?" Robert nodded his reply and left waving to Jayne, who was at another table. He walked over to her.

Jamie opened the first box. She gasped, "My dad's books. She slowly pulled out the well-worn volumes: REPERTORIUM AND WORD INDEX, the five volume MATERA MEDICA, KEYNOTES AND CONFIRMING SYMPTOMS, also books on flower remedies, a dosing guide and her flash card index of keynotes. "My Dad drilled me on these flash cards until I knew the two hundred common remedies cold."

Sophie asked "What can you do with these? Don't you know everything already?"

"Oh, no, Sophie it takes a lifetime of learning and still you know so very little. These books will help me continue to expand my knowledge and someday take on an apprentice."

"Please take me, I can study hard. You and Roz have callings that help the clan. I would love to be a healer. I want to help too!"

"Okay. Apprentice Sophie, we start today let's check my other boxes." The second box had more of her father's books and the book of stories he had read to her as a child. Her eyes moistened as she held that book to her heart. The third box was her mother's midwife books and her personal notes of observations and records of births. The last box had another several smaller boxes wrapped in paper. A smaller boxed surgical set, two round wooden boxes containing the glass vials and jars used to make the mother tinctures for the remedies, and more remedies. As Jamie pulled out the last wooden box her hands began to tremble. She very gently placed the box on the table opened it and removed her mother's tea set. Jamie began to shake and then weep. Her friends placed their arms around her shoulders and held her. Both had their heads on her shoulders. Jamie told her friends about the tea set and her foster parents, and her joy of receiving these unexpected gifts. Who could have known how much this would mean to her? Who would even have known where to find her? Then it dawned on her. It was the elders or more likely their wives. They were Roamy living secretly in the village and had always been so kind to her. She smiled, no longer weeping. She had never really been alone. She had been surrounded by friends all her life. She had not realized it until now. Now she had acquired two sisters she loved and most importantly she had Derek. She had a calling, and valuable skills to help her community and now the means to pass it on. Jamie thought she had never been happier.

"Our first task, Sophie is for me to check your aura. May I?"

"Please!"

"Mine to Jamie!" said Rosalind excitedly.

Jamie closed her eyes relaxing and reached out to her friends, their auras were bright white. Both had swirling areas of yellow and green. Sophie's very strongly green Rosalind blue green. "Both of you have healing colors in your aura. Sophie most strongly, you too Roz you could easily stand in a healing circle. Your gifts are strong too."

"I really don't want to be a healer but would love to stand in a healing circle, I really want to be head woman," replied Rosalind with a gentle smile, blushing.

Sophie was beaming with a smile. "Jamie I saw your aura when we touched and I saw mine too. But not with my eyes. It was weird. Is that what it is like for you too?"

"Yes. My parents could see auras with their eyes alone. I can't but they both agreed that I would someday. They would not tell me when and I often have my doubts. Roz you will gain that skill once you stand in a healing circle. It's a skill you must use with care. My parents often asked permission before using but not always. In some cases the person cured in the healing circle also gains the sight too."

The seasons continued to change and it was time to move the camp from the high desert through the mountain pass to Winter Camp on the east coast. The preparations and planning took weeks. They needed to take along enough food to sustain the group of about four hundred for nearly a month while traveling and to feed them through the winter. Fodder for the animals needed to be carried also as well as water. Many of the men would return once the river froze solid to transport salt from the salt basin to the storage barns returning to Winter Camp before the late winter flooding. This trip Winter Camp would include the new permanent settlement of Port Hope. The new Roamy Navy scheduled to arrive early spring. The fish monger guild would transport the season's catch of salted fish to imperil markets all over the continent. This trade provided much the needed cash that had allowed them to build the new port and settlement. The salt trade provided a cash stream during the warmer seasons. The scene was organized chaos. Roland was a wheelwright and he was very busy making sure all the forty plus wagons were travel worthy. Derek as black metal smith equally busy making and repairing iron tools and accouterments for travel. Rosalind was called to be Head Woman. Jamie helped in the delivery of two more babies and was very occupied in her role as healer. Sophie accompanied Jamie for the birthings and assisted. When they finally moved, the train was a mile long and they averaged about fifteen miles per day. Each night they made camp. They frequently had music or dancing at the camps. Feeding everyone took enormous organization. Children needed watching, cattle mending and the healer was in constant need. Derek saw very little of Jamie most days.

On the fourth day out they did have and evening together and were able to dance together. To Jamie's surprise Sophie and Rosalind were in the band. Sophie played a wheeled fiddle and Rosalind a bowed fiddle with a dozen strings and finger keys. Sophie and Rosalind also did several vocal numbers with Roland at the flat drum. Jamie especially loved the slow dances and clung tightly to Derek. "I really miss having you all to myself dearest brother!" Jamie whispered into his ear. Derek was just the right height to nibble her ear unobserved. "I can see why you like my nibbling so much and were so distracted when I nibbled you my love!"

"Really can't wait for our betrothal period to end little sister, I want you so much."

"We can formally wed in Winter Camp as soon as we arrive. Roland and Roz too. We can make it a double wedding. Because of the special circumstances of the colonization they are allowing the betrothal time to be advanced." This came as a happy surprise to Derek.

"I will be so happy and so complete when you are mine forever. Let's have ten children!"

Jamie laughed, "Didn't I tell you a long time ago you were a hopeless romantic?"

"Yes little sister and crazy too!" They continued to hold each other long after the music stopped. Only stopping when it was time to part for sleep.

Several days later a very worried Roland came to Jamie and

Derek, "Sophie's walker just came in and I can't find her." Her shoes were still tied to the saddle as well as her coat. A search of the camp then ensued and at dawn twelve grim riders left in groups of two to search. Their hope for success was very poor. Derek and Roland road out together.

Chapter 8 Sophie

Sophie slowly regained consciousness. She realized she must have fallen asleep and fell from the walker. She was freezing cold. Her shoes, coat and knife still on the camillid were gone. Sophie knew how to survive in the desert but without her knife and a way to keep warm she was doomed. She knew it best to wait for rescue. Roland would find her. She was so thirsty. She knew she could get fluid from the cacti but she had no knife so she removed her skirt and wrapped it around a cactus to cushion the sharp spikes and opened it with a rock. The pulp had fluid so she sated her thirst. The fluid was sticky so sand clung to her face and hands. Attempts to wipe it off only increased the area of stickiness and soon she had sand sticking to her eyes, ears and mouth. Feeling cold and miserable she rolled herself in a ball and wrapped herself in the long wool skirt hoping to conserve enough heat to survive until Roland found her. She prayed to the mother god for Roland to find her then added if he was not available let it be her man that did. The day saw some warming and she felt a little better but she knew the cold night would be her undoing. Sophie tried to sleep trusting in divine providence.

David's travels in the desert had done little to lessen his guilt. He usually traveled during the hours of darkness and rested during the day but as it had been getting very cold at night he reversed the pattern. He had initially thought that in the desert he would find peace in his soul but guilt and shame still plagued his sleep. He had been picking up wood while he traveled so he could have fire when he camped. Had accumulated quite a bit from the dry riverbed he had been traveling in. Then topping a small hill he saw red hair blowing about on the ground then he saw the little woman. She was huddled up in a ball on the ground wrapped in her skirt. An angel he thought so pale and beautiful so delicate and ethereal. She had no shoes, no coat and no knife. She was bereft of nearly everything even underwear. He could not find any sign or evidence of how she had arrived there before him. With bare feet she clearly had not walked. With the pitiful scarcity of belongs she could not have been there long. She must have fallen from the sky he mused. She was shivering. Her lips and her bare feet blue. She had sand caked on her hands, arms, face and mouth. She was barley lucid. David got out both of his blankets and wrapped her gently. Touching her shoulder her he asked, "Who are you, where did you come from?" Her answer came as a shock.

"I fell." She pointed skyward her voice thick and muffled.

"Are you an angel?"

She nodded and said "Angel Girl."

David, startled, started a small fire to keep her warm then set up his tarp as a lean-to to shelter her from the wind and to contain the heat from the fire. He removed his coat and then his shirt. Putting his coat on his angel he used his shirt to clean much of the caked sand on her face and hands. She looked so frail and beautiful with her pale skin and carrot hair. He offered her a little water and ordered her to spit which she did several times clearing the sand from her mouth. He told her to take some slow sips and she did choking at first. Then wetting his shirt he gently cleaned her face taking care to remove the sand from her eyes and ears. He offered her dried fruit but she refused. Her shivering continued unabated. He banked the fire and began to prepare a light meal. He had caught a snake and skinning it he impaled bits if on a stick to roast on the fire. He brewed some tea. David was able to get Sophie to sip the warm tea. Sophie was then able to eat some of the meat and accepted some of the dried fruit. She continued to shiver in spite of David's coat and the blankets. The sun was rapidly setting and the cold worsening. David was beginning to worry about his angel. She appeared dazed and confused. "What is your name?" he asked as he gently brushed her hair from her face.

"Angel Girl. Did the gods send you to me?"

"I believe so. I was sent to save you Angel Girl." He knew she was developing shock and he'd need to raise her core temperature fast or she would die. "Angel Girl I will use my body to keep you warm. I will do you no harm. Please may I help?"

"Is Roland here too?"

"No just me Angel Girl."

"I'm so cold. I can't stop shivering; please may I have more tea?"

David supported her to set up and got her to take another cup of warm tea. David stripped off his clothes and Sophie's tunic. He wrapped both of them together in the blankets. His skin was so dark compared to her pale bluish skin. She felt very cold against his skin. He pulled her body close to him face to face then slid her so her head just reached his chin and covered her head with the blankets. From his position he could man the fire and keep it going. She felt so soft and so right against his skin that his body reacted as a man's body does. David knew that she was helpless and vulnerable. His angel was not a consenting partner so he ignored his discomfort concentrating on keeping his angel warm.

    David was a man who had known women and was skilled in pleasuring women. When it had become known he was to become an officer in the guard he had had a series of lovers. Each one staying only until a better arrangement could be found for them. David initially thought these women had offered him their favors out of love that they found him handsome and clever. David discovered that while he would not be allowed to marry while in the guard, many in the guard had unofficial wives, often more than one. Some became camp followers. Some women collected men like men collected them. It was the lure of thirty years income that attracted these women. David soon became disenchanted with women in general. He wanted desperately to be part of something. As a child it was family he craved, as a young man love and acceptance. The guard, he hoped would be family, and that choice was a disaster. Now he realized what he really wanted was to give and receive love without expecting anything else, to be a family with a woman. Now he could never return from the desert without suffering death, so this dream of a wife and family was truly lost. All he had left was this moment and his angel. He would do his best to save her life and expecting nothing in return from her. He hoped for redemption. That by saving his angel he hoped he could save himself from his awful guilt and shame.

    Sophie, although only partially conscious was fully aware of David's hard body against her. She craved his warmth. She was so cold but her hard shivering had stopped. She pressed herself tighter against David wrapping him in her arms and legs. Finally she slept. David maintained the fire and held tight to his angel. Sophie awoke at first light. She felt warm, no longer foggy or confused. She saw David sleeping quietly still holding her. She just lay quietly enjoying the feel of David's warm skin and his scent. Eventually he woke and saw Sophie looking into his face smiling radiantly. Her eyes emerald green, angel eyes he thought. He loosened his hold on her and lay on his back. "My angel lives" he said smiling. Sophie then rolled on top of David looking into his face smiling, her long red hair falling to engulf both of them like a tent. The morning sun on her hair glowed like a fiery halo.

"Thank you for saving me. I prayed to the mother god and she sent you to be my man. I will love you forever!" Sophie then gave David a firm long enthusiastic kiss. Before she had finished the kiss she heard Roland's sharp voice.

"SOPHIE! What are you doing?"

Sophie turned and saw Roland and Derek standing. She smiled happily, "I knew you would come. Roland, Derek let me introduce you to..." whispering she said to David, "What is your name?"

"David."

Totally unabashed she continued, "David? David this is my brother Roland and a friend, my newest cousin, Derek."

Roland replied in a bad temper, "Sophie knock off this nonsense and get off that man!"

"Well I can't... I'm not decent... You both turn around and close your eyes. You to David." Sophie got off the blanket and dressed quickly. "Roland did you bring my shoes? My feet are getting cold."

Roland's mood foul he glared murderously at David "You get up and get ready to travel." As he got up Sophie made audible sigh and Roland barked "Sophie turn around."

"Aww Roland don't you think we are beyond..." Roland's glare silenced her.

"What are your plans for me?" David asked expecting the worse.

Sophie cut in, "Roland he saved my life. I'd of frozen. I'm keeping him!"

"Buy the gods Sophie I don't know what to do with you. We will go to the encampment and let counsel work this out."

"Ok, I'll ride with David you and Derek can ride together."

Roland was ready to fall into a murderous rage and rip David apart but remembering his covenant he closed his eyes, gritted his teeth and said, "No Sophie you will ride with me!" That settled they left.

Their arrival at camp was met by the entire community. All were relieved to see Sophie alive and well. She waved enthusiastically to her parents taking a mile on minute to parents and brothers behind Roland on the camillid. Roland looked angry and grim and requested council. Sophie was sent to the midwife to verify their story of no intimacy between them. Roland still very angry grabbed David tearing his shirt revealing the tattoo. The entire community gasped. He was Praetorian. The anger toward David was thick and simmering. The guards were hated for good reason. The Praetorian were hated the most. David, seeing the looks in the eyes of Sophie's family, knew his fate was grim. David was fed eating with the community. Sophie sat with Roland looking frightened and sad. Her face was blotchy red from crying. No one spoke to David or approached. Derek sat next to him but David saw him as a guard but had no intention to run. David was finished running. It would all end here, tonight. Then after dinner council was called. David was instructed on protocols by Derek before he was presented.

"David, what is your story? Lord Grandfather asked. David told his story of finding and saving a fallen angel he had found in the desert hoping for his own redemption then discovering it was Sophie. "That mark on your shoulder is that a mark of pride?"

"No, grandfather it is my mark of shame."

"Are you a deserter?"

"Yes, Lord Grandfather."

"Are you a coward son?"

"I was, Lord Grandfather, until I had the courage to run. I am a coward no longer and accept any sentence you give, I am under a death sentence so you need only turn me in. I fled into the desert to die and am resigned to death. The gods have answered my prayers and sent an angel. I have been forgiven and my heart is full. The awful guilt and shame I felt has been lifted because of an angel, your Sophie." Further questions brought out his role in the destruction of the village, his awful guilt and shame. His flight into the desert and what he had hoped to find there. Sophie was then asked for her story. Sophie spoke of her rescue and how she had prayed for her brother to find her and added in her prayer that if Roland could not come in time that her man finds her.

"And the gods answered and I'm safe. So could I please keep David?" Sophie's plea caused several present to smile and some quiet laughter.

Jamie gave evidence that they had not lied regarding physical intimacy. The counsel then met alone to decide while all waited.

Then returning Lord Grandfather stood before David. "Are you ready for our findings?"

"Yes, Lord Grandfather, am I to die?"

"Yes, David," Sophie gasped and collapsed in tears. Lord Grandfather continued, "But not today."

Derek and Roland walked Jamie and Rosalind back to the girl's wagon holding hands. "I am grateful to the gods for Lord Grandfather's gift of discernment. I almost broke the covenant in my anger." Roland said. The couples embraced as Sophie rushed passed them with her travel bag and burst through the door into the wagon. Her face still red from tears. She tossed her bag on an empty bed and flopped on another.

"Sophie where are your shoes?" Rosalind asked smiling.

"No idea Roz, but I'm moving in at last.... I got my man!"

Chapter 9 Winter Camp

The long trek to Winter Camp continued. Roland, David and Derek were becoming close friends. David accepted the calling as carpenter, although he had little carpentry experience. Then one morning a month into their travels word went out that Lord Grandfather's wife, Grandmother Phoebe had died in the night. Sophie's grief was apparent as she sat sadly while Jamie and Rosalind flanked her holding her while she wept. David was so tender with her. She had hugs for Roland, Robert and Derek. The traveling stopped as the little community prepared for the funeral. They gathered at the graveside for the memorial service. This was Jamie's and Derek's first experience with Roamy funerals. There would be three speakers. Sophie, the youth speaker was first, her composure and presence riveted the audience. She spoke of how much she loved her great grandmother. She told stories of their lives together, some of the stories very tender, some funny and the audience laughed and wept with her. She concluded with her knowledge that life does not begin at birth nor end with death, that she and her great grandmother were part of an eternal family and would they be together again forever. Sophie's father gave the second talk. It too was upbeat and full of hope. The last speaker was Lord Grandfather. He too spoke of his great love for Phoebe. He said that they were eternal partners, sealed together in the sacred covenant of marriage. He closed with his testimony that someday in the new world a savior would come. The savior's gift would be resurrection and eternal lives with each family sealed for eternity. The service over Grandmother Phoebe was laid to rest and the evening meal taken.

"Are all your funerals so upbeat?" Derek asked Roland and Sophie.

Sophie replied, "Yes, death is not so unexpected with older people. A child's funeral is much more difficult."

"What does sealing mean?" Jamie asked.

"That is what happens when the betrothal period ends. You are already married for life. You both did that when you declared yourself married before witnesses. We did it as betrothal and it is as binding as marriage. Lord Grandfather believed that having both of you experience the traditional betrothal it would strengthen your bond and give Jamie more time to strengthen her feelings of self-worth. You can't truly give love until you can love yourself. The next step is being sealed together for eternity. That is separate and is called the sacred covenant of marriage. We will do that together in Winter Camp," Roland replied, "Sophie and David too. We're planning a triple wedding."

"I like that dearest brother, sealed together for all eternity!" Jamie whispered. Derek held her close. She would be his lover for time and eternity.

"I like that too; I want to be with you forever my love!"

One weary afternoon as the wagons slowly continued their journey two year old Eric managed to fall from his seat next to his father and landed as the wagon wheel rolled over his head. The entire procession of wagons stopped and the healer was summoned. Jamie and Sophie arrived moments later. Eric was crying, his face was colored red and his nose was bleeding and swollen. His eyes were very puffy and closed and blood was exiting from his left ear. Sophie was near hysterical when she saw her cousin. Jamie faced Sophie, hands on her shoulders looking into her eyes, "You're a healer Sophie, take a deep breath, you can do this!" Sophie steadied herself closed her eyes and nodded. "Okay. Healer Sophie, how do we proceed?"

"We stop the nose bleed and check for signs of fracture. I would guess Arnica as a remedy?"

"No guessing Sophie, you know this!"

"Arnica," Sophie said with conviction. Jamie then allowed Sophie to proceed and watched quietly as she examined Eric with her hands. "The bleeding from his ear may be a fracture," she said to Eric's parents. "Let's keep him awake and we will look for signs of bleeding inside. I gave him a remedy for bleeding, now I will use a flower remedy to help him keep calm." Sophie looked toward Jamie who nodded approval.

They were then joined by Rosalind. "You wanted me?" she asked.

"We are planning a healing circle. Eric is bleeding into his brain. The Arnica stopped it but later it will swell inside. His temporal bone is fractured as well as his right orbit and nose. Sophie did a scan while laying her hands. Will you help?" Jamie asked.

After nodding her approval the sisters returned to Eric's side.

Jamie continued "We will stand in a circle you hold hands and put your hands on my shoulder. I will place my hands on Eric's head. You need only close your eyes and will me your life force. I will direct it along with mine and you will see in your mind how I direct it. You will also see all our auras." After a short prayer Jamie began. She could feel the energy from Rosalind and Sophie. All three energies were very different so she blended them into an energy chord much stronger than if just added together. Then visualizing the broken bones she directed them to heal. The swelling in the brain was harder to visualize, so she imagined it as a puddle of fluid between the sheathes covering the brain, and reduced its size. She then saw the red in Eric's aura fade and the color becoming more and more white. She then relinquished the energy and withdrew her hands. The healing had taken a little over an hour and all three were exhausted. That evening Jamie, Sophie and the child's parents kept a vigil reading to the child and periodically checking his pupils. By late evening Eric looked well. Much of the swelling down and no more bleeding. As Sophie returned to her wagon with Jamie she began to tremble and began to weep. Jamie held her close as Rosalind also sat next to her on the other side. "I was so scared Jamie. What if I was wrong? What if..."

Jamie replied "Shh Sophie. What if nothing. What if a bull frog had wings? You were great. You knew what to do. I'm so proud of you, apprentice Sophie. My first patient was hard too. You are going to be a first class healer. I love you little sister!"

"And I second that!" added Rosalind.

The next morning at breakfast Eric came to Sophie. He was clutching a book and motioned to be held. Sophie put him on her lap. "Soapy read!" Sophie and David took turns reading. Sophie looked radiant as she looked at little Eric. She really was a healer.

David whispered in her ear, "Let's have a little boy ourselves! Perhaps little girls too, all with red hair." Sophie held David closer and continued reading with her head on his shoulder.

The weather became colder as they continued to gain altitude in the high desert. Finally in the mountains they reached the Pass Of The Shepherds. "It's all downhill now, Jamie, and it will get much warmer, just five of six more days at the rate we travel." Sophie said cheerfully. In the steeper grades of the pass the wagons were unhitched from the haulers (small heavy camelids used as teams for hauling wagons) and the wagons were sent down the grade on rope and tackle. Those riding walkers went ahead arriving in Winter Camp the next day. When all the wagons got down they were re-hitched and progressed until the next steep grade. Haulers were much slower than the walkers. The trail was rough and rocky. A small river flowed down one side of the canyon. Numerous waterfalls dotted the walls of the pass. Sophie pointed out land marks. "That ridge of black rocks is called the dragon's spine. That's the Bridal Veil Falls; it's much bigger in spring." Winter Camp having learning of their arrival sent out additional teams to assist their arrival. They descended into a beautiful green valley by the seaside. The new town of Port Hope glittering white was visible in the near distance. Several clans having arrived earlier, they were directed to their traditional camping area. They set up in the same order and precision of Summer Camp. The six friends walked into the town of Port Hope. The town had large whitewashed dormitories. The dormitories were five stories tall and each unit had its own plumbing. There were single bedroom units for newlyweds, with a small receiving room and kitchen. These were considered temporary arrangements as many of the newlyweds would be immigrating to the new world. There were also three and four bedroom units. These were meant for the families who would occupy the town and run the town during the several decades the immigration was to take place. Also, the families of the Roamy Navy would be quartered in the larger units. Most of the people would continue the pattern of seasonal migration until they were called to immigrate.

"In three days we will be sealed. Each clan has access to the sealing rooms on different days. We will talk about that after dinner. This will be our last two nights in the betrothal wagons. Let's try and get adjoining rooms in the dorms, even if we need to go to the fifth floor." Rosalind said. At dinner they discussed the ceremony. "Wear your best clothes. We will be picked up early in the day and taken to a beautiful grotto down the Echo canyon. You will be given a white robe that's water proof to wear in the grotto as it's frequently wet. Can't tell you much about the ceremony as its sacred and I've never seen it, but it will be a foursome as Robert and Jayne will be joining us," Rosalind continued. The couples were very excited. They did manage to get adjoining rooms on the second floor and made preparations to move in the day they were sealed. They had very little in the way of furnishings so little preparation was needed. The apartment did have a bed and a small table with two chairs. Derek planned to build a plank and block book shelf for Jamie's books. They would only be in the apartment less than four months before departing for the eastern continent.

Jamie was very restless the next two days. She was grateful for a calling that kept her busy. She and Sophie had been busy treating several minor injuries from the trek in. The valley in which Port Hope lay was semitropical. There were date and fig trees everywhere. The town sat in a small bay of the bluest water. All the homes and buildings were white washed. The shutters and doors brightly painted. There were brightly colored birds, many of them with no fear of people. Many of the homes had trumpet vines or window boxes with numerous flowers. The harbor was surrounded by a rock break water. The fleet had already started to arrive with the two largest and fastest ships tied up at the dock. The town was surrounded by a thirty foot wall. The wall also painted white with red, dark blue and green striping below the crenulations. The excitement was palpable. Ship stores were piled everywhere. Tons of supplies needed to start three self-sufficient colonies of two hundred souls each. The town was abuzz with talk about the new fleet and the immigration schedule.

The day for their sealing arrived and after the morning meal the four couples were transported down the Echo canyon to the sealing rooms. They put on the white robes and entered the first grotto. There they were instructed in the oath they would take. They would swear total fidelity to their spouse forswearing any sexual encounters with anyone outside their marriage. Then they were taken to an inner grotto that had a curtain of white water descending from an opening in the rocks above, blocking the view of the next room. There they were told that as they are now the gods once were. That this sacred covenant of marriage was binding on the gods only if they kept their oaths. That by accepting this they were bound together eternally. That by keeping the covenant they themselves had the potential to become gods and goddesses. That when they stepped through the veil of water they would enter an area that represents the afterlife and if reverent would feel the presence of the gods. Derek was the first to take the oath with Jamie then stepping through the veil of water reached back then drew Jamie through to him. The four couples stayed a very long time in the grotto. It was beautiful with lighting from openings above. Many colored clear crystals in the walls were reflecting and scattering light. Beautiful orchids were growing naturally in numerous clefts in the wall. They did indeed feel the presence of the gods.

Jamie and Derek were out and about the next day. They visited friends, walked in the town; they lay on the breakwater soaking their feet in the warm water. They ate figs and dates fresh from the numerous trees. Derek purchased seeds and he and Jamie fed the birds. The birds were emerald green with dark blue head plumage. They would land in Jamie's hand to take the seeds. Some perched on her shoulder. Derek did not have nearly the success Jamie had. They walked hand in hand. Most of their friends were surprised to see them about as most newlyweds sequestered themselves with other activities in mind. But they were both so overjoyed with their now eternal union. They were to be together forever. Derek confessed to Jamie that this was the happiest day in his life, and she agreed holding him tight in her embrace. "When was the first time you decided you loved me dearest sister." Derek asked.

"I'm not sure, my love, you just sort of grew on me like a fungus," she replied with a mischievous smile.

"What about the time you tried to lure me into bed?" Derek asked equally mischievous

"Which one? I thought I tried repeatedly, but you were so dense, dear brother?" They both laughed and enjoyed a long enduring kiss before returning to their apartment for further discussion.

They lay together face to face embracing. Jamie looked sleepy, her eyes partially shaded by her long eyelids. Derek kissing her forehead and spoke, "Yesterday I thought I could never love you more, but today I find that I do. You fill my senses, your skin against mine, the way you taste, the smell of your hair!" Derek moved his hand through her long dark hair. "I love to pleasure you and I love the way you feel when I make you sweat. You fill my soul and make me feel compete."

Jamie smiled and looking into Derek's eyes, "You are a romantic, beloved husband. I, too, love you more than yesterday. When you pleasure me with your touch I feel beautiful and desired. When you react to my touch I feel powerful. I can alter your breathing." Kissing Derek's lips in a long deep kiss his breathing quickened and became shallow. She then, moving her hand down his abdomen, "With my touch I can make your body stiffen." Derek's body stiffened as she reached this belly. "I like feeling beautiful and powerful. Earlier today when our bodies were joined I felt our souls touch. I want so much to have your baby my love. I want to feel the quickening of new life in my body and know our love gave it life."

"Keep moving you hand and you never know what might happen next little sister." Derek said roughly. Jamie smiled mischievously, her eyes darkened and her face flushing she bit her lower lip, pushed Derek over and rolled on top.

After several days the three couples, also accompanied by Robert and Jayne took walkers and went for a picnic in the mountains. They carried lunch and several other packs that Rosalind, Sophie and her brothers were rather secretive about. Sophie said "We are taking you to our secret valley. It's so beautiful. We can only visit it for a few weeks a year as it will be snowed in soon." They climbed for about three hours, then hobbling, the walkers descended a barely visible path down a steep wooded valley. They finally arrived into an open area. There were flowers in profusion and a small stream of water poured from a cleft in the rocks. They followed the stream for a quarter mile when the stream became a waterfall. The waterfall was about five feet tall and cascaded over several steps ending in a small pool of crystal clear water. The river then continued about five hundred feet and disappeared back into the rocks. Huge rocks with flat surfaces looked like tiny islands in the pool. Large green and brown fish were swimming slowly about the pool. A rustic bridge connected the shore to the largest rock island. Sophie continued, "Roland and Robert made this bridge about nine years ago. We always come to our secret valley when we are at winter camp. This will be our last time. I'm so excited to share it with you." They crossed the bridge and set up for a picnic on the island.

Roland then spoke, "Our family has known about this valley

for generations. The bridge was Roz's idea when she first came here. The water is freezing cold but swim if you want." Jamie slowly extended one foot into the water only to withdraw it quickly.

"Freezing! You weren't kidding. What's in those bags you brought along?"

"Lunch," Sophie replied.

"Nice try, Sophie. The other bags you all have been so secretive about?" Sophie opened the bags and withdrew her wheeled fiddle; Rosalind's bowed fiddle, flat drums and several woodwinds.

"We decided that we would have a little music and singing after our picnic. I have a special song in mind for you, David," Sophie said smiling seductively. "And besides we are going to teach you to sing." Derek moaned and David blushed when Sophie mentioned a song just for him.

"I would love to sing Sophie! I'll be your apprentice." Jamie responded They ate a leisurely lunch then tuned the instruments. Rosalind and Sophie worked with Jamie and Derek. David surprised everyone with a deep baritone voice. They worked on several of the songs that had been popular in camp and on the road. Then as evening approached Sophie turned to David and said, "Now I got something special just for you!" She sat tailor style in front of him their knees touching. Jayne played the wheeled fiddle; Robert the flat drum; Rosalind a double reed woodwind. Sophie started her song slowly. Her words and gestures provocative and sensual. David blushing and smiling could not keep his eyes from Sophie as she sang teasing and touching him lightly from shoulders and face. Jamie and Derek were mesmerized by Sophie's skills. Then to Roland's surprise Rosalind took up the second verse sitting tailor style in front of him. Her performance was equally provocative and sensual. The song ended with David and Roland breathless locked in their wives arms.

"Roz you are the most surprising and sensual woman in the world!" Roland gasped breathlessly.

"Sophie taught me the song. I wanted to surprise you. Now, Jamie, we are going to teach you this little number."

"That would be wonderful!" Jamie said looking at Derek, her eyes dark and her face flushed. "What about Jayne?"

"Don't worry about me Jamie. I taught it to Sophie. And used it on Robert. I think that's why he finally got around suggesting we marry. Otherwise I fear I'd still be waiting."

Robert laughed. "It certainly sped up my decision making."

Preparations continued in earnest for the voyage. It would be two years before the ships could return to the colony so the preparations were very important. Sufficient stores of food for two years were essential. Also, fruit bearing trees of every kind, grains for planting, tubers and every kind of plant and vegetable, livestock for food, wool, milk, and work. They would need enough livestock to reproduce itself sufficiently, tools of every kind, grinding stones, looms, iron, bolts of cloth, leather for shoes and harnesses, nails, and books of every kind for instruction. Each of the three colonies would need to be totally self-supporting in two years. They would also need to discover products they could export so they could fund further immigrants. Those who would go had to have the skills needed to sustain the colony, those with multiple skills and those with agriculture skills were top on the list. It was further decided that the initial colonist would not bring children, but this was dropped as they needed the talent some of those with children possessed. That meant that much of those going were newlyweds and parents with small children. Admiral Casmir was released from his calling in the navy and was called with his wife, Ruth, to be Lord Grandfather of the colony. Life for the three couples settled in to a routine of preparation and planning. Jamie and Sophie would examine the flora and fauna of the new world for additional remedies and food. David would search the immediate vicinity of the colony for minerals. Derek would seek a water source for three mills and organize construction of earthen dams. Rosalind would organize the store house and method of distribution of household goods. Roland was called to be president of the first colony with David and Robert as his counselors. Rosalind was called to be headwoman, Jayne as her assistant. Two other colonies were similarly organized; Derek's calling had him serving all three colonies. One last task was left. That of bringing the next years supplies of salt to the storage facilities at Summer Camp. A general meeting was called to request volunteers. David was the first to raise his hand. Fifty men would go in as forty-eight sledge teams. The others acting as scouts and back up. The salt was already packed in sledges; they would pull them the two hundred miles to Summer Camp over the frozen river. They would use walkers for the first time hoping to increase the speed and perhaps allow a second load this season. Prior to leaving Derek had received communication that his family was aware that he was going to the eastern continent with his new wife and his sister Rosie. Derek was greatly relieved by their knowledge. Married less than a fortnight and three couples would be separating. This first separation would be difficult for all.

Chapter 10 The Ice Road

There was much sadness in the camp as the men bade farewell to loved ones. Jamie, Rosalind and Sophie huddled together and watched as the men slowly disappeared in the distance. Outwardly Jamie appeared composed and serene but inwardly she was not. Sophie had obviously been crying, crying a lot. Her eyes were red and her face blotchy, her carrot red hair and pale skin only served to emphasize the blotchiness. Rosalind who usually appeared as unflappable seemed frightened and sad. They had been married two weeks, now the men would be gone for at least two months, perhaps more. When the men were gone from sight they turned and returned to their homes.

This was the largest assembly of walkers yet. Each of the men had two walkers. On the road to the salt flats one walker would be used as the pack carrier the other ridden. Then on the ice road the animals would be used in pairs to pull the sledge. Walkers could easily make fifty miles in a day. The animals usually were worked about two and half hours rested and then worked another two and half hours. When Derek and Jamie had been rescued the walkers had been rode ten hours straight then rested for longer periods. But the truth was that no one really knew what the animals could do. They were susceptible to heat stroke and could be pushed until they collapsed and died, but this they needed to avoid at all cost. Walkers were not very prodigious breeders. The females did not breed until the age of fifteen and then only calf every third year. Roland was given the task of testing and pushing the walkers on the trip out so their future potential could be assessed. The haulers could only make fifteen miles per day. This meant that the trip from the salt flats to the storage facility at Summer Camp would take two weeks, with the walker four days, perhaps less. The distance to the salt flats from Winter Camp was about nine hundred miles. With haulers that would be at least two months travel with walkers about a fortnight. The calculations looked good but it had never been tried. Most of the Roamy's precious walkers were with them. This trip would test both man and beast to the limit. The stakes were very high. Roland then enlisted David, Derek and his older brother in his task. Two of their walkers designated as pack animals were hitched to a wheeled cart. This served to test the animal's ability to pull and teach the men how to use the walkers as a team. The cart also had a highly accurate odometer built into the wheels so accurate measurements of speed and distance could be made. Three other clans would also send expeditions to the salt flats. These would be larger groups and handled in the normal manner using the slower tried and true haulers. They would depart separately with four days between each group.

As they ascended up out of the Pass Of The Shepherds they came into heavy snow. The snow was very dry and blew around not accumulating. There was concern if the animals could find enough to sustain themselves so several tons of fodder were carried on the pack animals. Eventually they learned that had not been necessary as the desert had sufficient plant life. Water had also been a concern so tools were brought to break any frozen ice on the water holes. The biggest surprise was when they observed the walkers could find sufficient water in the snow. The men had been apprehensive of letting the animals eat the snow fearing hypothermia but there was no stopping a hundred walkers from doing anything. Their first camp was about twenty miles from the pass in the high desert. Roland's crew was also asked to act as scouts and message bearers. This was their first experience on the ice road so they deferred to more senior members for planning and decisions. Rumpole was the group leader. At fifty-nine he was the most experienced and senior member. This was his thirty-ninth ice road trip and he looked forward to many more. Usually his wife accompanied him but not this trip as they were pushing the limit of experience. Rumpole approached Roland, "Tomorrow have two of your animals leave camp about two hours early and run them as fast as you can for an hour, then rest your walkers until we catch up. We can measure the distance and check the walker's condition. Light a smoker flair so we can come and find you easier."

The next morning, after eating, Derek and David left the camp pushing their walkers into a galloping run. They felt like they were flying. The animals gait had become increasingly rocking then at full gallop it became smooth which made it really feel like flying. As they approached the hour mark they noted the animals were foaming at the mouth so they slowed them for the last few minutes. When they stopped the walkers squatted down. Derek and David carried large warming blankets but since the animals were not sweating they did not cover them. David lit the smoke flair and they waited. A little over three hours later the caravan caught up with them. Rumpole was pleased, "You made thirty-four miles. How did the animals react?" He then inspected the walkers and became even more pleased. Roland and his brother had taken the cart. The walkers had not responded well to the use of reins so they ended up with each of them riding mounted on a walker and the animals were easy to control. They had no problem pulling. Tomorrow they would increase the weight of the cart and other teams of men would ride the cart animals. Derek and David's walkers had stood at the approach of the caravan so they were apparently ready to go on. The caravan decided to go ten hours then stop for the night. They made exactly fifty-three miles that first day. The men were elated that night in camp.

It took sixteen days to reach the storage area. Two days longer than they had hoped but still excellent timing. They had learned a lot about their walkers. They were fast and by establishing a series of relay stations they could link the semaphore station at Eastedge village to Summer Camp then to Port Hope and get and receive messages in two days instead of weeks. This would greatly increase their ability to listen in on Imperial activities and do counter moves. They had already implemented this by sending a speedy messenger back to Port Hope.

They also had some disappointments as the walkers could not match the pulling capacity of the haulers. They were much faster but could only manage a third of the load. Even by increasing the pulling team to four walkers it only increased the hauling capacity slightly. It was good that the other clans were using the haulers or they would not have sufficient salt storage. Rumpole sat in counsel with the men "We need to lessen the load in the sledges by two thirds and we need to be on the ice day after tomorrow. We need to start slow and maintain sufficient space. I will lead. You need to stay in my tracks as I will follow the thickest ice. If you go too fast the ice will blow out. When we stop leave the sledge on the ice but get the walker off as we will not camp on the ice." The men nodded in agreement and they began to remove some of the salt cakes from the sledges. The salt cakes were formed into cake shaped wheels each weighing about forty-five pounds. They could easily be carried or rolled and stacked easily. Once the unloading was finished and the sledges weight adjusted they began the placement of the sledges on the ice using a block and tackle. The sledges were then positioned along the ice road and the men settled down for the evening meal and rest.

The next morning teams of walkers were hitched to the sledges. The animals growled loudly with displeasure but the task was accomplished. A rider would mount one walker and control both animals. They had forty-eight sledges in the ice. Initially many riders had difficulty getting the walkers to pull in unison but by the second hour all the kinks had been worked out, and by the end of the day they had made forty-eight miles. It took only six days to reach the storage facility at Summer Camp. The men made quick work of unloading. Then they began to disassemble the sledges and pack them as they would be floated back to the salt flats in the spring during the high water on flat boats. Rumpole discussed the possibility of a second trip to and from the salt flats but an urgent messenger from Port Hope arrived with other orders.

The Imperial army was to be dispatched against a fishing guild village. The village was on a lake that fed into the River Skell via the Red River. They would have easy access to the village over the ice, and Lord Grandfather has requested the village be evacuated. The village consisted of forty adults, about eight were Roamy living inside Imperial territory. The village was under forfeiture as the Imperial City wanted to make them an example to reduce costs of the fish they imported. They believed other fishing villages would see this and either increase production or sell below costs. The population was to be culled and the rest sold into slavery. This would be a race against time. The sledges were unpacked and reassembled and the party resumed the ice road trek.

Derek and David were riding scout the day of their arrival at the village of Lake Pleasant and entered the village a few hours before the main body of walkers. Most of the population had never seen walkers and were standing in the village square with expressions of awe. Still mounted on his walker Derek began to explain their plan to evacuate the village as Imperial forces were planning their destruction. This information was met with disbelief and refusal to leave by most of the population. The village counsel chief was the most loudly vocal, "We have nothing to fear from the imperial army. They are pledged to protect our lives and property. They would never be allowed to..."

While he spoke David removed his coat and shirt to reveal his tattoo. The effect was riveting and all eyes were on David as he described the action of the guard on the small village of Holly he had witnessed. His narrative ended as he wept and told of the valiant little blonde girl that dared to resist. The effect was like ice water was pored over the crowd as mothers clutched their children closely. Even the counsel chief sputtered on his words. David continued, "We have forty-eight sledges that will arrive here in a few hours. You will be only able to take essentials. We need to be off by first light so please go and make ready with haste!" They then began a door to door canvassing of the village to ensure everyone was aware of the evacuation. One home looked vacant and was posted with a yellow cross on the door. Derek pushed the door and slowly entered.

The smell of death in the home was clawing as Derek entered. It was winter yet the loud buzz of flies filled the air. As he moved slowly through the house he found the bodies of an adult male and female and two boys not yet ten years old. The woman had been dead only a few hours the male and children much longer. As he made ready to leave he heard weeping and went to the kitchen. A young woman (or girl he thought) lay on the floor. "Please don't leave me alone!" she cried in mortal anguish. Derek lifted her into his arms and exited the home as David arrived.

"Don't go in there David it's a death house!" David reached to take the girl but Derek shook his head. "Please, no David, we can't afford to expose both of us. You go ahead and organize the evacuation. I will stay with her until we can catch up. Leave me a walker in the stable and we...I will leave before the troops arrive." The look David gave him was of pain; David did not expect either to survive. He walked with the girl in his arms to the adjoining home only to have the door blocked by an angry village chief.

"You can't bring her in here, she's dying. This is my home!"

Derek responded with a menacing growl "You are just leaving. So go!" The chief and his family quickly left as Derek laid the weeping girl on a sofa and covered her with a blanket he took from a bed. "I got you here now. I won't leave you. Can you tell me your name?"

"Rebecca, but I prefer Becky. You should have left me. I'm so sorry. I'm going to die and I was so scared. Please you can't stay or you will die too!" Becky continued to weep quietly. She was shaking and her breathing labored. She was sweating and her hair was wet and plastered to her scalp. She convulsed with a bubbly cough and finally slept. Derek explored the house and found a small bed which he disassembled and brought into the kitchen and assembled near the hearth. Then he gently placed the still sleeping Becky on the bed and covered her. Then he began a careful search of the home. A meal was still in preparation in the oven and a small cake was cooling on the table. Tea was brewing and a dark beer sitting on the table. He also found additional linen and blankets and moved a rocking chair into position next to Becky's bed. Then he watched as the sledges arrived in the village and were loaded and preparations made. He saw the counsel chief pointing at his home and gesturing angrily as Rumpole and David spoke to him. Rumpole just threw up his arms and walked away. David stood looking at Derek through the window, he said nothing. Night fell as Becky slept on. Derek watched as the sledges left at first light. Roland, David and Robert stopped by as they spoke through the window. They tried their best to appear hopeful but sadness radiated from his friends. Then he and Becky were alone.

When Derek returned to the kitchen Becky was awake she had been weeping until she saw Derek. "I thought you left me like everyone else! Please you must not stay!" As she looked around the room she stared with surprise at Derek, "How did you manage the chief's house, he refused to help us when my Dad got sick, he refused to send for a healer!" Derek sat on the bed and took her hand.

"My name is Derek, I will not leave so consider yourself stuck with my presence. Would you like some food?"

She shook her head, "Been unable to eat for a couple of days but I am so hungry!" Derek poured a small glass of the dark beer and got a small bowl of the thin stew and set Becky up in the bed using pillows.

"I'm reluctant to give you the beer sweet thing as you're so young, I'm guessing, but you look about thirteen. The beer will stimulate your appetite and has a lot of calories."

Becky smiled, "My Da always called me sweet thing. I will...or would have been sixteen next week. Oh, I wish so much I could have one more birthday!" The last words brought a sad look to her face but she quickly recovered and tried to spoon some of the stew to her mouth but her hand shook so much she stopped. Derek wordlessly picked up the spoon and began to feed her. "Sweet thing was our private joke because I was the village hoyden."

Derek smiled, "You a tomboy? Why you're just a feather of a girl."

"I could out run, out swim and out climb all the boys. I was very popular until the chief discovered we were Roamy. Then we were alone. Only a few families would speak to us. The last three years have been so hard. My older brother died last winter. Now all of my family." Derek continued to feed her and then got her to drink the dark beer. "My Da would let me drink beer. Ma would have been scandalized!" She smiled at Derek. "You are so kind. I wish..." She was asleep before she finished. Derek then continued his search of the home as she slept. He found some willow bark which he knew would help Becky's fever, but he felt impotent to do much else. He wanted Becky to live more than anything. He felt his eyes water as he looked at Becky.

Derek dozed off on the rocking chair next to Becky and was awakened late that afternoon by her coughing and quiet weeping. "I'm here sweet thing. You're not alone!"

"Oh Derek, I'm so sorry but I've soiled myself, I didn't want to tell you but I'm so uncomfortable, I'm so sorry!" she wept.

"Not to worry Becky, I helped take care of my sister when she was sick. I can handle this." Derek got a large basin, he had been warming water for tea but used the water to wash Becky. He covered her with a soft blanket and only exposing a little of her at a time bathed her and washed her hair. He found a shirt (the village chief's he hoped) and dressed Becky. It was huge and covered her well below her knees. Then remaking the bed used pillows to set her up and combed out her hair. She had thick strawberry blond hair and blue eyes. She watched him quietly with her large expressive sad blue eyes as he took care of her, her long wavy hair spread over her pillow. She possessed a terrible serene poignant beauty despite the gauntness in her face. Needing to break the stillness between them Derek asked, "What happened sweet thing?"

Becky began her narrative. "My Da had returned across the ice from a visit to a village in the north. On the way back he had fallen through the ice but managed to free himself and make it home. He had taken a terrible chill and developed a cough and fever. My Ma went to the village chief to summon a healer but was refused. My home was placed in quarantine and the village ordered to shun us. Our friends continued to bring us food usually late at night to the back door. Da died several days ago but not before my little brothers took sick. Ma cried a lot, she was so sick herself, and begged me to run. I lied and told her I was okay. I took care of her and my brothers. Ma died the day before you came, my brothers a day or so before. I didn't get to coughing till very late so Ma thought I was okay. I felt so alone and frightened. I just lay on the kitchen floor hoping to die quickly. I lay there for hours before you came, why are you so good to me Derek? You could have run. You still can. I won't blame you."

"My brave little Becky, how could I leave you? I will not give up easily. I want you to live sweet thing!" Derek said as he lifted her into the rocking chair and she rested her head on his shoulder as he kissed her forehead. He quietly rocked her as he stroked her head. Becky slept again. Her breathing less laborious when Derek sat her up. She still was racked by a bubbly cough. In his heart Derek knew Becky had very little time. So he considered ways to bring her a little joy. He gently returned her to the bed them went into the kitchen with a plan.

It was very dark in the house when Becky woke again. Derek was in the rocking chair. "Hello sweet thing, I've got a little stew and more of the beer for you and a surprise dessert, would you like to eat a little?"

"Life is short, so let's have dessert first!" She said with a bright smile as she watched Derek with her hauntingly blue eyes.

"Well, I got you a cake, compliments of the chief, frosted it myself." He brought out the cake, it had candles on it and Derek lit the candles. "Happy sweet sixteen Becky!" The look in Becky's face made Derek glad of his decision. There was sadness mixed with joy. She smiled looking into his eyes. Derek kissed her forehead, "Happy birthday..."his voice choked and he could say no more.

"My noble Derek, you are so sweet! You will have to feed me again but I would love some cake." Becky was smiling with tears in her eyes as she managed a tiny bite.

"You are so brave sweet thing. You are noble, not me."

"I'm not as brave as you think my dear Derek. I'm still scared. But it's...I know that I will be okay. I accept that I'm dying. I pray for you. I want you to live and be happy. My fear is for you." Derek lifted her into his lap and rocked her. "I so much want to see the sun rise just one more time," she said. Derek moved the rocking chair to a large window facing east across the lake. Then he resumed rocking Becky in the chair as they wordlessly watched and waited for the morning sun. The sun rose majestically into a red and purple sky. The gods apparently sent a special sun rise for Becky Derek thought.

"Look sweet thing, it's so beautiful. I had forgotten how much beauty there is in the world! I'm so glad to share this with you."

Becky reached up and gently stroked Derek's cheek. Looking into his eyes she said "You are beautiful, Derek...I've never been kissed by a boy?" Derek paused then kissed her forehead. "No silly, here," and she touched her finger to her lip. So Derek smiled and very gently kissed her lips. She smiled back at him and slept.

It was still early in the morning when Becky awoke still in Derek's arms. "Look Derek, my Ma and Da are here. All my brothers too. I'm so happy. Ma says the gods heard my prayer. You will get very ill, but you are married to a gifted healer. You will be okay. She will find the cure so no one else will die from my illness." Becky put her arms around Derek's neck and buried her face in his shoulder. "I love you Derek. Please don't forget me. Be happy my love!" She slept again and Derek continued to hold her. He held her until he was alone.

Derek then returned her body to the bed by the hearth and spread lamp oil about the kitchen and set the home on fire as he left. Then moving house to house he set the other homes ablaze. As he walked to the town shed he was met by Roland and David. "What are you doing here?"

"Did you really think you could just wave us off? We have been waiting for you," Roland said smiling.

David interrupted, "The Imperials are about three hours away. I spotted them earlier this morning. Your bonfire will bring the pickets and scouts here earlier. We need to get." The walkers were already prepared so the three friends left. Derek's heart ached as he rode past Becky's home. It took four days to catch up with the sledges. By the time they arrived the villagers had been taken in by several Roamy fishing communities along the River Skell.

By the time they had returned to Summer Camp Derek was having chills and fever. The sledges needed to be broken down once more and packed. They kept one to carry Derek home. Roland, David and Robert assumed the role as caretaker as they headed to Winter Camp.

Chapter 11 Three Sisters

The men had left for the salt run and the new wives were left alone. Jamie was acutely aware of her loneliness and having had slept with Derek found the loneliness much harder to bear. That morning she received a surprise, Rosalind and Sophie showed up at her door with cots, bedding and travel bags. "We decided to move back in with you sister girlfriend, it's just too lonely without the men." Sophie explained. The three hugged and all talked about their loneliness after being married then so quickly separated. Rosalind and Sophie could not decide who had first thought of the plan but Jamie felt in her heart it was divinely inspired. The three of them together would be a tremendous support for each other and help the time to pass quicker. Sophie was so much more subdued since marrying David and becoming her apprentice. Frequently she was the stalwart pillar of the team.

"You are both welcome, sister girlfriends. I truly love you both and it was very difficult to let Derek go. I wanted to scream and cry and beg him to stay, but I held back so he wouldn't have to worry about me. I was nearly at wits end and you both came. I'm so happy to have you here!"

"I did a lot of blubbering on David's shoulder, but he was so kind and gentle I finally relented. I was really starting to enjoy him." Sophie said blushing. Rosalind then began organizing the small apartment to accommodate all three.

"Think of this as a big slumber party!" Rosalind said smiling.

The days did not pass quickly. Jamie and Sophie were able to keep busy with their calling as healer midwife, and Rosalind with planning for the colonies physical requirement that needed to be packed, but the days dragged on and on. Many a night found the sisters in tears usually with Sophie in the center holding both of her friends. They had regular contact with other young women many of whom were also newlyweds. Some of the young women also had small children so Rosalind set up a support group and assisted with baby care. They also spent a lot of time holding lonely weeping women. The Three Sisters became their unofficial title as they helped rally the sagging morale of the young women left behind.

Sophie organized the young women in singing. She would play the wheeled fiddle and Rosalind would lead. Jamie, after gentle encouragement, joined in and was startled to learn that she could sing well. Jamie, after instruction, became adept with the flat drum. The music had a strong therapeutic effect on the lonely women. Sometimes passing people would stop and sit near the dorm just to enjoy the singing. The sad songs were the most often sung, but Sophie also knew a number of seductive and lively songs and these were included each night. The song Sophie had sung to David was one the young women were enthusiastic to learn and eager to perform when the men returned.

Then they received news that all was well with the men. They had just entered the Pass Of The Shepherds and should start arriving late the next day. There was much excitement and happy rejoicing amongst the young women when Rosalind noticed Jamie sitting, looking very pale and weeping quietly. She and Sophie rushed to her side. "It's Derek, he's dying. I just felt it in my soul. I don't know what to do!" They quickly surrounded her and waited for her to finish weeping.

"You and Sophie are healers and damn good ones!" Rosalind said with conviction.

"I need to compose myself!" Jamie whispered. "Can't have Derek see me like this!"

When Derek did arrive on a stretcher bore by his closest friends, Roland and David, his friends looked worried and grim. "I got this little lung infection, little sister," Derek said wheezing and barely able to talk. "So here I am, some of the men said I'm dying but they have no idea what a gifted healer you are, my love, feel much better just seeing you!"

"And I seeing you dearest brother. We are here just for you." Jamie said smiling, giving no appearance of the utter panic she was feeling. "David and Roland, please put him on our bed and get some rest yourselves. We can handle things from here." The men nodded then hugging their wives left. As they undressed Derek, Jamie noted he was burning with a fever. "First thing my love you are going to get a cool bath so we can break the fever!" Jamie's mind raced as she mentally reviewed the keynotes of symptoms but to no avail. Now she was really panicked. Then as Derek slept the women prayed. They prayed for Derek and they prayed for guidance.

Jamie's first choice of remedy was Kali Bichromicium. This she administered to Derek and waited as she explained to Sophie that while her choice did not really fit the symptoms it was a remedy that was used successfully on lung infections. After four hours and no response to the remedy Derek developed a severe racking cough and his fever continued unabated. Jamie then tried Ipecacunha and this stopped most of the coughing. The next series of coughing spasms were not nearly as severe but Derek had greenish sputum. Jamie tried two additional remedies based on keynote symptoms, but Derek seemed to be slipping farther away. "Derek are you getting enough air?" Sophie asked.

"I'm breathing okay just so very, very tired." Derek replied. Sixteen hours had passed and there was no significant change in Derek. The three sisters continued the sponge baths and were relieved regularly by David and Roland. The three sisters were back on duty while the men rested when Jamie looked up with a startled expression.

"I've got it, I know what to do. Roz get the men back and get some sleep. Sophie you follow me and bring that piece of linen Derek coughed into. We are going to try something unorthodox, Sophie. My dad never did this in his practice but we did talk about it. We are going to create a new remedy. A sort of nosode based on Derek's own sputum. You will help me make it." Sophie assisted as Jamie got out the glass vials and measuring instruments. She also got water and grain alcohol. As she measured and poured Sophie succussed the mixtures. This procedure continued until Jamie had three different doses. "We will mix these and make a remedy chord. This is also my first time using LM potencies. This remedy will also take care of anyone else; we can use it as a vaccine"

"I followed your choices in the other remedies and could understand your choice and logic, but this I don't understand!" Sophie said.

"I will explain the theories later. Now we begin to administer." Jamie and the team met at Derek's bed side." We will be using a liquid remedy and administering a dose every twenty minutes. Once the fever breaks the men can take a break. I would suggest a nap. We need to continue the sponge bath until the fever breaks. We will continue the dose for as long as Derek is awake. Let us begin!" The group commenced the plan. Five hours later the fever broke and David and Roland left to rest. They continued the dosing another six hours then Derek finally slept.

"Now we are ready for the healing circle," Jamie said. "I had to clear as much of the infection as I could first. We will start with a scan then proceed. As Derek is so ill I could easily die while laying on hands. If you feel me passing you must break the circle or all of us could die. It will feel like a punch to your heart to break but you must let us go."

The sisters grimly nodded and Jamie started with a scan. "His infection is contained but both lungs have areas of collapse or consolidation. His life energy is very low his aura gray to black. I'm scared out of my wits. Let's pray together first then proceed." The sisters took their position in the healing circle and Jamie placed one hand on Derek's solar plexus the other over his navel then willed their life force to Derek. She visualized Derek's lungs as a great tree in his chest. It was upside down with two great branches. She followed the branches as they continued to part into smaller and smaller branches and finally into leaves. Then she sent green energy into the millions of leaves until all were glowing green. She was sweating heavily. Derek's aura now began to glow a faint white. Over five hours had passed and Jamie knew he would live. She untangled the energy chord and relinquished Sophie's and Rosalind's life energy. She then willed her life energy to maintain a connection to Derek. Then she broke the circle. Rosalind and Sophie collapsed on to their cots and slept and Jamie removed her skirt and climbed into bed with Derek. They all slept exhausted by their efforts.

Derek was the first to stir. He had felt Jamie lying beside him for some time before waking, "It's so good to see your face, my love. Just seeing you and I feel so much better! You are glowing my love I see white light and green light flowing around you. You look so very beautiful. I see a white light connecting me to you...what happened?"

Jamie looked with sleepy eyes into Derek's eyes and smiled. Her heart raced with joy leaving her speechless. Rosalind and Sophie awoke when they heard Derek's voice and Sophie sat on the foot of their bed. "Oh my! Jamie, Roz look at Derek's hair." They were shocked to see Derek's blonde hair was now totally gray. Derek felt his head.

"Have I gone bald or something?" he asked anxiously.

Rosalind brought him a mirror "What happened? Looks like I aged fifty years."

"It means you will live my love. We have by the grace of the gods brought you back from the brink." At that point Jamie began to sob quickly followed by Rosalind and Sophie which in turn brought the men rushing in expecting to find Derek dead. David and Roland, at first shocked by Derek's gray hair, then gathered their wives in their arms much relieved by Derek's recovery.

"Hey guys, what does a man have to do to get something to eat?" Derek asked. That brought a chorus of laughter. Sophie made a tray of hot soup while Rosalind brought bread and cheese. Jamie just stayed in bed clinging, looking so happy she literally glowed. Derek served, the friends took their leave, leaving the couple alone. "Little sister you look so tired, your hair is wild, your face is smudged and you are in bed with me and nothing between us except that scant shirt of yours. I have never seen you so beautiful or desirable."

Derek's full recovery took weeks. He tired very easily and slept a lot. He was able to walk short distances by the second day. He ate a great deal. He had lost over twenty pounds while ill. His hair color never returned to its original blonde, but Jamie loved him; that is all he cared about. He told her of the rescue run to save the little hamlet. He told Jamie about the brave little Becky and her passing. Later his friends would tell him of his illness and their labors to save him. Jamie relinquished her gift of energy slowly over a few days and then mourned the loss of the intimacy of that connection. Derek had a deep gratitude to his friends, and an even deeper gratitude to his wife's skills as a healer. Jamie was grateful too, to friends who she loved dearly and to the gods that had inspired her. While Derek convalesced he was given books to read on dam building, water wheel construction, water management, plant husbandry and related subjects. Jamie also allowed Sophie greater reign in handling the more routine care, allowing her more time with Derek.

Chapter 12 Port Hope

Sophie laughed and twirled with delight as she and Rosalind escorted Jamie to a special meeting they had arranged. Jamie had no idea why her friends were so giddy. Derek was still convalescing but her friends had been so excited and insistent that she was finally persuaded to go. "Okay Sophie, Roz where are you taking me?"

"Our lips are sealed!" laughed Rosalind. The excitement of the pair was palpable as they made their way across the harbor to the large whitewashed dorm buildings. Three more of the ships had arrived including the admirals flag ship. Jamie knew nothing of ships but it was big, five masts. There was a lot of activity on board as carpenters scurried across on thin planks.

"So you got me out to see the boats?" Jamie asked, a little peeved.

"No!" They replied in unison. Refusing to say more the trio continued to walk in silence. They finally arrived at a door painted red. There were red window boxes on the two windows that flanked the door with red and pink impatients growing and trailing down. Rosalind knocked and the door was opened by a tall bald well-tanned man. Sophie and Rosalind drew Jamie into the apartment smiling with great delight at the man in the door. Rosalind started "Jamie, we would like to introduce you to Admiral Casey, your grandfather." Sophie and Rosalind hugged the admiral and his wife as Jamie stood, mouth agape, looking at the admiral and her two friends. Admiral Casmir took her hand holding with both of his and looked deeply into her eyes.

His voice cracked as he said, "You have your grandmother's eyes and hair. You look so much like my dear Elly." Then he folded her into his arms for a long hug. "I never knew you lived until these two sweet girls found me. Elly died in childbirth and your mother was fostered to my cousin as I was in the navy and at sea. I knew Elly had died, I was unaware of you. I am so delighted to see you."

"That's only half of it. Jamie, his cousin is Lord Grandfather, my great grandfather! Jamie we REALLY are kin, sisters by blood and marriage!" Sophie blurted twirling.

Admiral Casmir continued, "This is your step-grandmother Ruth." Ruth, smiling with absolute delight, hugged Jamie; she was short and plump and Jamie enjoyed the softness of her warm hug.

"I can imagine this must be overwhelming to you Jamie." Jamie unable to speak just shook her head yes and hugged her grandfather again.

Ruth was the next to speak, "They call you the three sisters, so can I just call all three of you my grandchildren?" The reply of yes was unanimous.

Casmir, smiling at his wife said, "You have a knack for collecting children, my dear wife." Then he spoke to the three sisters, "Every officer in the Roamy navy and some in the Imperial navy call her Mother Ruth. She is loved by every young man that has sailed with us."

"Now I have some girls too! Please sit, I have tea and cucumber sandwiches for us all." They spent the afternoon talking. Jamie was surprised Admiral Casmir knew so much of her history. She knew she had Roz and Sophie to thank. Admiral Casmir spoke of his first wife Ella who had died in their first year of marriage. He had been given his first command and had married Ella shortly before returning to sea. He met Ruth five years later and they were wed after a three month courtship. Ruth had been at sea with him since the wedding. While they had no children Ruth collected foster children whom she loved dearly. The three sisters were her latest acquisition. "Have you ladies any plans for the talent contest next week? I have heard from Lord Grandfather that you had organized the young women into singing sessions while the men were gone. I know how much music can stir the soul. That was an inspired service you did for those grieving women."

Jamie replied, "Yes we are planning a song would you like to hear it. We have no music now but could do it, music adds a lot of drama but you would get the feel." After they were given a nod the three sisters sang their song and explained how they would use drums, wheeled fiddle and woodwinds to add drama and depth to the song." Ruth was delighted; she suggested they perform the song standing and dance at the same time. Rosalind blushed, but Sophie was excited by the suggestion.

Ruth demonstrated some of the slow sultry dance moves that were from the southern islands and volunteered to help with costumes, "I actually sew quite well; just ask any of my young men. It would be fun to sew for girls; you are all such pretty girls!" That led to a long discussion in possibilities for appropriate costumes and all four of the women were so excited and energized by the discussion that Admiral Casmir just sat and watched his beloved Ruth. He never knew how much she had wanted girls. These young women were just what she needed now that they would separate from the navy. Ruth needed a focus for the tremendous reservoir of love in her heart.

When the three sisters left Jamie felt as giddy as the others, "Thank you so much Sophie and Roz," She said. "If not for you we would have never met!" Jamie continued, "If we dance like that...Derek will go nuts! I can't wait to see his face! All the others will be sitting or standing for their numbers."

Sophie exclaimed, "This could be more fun than I ever dreamed. Roz why are you blushing so?"

Jamie put her arm around Rosalind and Sophie joined her. "Roz you are a beautiful woman, it can be fun to flaunt it once in a while. Roland really liked that song you did at the picnic!"

Rosalind blushing an even deeper shade of red laughing, "He really did. Done it several more times since, won't discuss what I wore or didn't." Rosalind looked much happier as the trio continued their discussion. They would keep their plans secret until the contest. It was wonderful to have such an interesting and unusual grandmother. They met several more times with Grandmother Ruth and worked out the costumes and the dance. Grandmother suggested they have two additional numbers ready in case more were requested. The three sisters stated that would never happen, but they did prepare the additional songs and dance numbers.

When the time came for fitting of the costumes Grandmother Ruth was as excited as the three sisters. "You three are so tiny and pretty. We need to take advantage of your gifts, not hide them." They all had ankle length dresses. The dresses were a chestnut color with some red in it to emphasize Sophie red hair and the red highlights of Jamie's and Rosalind's. The dresses had a square cut along the bodice and were cut a little lower than Rosalind usually wore and were off the shoulder with long sleeves. The dresses where tight fitting and emphasize their small waist and flat stomach. The sides of the dresses were open on both sides to the knee to facilitate their dance moves. Each had a wide silk sash around their waist which lifted and supported their breasts. Jamie's and Rosalind's were red and Sophie's emerald green. Sophie also had a wide emerald green belt to hold her wheeled fiddle just below her waist so she could dance while she played. Grandmother Ruth also made head gear for them to give them a little height. The head gear fitted on their head from the crown to the nape of the neck. It basically was an open cone about a hand span deep and looked like it was made from a wound silk scarf. It had long colored ribbons that would trail down their back. Their ears were uncovered and three long braids trailed down in front of their ears to their waist. The rest of their hair exited the back of the head gear in a mix of braids, curls and ribbons. The head gear matched their sash in color. Grandmother Ruth also showed them how the women did their makeup in the southern islands. The brows and lashes were darkened and a dark line extended past the outside end of the eye and a short vertical line extended down toward their cheek from the inside edge. The effect would enhance the size of their eyes under the lime lights. They wore anklets with bells to give then an additional source of sound and rhythm. They also had a mock diamond affixed to their forehead just above the brow ridge.

The night of the music contest had arrived. The three sisters were slated to go last. It had aleray been a long night and much of the audience was tired. The stage was dark as they entered and assumed their starting pose. They had ditched their shoes just prior to getting on stage as Sophie could not bear to keep her shoes on. When the lime lights were lit it revealed the three. Rosalind stood in the center flanked by Jamie and Sophie. Jamie held a large flat drum high in the air, Rosalind a long deep drum and Sophie the wheeled fiddle. Sophie started by sounding only the drone stings. Then Jamie started with a slow syncopated rhythm, a little later Rosalind added the counter rhythm. Once the music was started the trio began to dance. Their dance movements were slow as they swayed their hips and abdomens with the music. The open sides of the dress emphasizing their bare feet and shapely calves. Then they started the song. At the end of the first verse they paused the music for several seconds then Jamie gave a loud boom, boom on the drum and they began the chorus. This was much faster than the verses and Sophie cranked the wheeled fiddle faster to produce a buzzing rhythm. They made several instrument changes with

Rosalind playing alternately the double reed pipe, and her bowed fiddle. With each instrument change they altered their dance and position to feature each instrument. Sophie played bag pipes and single reed woodwind, Jamie the tin whistle. Several verses were sung, followed by the chorus. Derek, David and Roland were in the audience and were overwhelmed by their wives beauty and exotic sultry dance moves. The reaction of the audience was an explosion of approval. The girls were positively giddy as they left the stage; the stage manager earnestly motioned them back.

"Can you do another song, they loved it! Can you hear that applause?" The three sisters returned to the stage to the thunderous approval of the audience. Their second song was from the pirate islands. The song was exotic and seductive as the trio danced and sang, their movements fluid and slow. Then in response to the continued applause they started their third, their swan song as Grandmother Ruth called it. It was an old song and well known by the audience. A song of lament over lost love. They had sung it a lot themselves with the young women while the men were on the ice road. Grandmother Ruth had found a much older rendition of the song with a more lilting rhythm and the words in the old tongue. These simple changes gave the song even greater power to stir the emotions. Rosalind asked the audience to join in the chorus. They began with the drum, and then they began to dance with the anklet bells adding to the rhythm. Sophie began the melody on the wheeled fiddle and the audience joined. The song had great beauty; most in the audience had never heard it in the old tongue. Some were moved to tears. Rosalind directed as well as sang as they alternated between the modern verses and those in the old tongue. Rosalind played the bellows blown bagpipes while singing, dancing and directing.

The three couples walked back to their dorm after the music ended. The three sisters should have been exhausted but instead were giddy and energetic. They skipped and twirled and demonstrated some of their dance moves to their husbands as they walked. People passing smiled and voiced approval for the performance. That night no one slept.

The next morning the trio, now very tired, were again walking to visit Grandmother Ruth when they encountered Sophie's mother. Sophie greeted her mother with a hug and a kiss. "Sophie... all three of you were certainly...different... last night. I'm so grateful you girls are married. Dancing like that would have been a scandal if you were single. You all were so seductive, where did you learn that?"

"Ruth, Admiral Casmir's wife, helped a lot. She is such a neat lady Mom." Sophie replied.

Sophie's mother gave them all a shocked look, "Do you have any idea who they are. You need to keep your distance; He is to be the new Lord Grandfather in the colonies!"

"But Mom, I've never treated our Lord Grandfather different!"

"Sophie, I don't know what to say. You're a grown woman and you still can't keep your shoes on and you flirt shamelessly with everyone. I'm surprised with you too, Rosalind, you should have known better. Jamie I understand...growing up a hoyden. All of you dancing like sirens from a brothel." The happiness of three sisters that had been glowing in their heart was shattered. Sophie was crying softly as Jamie and Rosalind walked with her with their arms around her shoulder. Rosalind was also deeply hurt, but swallowed it as usual. Jamie was just plain angry. They arrived at the admiral's home and Grandmother Ruth knew immediately her girls were hurting, her response, tea and cookies along with hugs.

"You can't expect universal appreciation when you try something new. Sometimes the critics that hurt the most are those we love." Grandmother Ruth whispered. As they discussed the performance and the response they received the mood of the group improved and Sophie became more like her bubbly self. Rosalind remained more reserved.

"Why didn't you tell us Grandfather Casey was Lord Grandfather?" Jamie asked.

"He's not yet, and besides I was afraid you would become more distant, and I do so enjoy your visits and helping you and mostly I just love having grandchildren."

"You were probably right. I'm glad we can still be close," Jamie said with the others agreeing. "How did you learn to dance like that Grandmother Ruth?"

"I was a dancer a long time ago. Our village was culled by the Imperial Guard. I never knew why, I was only thirteen. I had red hair and blue eyes and had always been told I was beautiful. My beauty saved me that day as I was spared. They murdered all the very young and old keeping a few of us to be sold into slavery. I was sold to a brothel and trained to be a dancer. They were evil and the other women beaten regularly. My master would not allow me to be beaten or branded as it would lower the price he could get for me. I owned nothing. My body was his to use or sell as he wanted. I didn't think I even had a soul. I tried very hard to please him and was terrified of him too. When I became pregnant he had the babies aborted and that damaged me somehow. When I was twenty-three he decided I was too old and sold me. He was an Imperial Magistrate, and he owned a brothel. The new buyer was a pirate from the southern islands who often had dealings with this magistrate. While on route we were stopped and boarded by the Imperial Navy. Captain Casmir ordered the slaves released but the pirate captain had papers listing us as imperial chattel and exempt from seizure. Casmir threw the papers and the captain overboard and rescued all of us. He returned us to Lands End and helped the other former slaves to find work and a place to live. He didn't know what to do with me as I really had no marketable skills. He was so handsome in his Navy Blues. He always wore a hat; I think his baldness troubled him. I was deeply in love with him but knew he was far above my station. He put me up in a boarding house then courted me, I refused him many times. I could not in my heart burden him with my past. But he persisted, I relented. He has always treated me with tenderness and love. We have been at sea all of our lives. I still love him deeply."

"So we were dancing like sirens from a brothel!" Sophie said laughing.

"Well, yes and no. You were seductive but not like a brothel. You are beautiful young women, and as such you are attractive to men who will find almost anything you do somewhat seductive. It's what's in your mind that counts. You also danced with modesty and innocence, not at all like I was forced to do. What you did was just plain fun!" The trio voiced their agreement.

"I don't think singing contests will ever be the same." Jamie wistfully said and the rest laughed. They continued their conversation as Grandmother Ruth shared stories about life aboard ship. They also speculated how their performance would impact the music as it would be handled for the next dance scheduled for the end of the week. The three sisters thought it would be fun to wear their costumes to that dance. As the conversation was winding down Grandmother Ruth looked at Rosalind. Taking her hand gently she said.

"You look so stricken child, would you like to talk?"

Rosalind responded with quiet tears, "I'm such a failure, I was so prideful and wanted to be head woman so bad, now I find I had no idea what was needed. I can't even keep Sophie out of trouble! I'm afraid the colony will suffer because I'm so very incompetent!" Grandmother Ruth held Rosalind as she wept, her friends closing ranks around her. They were surprised that Roz, the strong one, was hurting so bad. Sophie and Jamie started with some rather unkind statements about Sophie's mother but Rosalind quieted them saying it was only the last straw and her feelings of failure were long in coming. She implored them to forgive and forget. "I want so much to be like you both, to be sure of my abilities and at ease with my body. It was so much fun to dress up and perform with you. Roland has always said I am pretty and smart, why don't I feel it?" The four of them just sat and listened as Rosalind shared her deepest feelings and fears with them. There were plenty of tears from all sides. Rosalind was surprised that all of them had similar feelings and fears. She was aware of Jamie's struggle but Sophie and Grandmother Ruth too!

"Being a good head woman is not doing everything yourself. It is delegating, finding people with the skills and knowledge and giving them the means to flourish." Grandmother Ruth continued, "Your special skill Roz is you can motivate and inspire. You can see in others their skills and needs to achieve, which is why you were chosen. No one person can come near to handling all that must precede the colony."

"But Sophie's mother is such an organized and dynamic head woman. I'm not at all like her. I enjoyed dancing like a siren. I liked the way Roland looked at me. I can't demand order or even guess at the tasks that are needed." Rosalind looked at her friends, "I have no idea what needs to be done!"

"That's where I can help! I've functioned as ship's warrant officer for decades." Grandmother Ruth responded. "We need to meet at least biweekly with the other headwomen and their assistants. Jayne is yours?" Rosalind nodded. "We will also need the colonies healers at the meetings. I'm afraid that is just you,

Jamie and Sophie. Others will be called, but not until the second voyage. Roz, I'll leave the arrangements in your hands. By then the Admiral will be Lord Grandfather. Let's plan for our meeting on the day before the next dance. I suspect all three of you will be too exhausted the day after."

The meeting had been a great assistance. Rosalind's feelings were similar to those felt by all involved. Lord Grandfather as well as Admiral Casmir had stopped by to pray with the group and to encourage them. The task was daunting but they would succeed. The dance was a pleasant interlude amidst the chaos of preparation. The three sisters wore the dresses they had worn for the singing contest. Escorted by their husbands, they received continued accolades from most of their clan. Sophie's mother and a few of the older woman did look askance at them. Rosalind did her best to look regal and serene. Sophie, excited by the sound of dance music, grabbed David's hand in both of hers and led him off to dance. She was bubbling with energy. Roland continued to walk holding Rosalind's hand. "Something about you is different Roz. You have always felt so frail beneath the pillar of strength you appear as. I love you so much, and I admire you too. Now it feels like there is steel in you. What has changed?"

"It's hard to explain. I feel stronger. I feel loved. I'm happy Roland! That's what it is. I'm happy!" Roland held her in his arms very tightly.

"I'm happy too!"

The dance lasted well into the night. The band changed often with Roland, Rosalind and Sophie taking turns in the band. Then just before the dance ended a cry went up to have the three sisters do their songs again. The trio performed the songs then assisted many of the young women to learn the dance moves. The last dance of the night was the young women in mass performing the pirate song to amused spouses. Later that night Roland lay in bed with his wife. "I'm so happy you noticed that I am feeling stronger. It excites me the way you look at me. Tonight, I'm in charge!" Rosalind whispered as she began kissing her husband.

Chapter 13 The Long Voyage

Derek and Jamie were running late. They had meant to meet their friends for breakfast at the clans eating tent. Jamie had managed to look presentable but Derek's hair was tussled and his shirt miss buttoned. As they joined their friends, Derek began to re-button his shirt and Sophie noticed a large dark red mark on his neck just below the collar line. "Derek what's that on your neck, it looks really inflamed, Jamie you need to look at it!"

Her face coloring, Jamie said, "It's just a bug bite Sophie."

"But it's huge and red what kind of bug could do that?" Sophie continued. "Look Roz, it's huge!"

Derek looking directly into Jamie's now reddened face with a wicked smile said, "It was a bed bug, a really big bed bug."

Sophie continued, "Eww, do you have bed bugs? They are so hard to get rid of we need to..." While she prattled on Rosalind took a glance at Jamie's stricken red face and made a snorting sound and began to laugh.

"You're the bed bug Jamie!" At that they all erupted into a laugh and Jamie was tempted to crawl under the table. Then she joined the laughter. "Uh-oh Sophie, we've caught some attention from your Mom's table." Sophie looked to her mother. She was wearing her are you trying to embarrass me look so Sophie waived.

"Love you Mom!" Then turning to her friends Sophie started a new round of laughter. They continued to eat and tease Jamie. Sophie then looking at David with devilish smile, "I think I'm going to mark my man too!" David looked at her and shook his head indicating 'no' but Sophie continued, "You know you find me irresistible!" As she slid closer, a gleam in her eye.

Rosalind intervened, "Now children we must not embarrass the adults. Just mark him where no one but you will ever see...right Roland?" Now it was Roland who was blushing and the laughter renewed.

Derek arrived on the Admirals flag ship for his interview with Admiral Casmir. "Not sure how to address you, sir; is it Admiral or Lord Grandfather?"

"Hello, Derek, please walk with me. I've not been set apart yet so Admiral will do. What do you think of the accommodations? One of the lower decks has been modified on all three first raters and on four of the frigates. We have birthing space for over six hundred below decks. None of these accommodations are permanent and it all breaks down for storage later. Ventilation is good but lighting will be a problem. We will have under a hundred on each ship. There is a lot of space above deck, so I expect lighting to be manageable below." They strolled down a long corridor that ran the length of the ship. There were twenty four rooms total, twelve on each side. Each room had a single birth under which there was storage. Two pipe births that rolled up to store were above the main birth. The room had a small table, two chairs and a small locker. There was also a type of window. It consisted of a thick panel of glass that went through the hulls outer side, and a sliding shutter on the inside ceiling of the hull. The Admiral demonstrated how adjustments were made for light and air. The frigates have space for ten such rooms. For large families we can remove part or the entire adjoining wall. I've taken the liberty in having you, Roland, David and Robert assigned to this ship. So you can indicate the ones you like."

"Is that why you asked to see me Admiral?" Derek asked puzzled.

"No, I have a request, I am aware of your calling and this will not complicate it. By the second year you will have accomplished most of the work. What I want is to set up a university in the colony. My granddaughter has told me much about your education, so I would like to have you called to that position. Pray on it son, I would like to have you set apart before we leave."

"Your granddaughter? Oh, my Jamie. I accept the calling. Are we bringing books?"

"Books of every kind. You can talk to Ruth; she is handling book acquisitions. Thank you Derek." The Admiral continued how they would start with a library then grow it into a university. Math, law and natural science were to be taught. Derek was excited to be given a roll in the new university. His years of studying finally having found some practical use.

There was a huge gathering the day prior to embarking on the boats. Admiral Casmir was formally set apart as the new worlds Lord Grandfather as well as all other offices confirmed. The blessings of the fleet were handled by Lord Grandfather Casmir. Then the boats were boarded. The fleet consisted of three first raters including the new maxi, four frigates and over a dozen smaller craft commonly termed luggers. They would leave in order of size with the luggers going first, (some had already left), then the faster frigates and then the first raters. They would all meet at a large island about three hundred and fifty miles out from isthmus to regroup and find a good location to land. Jamie and Sophie, realizing that sea sickness would be a problem, had instructed all of the women on how to make a bracelet that when properly fitted would stop the worst of the symptoms. The voyage was long and tedious. The food monotonous and the accommodations cramped and smelly, they had a lot of time for reading and studying. The four couples partially removed the separating walls of their cabins so they could eat together. The colony's leaders ate with the captain and Lord Grandfather regularly. The women took turns assisting with the cooking. Most spent as much time as possible above decks, sleeping in blankets when weather permitted.

The sisters had lunch regularly with Grandmother Ruth, Jayne frequently joining them as she became Grandmother Ruth's fourth foster granddaughter. They truly enjoyed their time together as Grandmother Ruth was full of stories about her life. One evening Grandmother Ruth was discussing some of Lord Grandfather's plans. "Casmir wants the colonist to own their own land. He thinks that having full stewardship will encourage greater success and happiness." She continued, "There will be greater risk but Casmir thinks greater individual autonomy is needed to succeed. That will be very different than the cooperative sharing everyone is used to."

Rosalind asked, "Will everyone still draw supplies for their needs from the head woman's stores."

"For a while yes, but your task Roz will be to make your position obsolete. Once established, individuals will purchase their supplies from a store like in the non Roamy villages," Grandmother Ruth said watching Roz carefully. "We will have supplies for the needy of course, but Casmir has not decided how to handle this yet. He was hoping you might give it some thought."

Rosalind smiled, "Yes, I would like that. I will give it thought."

Grandmother Ruth smiled warmly, "I was hoping you would. By the way we have a storm coming."

"How do you know that?" Sophie asked.

"Years at sea my dear. We will be just fine." And they were. The ships rode out the storm. The passengers had a more difficult time.

Jamie and Sophie delivered two babies on the voyage with Sophie as healer and Jamie assisting. Sophie's level of skill and confidence continued to improve. Rosalind also assisted in the births and was a valuable asset to them. They had music every evening on the boats and dancing when the sea was quiet. The daily routine included unending cleaning and repairs. Derek started teaching math to anyone interested. The ships officers added piloting and navigation skills to the math lessons.

The sea and sky were beautiful. The moons were huge and bright in the night sky. Jamie and Derek sat out on the deck in a secluded section of the stern castle admiring the view very late in the night. Jamie sat on Derek's lap with her arms around his neck. She was pressed into his chest her breasts crushed against him. She had her legs wrapped around his waist. It was cool and they were covered in a blanket. They had been kissing and Jamie's hair and clothes were in considerable disarray. "Did you ever believe we would really get to go to the new world together my love?" Jamie whispered breathlessly, her face flushed.

"There were times when I thought not. Having you with me makes it so much better."

"I still remember when you said you'd pay my passage."

"You gave me my first kiss!" Derek laughed and renewed his kissing of her neck and bare shoulder.

"Derek, I think I'm pregnant!"

"How?"

"You don't know?" she laughed, renewing her kissing.

"That's wonderful! Are you sure?" Derek held her closer, his joy apparent. "I would like a little girl that looks just like you, little sister!" Jamie's only response was a smile. She slipped her hands under his shirt and stroked his back and chest.

"We have the deck to ourselves!" her whisper soft and seductive.

"How did you find this spot on deck? We're invisible here!"

"Roz discovered it, she showed me and Sophie."

"Rosie, my little sister?"

"The very person."

"Jamie, you glow when I touch you!"

"You're seeing my aura my love, I'm glad you can. I've always enjoyed yours." Jamie then pulled Derek's shirt off over his head. Derek adjusting her skirt and slip began slowly stroking her leg moving up her thigh, suddenly he paused.

"You're not wearing any..."

"Shh!" she silenced him with a kiss, "I got the idea from Sophie. Thought you'd be surprised."

"You never fail to amaze me, my love!" They were lost to further conversation.

The fleet met in the natural harbor of the island as planned. It took two and a half weeks for the entire fleet to arrive. The island had an excellent water source and a large rookery, so they began gathering eggs and brewing beer. The birds, called mutton birds, were also very tasty and a welcome change in their diet. The three luggers sent to the isthmus had not yet arrived and there was some worry over the delay. They had been expected there before the fleet. One morning two ships were seen approaching from the east so the three first raters were sent out to engage. Loud drums beat the men to quarters as similar sound echoed in the distance as the approaching ships also drummed. Imperial warships? Pirates? The crew was alert and organized as the huge crossbows were made ready. "Lord Grandfather, they look like navy; pirates never beat to quarters and would run from a force this size," Captain Ron said as he looked through his glass. The situation rapidly defused as the approaching ships raised their colors, Roamy Navy. Shouts of joy could be heard on the approaching ships nearly a half a mile away.

The new arrivals signaled a request for a healer as the smaller ship pulled alongside matching the speed of the Maxi. Heaving lines were exchanged and then heavy cables set up between the ships. A chair was rigged and the three sisters were prepared to go over. The chair was a canvas sling attached to a roller that rested on the cable. Lighter lines ran from either end of the roller to each ship. Jamie was the first to go. The sailors were very gentile as they strapped her into the chair then lifting it to the height of the cable she was sent across. Jamie closed her eyes and bit her lip as she went overboard and across. The exchange went quickly, however, to Jamie it was endless. On the other side she again received gentle assistance, however, some helping hands did linger a little long on her exposed legs. Sophie was next who apparently enjoyed the crossing. She shouted "Waahooo!" swinging her legs as she went across. Rosalind was the last to transfer and her crossing a less boisterous version of Sophie's. On the deck they were met by the first officer. "Thank you all for coming, we have an injured sailor, his leg was crushed weeks ago and he has refused amputation."

The ships surgeon then escorted the sisters to the injured sailor. "He refuses to let me near. I could have saved him. I don't think you can do much, but please try." Jamie was struck by the age of the man; not quite sixteen she thought. He was in obvious pain and the smell of gangrene heavy in the air. "I know the gods sent you. He has three older sisters; he has been calling for them. See what you can do. The leg needed to come off, now I fear it's too late." The sadness in the surgeons face was very visible. "He's my nephew, Ned, I hope my sister will speak to me. I encouraged him to come." Jamie gently touched the surgeons shoulder then they approached. Without waking Ned, Sophie did a scan as did Jamie. Rosalind watched quietly then took Ned's hand into hers as he stirred.

"Clare, you came. Betsy, Deb, you too!" Ned whispered, he looked at her terrified, and then closed his eyes.

Sophie with a determined look asked, "Jamie I want to do the laying of hands!"

"Okay, Sophie, be careful his life energy is very low. We will assist." Jamie whispered, then adding, "You may not be able to do much; I've got a very bad feeling." The sisters then began the healing circle after a prayer. Sophie placing her hands on Ned's chest above his heart, Jamie and Rosalind holding hands with one hand each on Sophie's shoulder. Sophie called forth and joined their energies weaving them into a chord as Jamie watched her. She then directed the energy into Ned. Then everything went wrong. Jamie saw in her mind that they were standing at the edge of a dark hole that sucked fiercely at their combined energy. As she watched to her utter horror Sophie stepped into the void. Jamie shoved hard at Sophie and Sophie broke contact with Ned. The three felt a flash of energy as each felt a blow as if kicked in the chest. Sophie fell to the floor unconscious. Ned remained unresponsive. Slowly Sophie became conscious. Her eyes large with fear, she was shaking and on the verge of tears. Rosalind and Jamie hugging her then assisted her to the deck for fresh air.

"I failed!" Sophie wailed,

"No Sophie, there is actually very little that we can do. Our skills are limited, death always wins. We can do great things, but we have limits. We came close to losing you!"

"I wanted so much to cure him, I saw it was hopeless but threw myself into the darkness anyway."

"That was foolish, but I've been there too. Now we need to decide what to do," Jamie said softly.

"Did you see the terror in that boy's eyes, I had to try to comfort him, and I let him believe I was his Clare," Rosalind said with sadness.

"Well healer Sophie what do you recommend?"

"Arsenicum, it will reduce his fears and help his transition, I think we should be his sisters and be with him," Sophie said firmly.

"Arsenic!" Rosalind gasped, "You can't be considering poison!"

"No Roz, it's a remedy, it can't hurt, I can take it with no effect, but Sophie is right, it will limit his terror. As for continuing as his sisters I agree. We can also use the laying of hands to bring peace and comfort. I will show you." Jamie removed a vial from her back pack containing the remedy and they reentered Ned's bunk area. Sophie administered the dose and then per Ned's request he was taken out on deck.

"Clare, Could you hold me?' Ned asked. Rosalind sat on the deck supporting his head on her thighs. The surgeon explained how Ned's sisters had kissed his forehead holding his head when he shipped aboard The three sisters repeated the gesture. Jamie and Sophie sat next to him, each taking a hand. The crew gathered watching the three sisters.

"Roz, you need to take our hands. All three of us need to contact Ned and each other. It's just like a healing just will me your energy and I will direct. Roz this is something you will be able to do yourself after you experience it." They closed their eyes and willed their energy to Jamie. Like in the healing she blended it, but this time it glowed blue and yellow with only a faint green along the edges. Jamie used the energy to surround the four of them wrapping Ned in an envelope of love and comfort. Some in the crew could feel the power some could see the faint light. They held the energy for a long time. Ned spoke to each of his sisters expressing his joy at seeing then one more time. Then he passed. When they finally stood the crew removed their hats and bowed to them in utter silence. Feeling tired and exhausted they returned to their ship via the chair. Sophie broke into tears as she ran to embrace David. The three sisters each seeking comfort in the arms of their lovers.

Later that evening the men were meeting with the captains and Lord Grandfather so the women were alone. Jamie and Rosalind walked to their private spot on deck. "Sophie, we knew we would find you here. You look so much better. We were worried." Jamie said.

"David really helped. He sort of gave me his strength; I thought I would feel hollow inside forever. He was so gentle, he..." blushing brightly she broke off.

Rosalind hugged her saying, "You just experienced the healing power of love Sophie!"

Jamie laughed, "Nothing like a little tumble to raise one's energy!"

"Seriously Jamie, I understand what happened. I just don't know what to do. How I will face the next deathly ill person? Will I over extend again? I'm trying to sort it out." Sophie said slowly.

"I reached that same point in my training, I almost quit I was so upset. I cried for a whole day and refused to get out of bed or eat. You are handling it so much better than I. Finally, my mom told me healers can only help a little. There is so much pain in the world yet we can help with some. My mom said promise little and try to give more than expected. That is what we did with Ned. We did our best; we gave comfort to a dying man."

Sophie's voice was very low, "What was that energy we made? It was so very different than the healing energy, and I too felt a comfort in it. I can reproduce it but can't see where it comes from."

Rosalind sitting down between her friends put an arm around each of them and her head on Sophie's shoulder, "It was love, Sophie. That is what it was. In a healing we use all of our life energy unfiltered and strong; that was love. It's the strongest force in the universe and fragile at the same time, like life itself."

"Roz, you should be a philosopher!" Jamie said.

"I have decided I want to be a healer too, Jamie, I love being head woman but once our colony is established I won't be needed. What we have done together is...is like magic! I want a bigger part in it."

"Okay, Roz, you are my apprentice too!"

The future leaders of the colony met for dinner with Lord Grandfather, Captain Ron and the other captains including the newly arrived. After the dinner they received reports. The crossing of the isthmus had been accomplished by way of log rails. One of the luggers fell from its cradle breaking its keel and crushing Midshipman Ned's leg. The ship's contents were salvaged then the ship was burnt to secure the iron nails. There were other settlements on the east coast of the new world south of the isthmus. These were colonies from the southern islands. The isthmus was not suitable as it was wet and marshy and fever ridden. The other colonies would be sources of future trade, however, they would settle the west coast several hundred miles further north. They wanted a good distance separation from the existing colonies. A large bay had been located that offered an excellent deep harbor and river. It was protected by barrier islands and was large enough to meet their needs. It was rich in timber and other resources. By vote the bay was named Bountiful Bay and they decided to begin to move the fleet north. Once the provisioning was completed the fleet sailed arriving in the bay in late summer. The three barrier islands were named the Sister Islands by the discovering crew in honor of the three healers who had come to the aid of Ned. The river had an additional bay that was about twenty miles from the river's mouth. This little bay named Turnagain Bay as it was where the exploration team turned again to return to the fleet. Two large Islands lay in the mouth of the river they were about a mile apart and close to the southern shore of the river. The first named Grand Isle would become home to the colony's harbor, business and governmental capital and the village would be named Harbor Town. The second they named Bell Isle would be the cultural capital of the Colonies of Bountiful. Turnagain Bay had excellent sources of running water for mills and would still stay ice free in winter as it still felt the influence of the tides. This would be the third colony. When the exploration team mapped the area they had indicated possible sites for mills. The mapmaker used the symbols

No. I, No. II, and finally, No. VI for the fifth site. When the third colony's leaders saw the map symbol they read it as Novi, so named the town Novi. The river itself was very wide with extensive estuaries all around. Upstream from Turnagain Bay the river had steep banks of hard rock several hundred feet high. All colonies would use the river for transportation.

Chapter 14 Landings

The fleet divided with each of the first raters anchoring at the site of their colony with their accompanying ships. Work parties went ashore and began to cut timber to produce a clearing. The trees cut were sawed to uniform size and squared for drying. Teams of haulers were engaged in pulling stumps. There were wild hogs and deer on the islands and these were hunted and salted for future use. The first construction for each colony was a deep water docking area for the ships and storage facilities at the docks. The dock area could accommodate two ships at a time and had eighteen feet of water at low tide. Each village site had docks and storage. Tent villages were set up as soon as sufficient land was cleared. They followed the same pattern of arrangement as was traditional with Roamy settlements. Then lots in the village and farm sites were also designated. As planned, the three sisters and Jayne had arranged for adjoining lots in the village of Bountiful. The site of Novi had experienced an extensive fire a few years prior so the clearing and planning went faster and they began house construction weeks before the other colonies. Most of the farm sites would be at the Novi site and they were able to get the fruit tree and grape vine cuttings in early. The cattle would also be in the Novi area and it was a great relief to get all the cattle ashore and secured in fenced fields.

Derek's first project was to plan the site of the mills. A good sized stream wound through the village of Novi dropping several feet as it emptied into the bay. Derek drew plans for construction of four dams and mill ponds through the village area and construction was started. The mills construction would be completed in the winter and scheduled for operation next spring. One grist and one lumber mill would be the first constructed. The labor force of the colonies was large and well organized. The three sisters were frequently seen pulling stumps behind a team of haulers, assisting in the cooking tents all while still acting as healers and midwives. The work was exhausting, but the colonists found much joy in the work. They had music with the evening meal and dances every week. The three sisters were often requested for singing in the evenings. Derek's work kept him in Novi for prolonged periods and Jamie complained bitterly of loneliness to her sisters. Finally, she had enough and demanded to taken to Novi on his next visit.

"Dearest love, please come, I hate being without you. I wish you had asked earlier. I'm so glad you spoke up!" Derek said holding her close. He was cupping her face in his hands and looking into her angry gray eyes. She softened as she drew closer to him. She turned her back to him leaning against him. Derek reached around placing his hands on her slightly swelling belly, laying a string of kisses along her neck. "You are so very beautiful, my very pregnant wife!" He whispered.

"Sophie can manage without me for a few days. I can't stand to be without you!" Jamie's voice shuttering in response to Derek's attention. When the longboat made the next run to Novi Jamie sat in the bow. She held Derek's hand as they made the run. As the tide was coming in they made their way across in less than an hour. The village site already had the homes framed in and the roofing made of bundled reeds was in progress. "Novi is far ahead of us, we won't start framing for at least a few more days. I really hope our home is done before I give birth."

"I'm glad you're here, I want so much to show you what I've been doing." Derek led her to the string of mill ponds they had constructed. "These will be the mill sites. After tomorrow I won't need to return here until the mills are finished. Once we finish framing out our home we can move in. The frames go up in a day, then the roof the next. Then we get to play in the mud. I'm really proud of the work we've done here." Jamie walked hand in hand with Derek as he visited the work sites. The framing for the mills were stacked at the sights. The workers had burned huge piles of sea shells then mixed the burnt residue with more shells and water and constructed the foundations of the mills, pouring the shell cement into wood forms to make the walls of the foundations. The construction managers spoke briefly to Derek indicating that no revisions to the plans were necessary. The couple then made their way to the eating sites for the evening meal. Jamie was greeted by a young couple carrying a rather large puppy.

"We know you're the healer so we brought you our puppy. She got her back leg crushed so we removed it but now it's gone putrid. Would you take the dog? We were going to put her down, but perhaps you can help her." Jamie stroked the dog's head. The dog moaned looking at Jamie with large brown eyes. "She's a farm dog, but now useless with only three legs. We have several others. The breed is called bear dog."

"How big will it get?"

"The parents weigh about one hundred and seventy pounds. She's almost full grown now. They pull wagons, carry stuff and swim very well. They've got webbed feet. They are gentle dogs. Hate to put her down." Jamie looked at the dog; its coat was black streaked with brown. Its head was massive and kind of square even as a puppy. Its feet were very large. The tail had a white tip and its face was wrinkled. It was a truly ugly dog. The dog returned Jamie's gaze with large brown tear filled eyes. Jamie's heart melted.

"Yes, I'll take the dog. Did you name her?" The young woman sighed with relief.

"You get to name her."

Derek's work finished in Novi they returned to Bountiful with the dog two days later. Rosalind and Sophie were very excited to have a dog. They decided to name it Stub. However, even with their love and attention Stub's condition continued to decline. The infection in the dog leg was not healing and Jamie had no clue as to what remedy to use. Rosalind, suddenly inspired, said, "We can do laying of hands on Stub! I don't see any other solution." The dog thrived with all the attention and care it received. Stub became the three sister's constant companion. It quickly put on weight and carried a back pack for the young women.

Framing day was a great success as teams of men raised the pre-assembled log frames for the village homes. The homes were closely spaced along a plank road that was named Central Street. This was crossed by a second street named Main which came up from the dock area. An additional plank road made an ark around the docks and storage sheds this was as yet unnamed. The land extending west from Central and main was divided into ribbon farms on either side of the road. A few large cedar trees that had died many years ago were found and it provided enough cedar shakes to roof the homes in the village. The farm homes used the traditional thatch roofs. A great number of thin willow branches were cut and these were woven together to fill the space between the log frames. A great pile of stones were gathered from the beaches and piled close to the homes. Then a great deal of sand and clay was also piled near the homes.

Mud day had arrived. The women rolled up their skirts and pinned them to a height just above their knees. The all wore head scarves to keep their hair out of the mud. A shallow pit had been dug and lined with a discarded sail. Sand, clay, straw and water were poured into the pit as the women mixed the material with their feet. There was a lot of excitement and laughter involved. Grandmother Ruth knew some working songs from the southern islands and joined in the mud, leading in the songs. The men routinely scooped up the mud and used it to plaster the areas between the log frames that held the woven branches. The homes were plastered inside and outside. The work stopped for lunch, then resumed. At the end of the day everyone was exhausted. Sophie, trying to get out of the pit, fell backward taking Jamie with her. They both landed on their backside in the mud. Rosalind witnessing the fall made the mistake of laughing, only to be pelted by mud balls from Jamie and Sophie. A mud fight ensued with the three sisters laughing and throwing mud at each other. David had entered the mud to assist Sophie to her feet only to be pushed into the mud by Sophie. When Roland arrived at the site he too was pelted with mud balls from both Sophie and Rosalind. Derek wisely stood off out of range until the three sisters had climbed out of the mud. Thinking all was clear he approached. A very muddy, laughing Jamie ran up to him. She gave him a very muddy full body hug and kissed him with a very muddy face running very muddy hands through his hair. Mud day had been an outstanding success.

    The homes were twelve by twenty feet. Each had two rooms with a hearth wall dividing the home. Jayne was an artist with stone and helped with the hearth construction. Each hearth had a small oven built in. Derek had designed the ovens which were made of iron. The homes were moved into after mud day and construction continued. Each home was given three windows. These had been secretly packed and transported in the smaller ships. They were a gift to the colonists from home. The homes had wood plank floors and a loft. The main room was the kitchen sitting room, the other a bed room. Those families with children used the loft for the sleeping children. The three sisters white washed the inside walls to brighten up their homes. All of the furniture from the ship was taken to the homes giving each home at least a bed, two chairs and a table. Derek made shelving to hold Jamie's books and their kitchen utensils. The homes permanently altered a Roamy tradition of eating in a common area and cooking for large groups. Each family now would manage its own meals. This was uncomfortable at first, so the seventh day dinner was still handled in common. This too, would become a tradition.

Once the houses were up construction began on the library. It was located on Main near the dock road. Its construction was similar to the homes but double in size. It had a single hearth and shelves for books. Benches were set up for lessons and Derek resumed math lessons. Jamie taught a weekly first aide and home remedy class. Jayne taught art and needle craft classes. Other colonists with special skills were also encouraged to share their skills. Soon pottery and cooking classes were added. The new university began with less academics and more practical instruction. History, law and natural science could wait.

Less than a mile of water divided the colonies from each other. A semaphore station was erected at each harbor so messages could easily pass between the colonies. On a clear day messages took only minutes. It was decided that two of the luggers would remain with the colony. No boats could be built until sufficient dry lumber could be had. Enough seasoned timber had been included in the fleet so a number of dories were built for fishing and with each colony received two long boats for river transportation. A sandy beach was located near Grand Isle so the ships could be grounded and careened on the low tide for cleaning and inspection of the hulls. The ships would winter with the colonies and return to Port Hope in the spring. It would be two years before they could return. The ships were given a water tight door in the bow to allow loading of the squared logs for the return trip. To ensure success the colonies had to show a profit. The timber they cut for the villages and farms would net an excellent profit for the first trip. The next return trip the colonies would export sawed lumber, salted fish, pickled eels and more.

A healer was requested for possible delivery in Harbor Town so the three sisters along with Stub were taken across in a long boat. The woman was known to them as they had been seeing her for her pregnancy during the voyage. The delivery went well and the infant was healthy. Having time on Grand Isle the sisters decided to view the colony as they would be unable to return until the tide turned. The town itself was very similar to Bountiful. With ribbon farms and village homes along plank roads. The harbor was much bigger. The harbor had a double bowl. The larger bowl set for shipping and receiving goods. The warehouses and docks more than double those of Bountiful with more in the process of being built. It would accommodate eight ships when completed. The smaller bowl had a sandy beach and there the fishermen had organized fishing shacks and drying facilities for nets and fish. The dories were nestled and stacked one on top of the other. The dories were twenty-six to thirty feet long and easily launched across a series of rollers by block and tackle. The dories were brightly painted and could be sailed or rowed. The fishermen used nets as well as hooks and line. Thousands of small silvery fish were drying on racks set about the beach area. They could see numerous dories out in the bay working nets. Another boat was unloading eels. The sisters had never seen such an abundance or variety of sea life. Stub walked along with them wagging its tail and sniffing intently at all the variety of smells. David had made a wooden leg for stubs and she walked easily.

Captain Ron's wife, Phoebe, was in the village and asked the sisters to dine with her aboard the ship and they accepted. They were all seated at the captain's table. The food was excellent. They were served a variety of local sea food including eels and lobster. Phoebe demonstrating how to get at the delicious lobster meat. "This is so much better than our regular fair of ship's food." Phoebe exclaimed. The sisters nodded with agreement. They finished with tea and ginger beer.

"I understand you will be wintering with us," Jamie said sipping her ginger beer.

"Yes, the captain does not want to risk a winter crossing. All the cabins have been removed so we can take on cargo. It's been so very hectic." After a pause and blushing slightly, Phoebe continued, "I had a reason for asking you hear for lunch. I wanted to speak to you alone without Captain Ron." Phoebe paused for a long time searching for the right words. "I have been unable to conceive, we have been married nearly five years. Jamie, I want a child badly." Jamie could see the pain and longing in her face.

"It might not be your fault, Phoebe. May I perform a scan?"

"Please!" As Phoebe lay on the bed Jamie performed the scan. Sophie and Rosalind assisted so they would also learn and see.

"Do you have regular periods?"

"Not always, I thought it was a blessing when I was young with them being infrequent, now they are regular and heavy."

"You apparently had an infection a long time ago, perhaps as a child. Only one of your ovaries functions and I see a blockage. We could do a lying on of hands and fix the blockage." Phoebe was close to tears. The stress in her face was replaced with relief, a smile brightened her face and the fatigue and years in her eyes softened.

"I would be so grateful Jamie!" Jamie, assisted by Sophie and Rosalind, did a lying on of hands and corrected the blockage. "I will name my first Jamie, be it boy or girl!" Phoebe hugged the three sisters as they left her. "Sophie and Rosalind too, if I may?"

The three sisters smiled at Phoebe and felt a flush of excitement at being able to help. "We hope you conceive soon; we would love to deliver your child," Jamie said as she kissed Phoebe's cheek, Rosalind and Sophie responding in the same way.

The building projects continued through the summer season. A shop for black metal work was built near the dock area as well as one for woodworking and for the copper. Derek spent much of his time at the black metal shop as the mill project was on hold for the winter. The mill buildings were up but Derek needed to do a lot of iron work for the water wheels. This kept him and three metal workers busy. David worked at the woodworking shop making furniture and a special project for Derek, Ronald and Roland. It quickly became apparent that while Derek and Jamie's home was more than adequate for their needs it was way too small for the healer practice. The solution was to add another twenty by twelve addition with a separate door and hearth. The addition had two rooms and a full loft. Jamie's books and remedies were moved in and the second smaller room was used for remedy production and storage. Jamie and the sisters kept a ready supply of herbs and other remedy mother tinctures on hand. The three of them were ecstatic to have a place for their practice and study. They planted window boxes on their homes and soon had beautiful flower displays for their homes. Root cellars were dug for each of the homes for food storage. The colony had brought tons of wheat berries with them and these were distributed to the farmers for planting and the families for consumption. They had several hand grinders for the wheat and these were rotated throughout the homes. They had classes at the library on making wheat bulgar and bread making contests to encourage innovation. Rosalind won a prize for her no knead bread method.

Rosalind was in her home assisting Jamie, Sophie and Jayne in her no knead bread method. They were so busy and having a very animated discussion regarding their men folk that they failed to notice the arrival of the said men folk. "So, this is what you four talk about all day!" Roland said laughingly as he hugged Rosalind.

"You were eavesdropping, that's hardly fair!" Rosalind said as she returned the hug and kissed her husband, "Besides it's all too true, you all are impossible!"

David smiling as he held Sophie and tickled her until she kicked him said, "We smelled bread baking, so we came running!"

"I guess we need to feed them, Roz," Jayne said as she and Jamie began slicing the warm bread and opening a jar of jam. "You and Sophie need to take that outside, David!" She continued with a laugh.

As they ate, Sophie, with her most seductive smile, slid very close to David, "So what's that special project you've been working on Davey?" she asked as she stroked his chest and played with his hair. David choked, then gasped.

"Special project? How did you hear? No... I mean what special project do you mean, angel girl?"

"The crossbows, you know, the ones for us girls." The men were stunned silent. They looked, open mouthed, as the women looked at them smiling innocently. "You know you can't keep anything from me," Sophie purred, "I have my ways. You talk a lot after we...you know..." David blushed.

"You took our arm measurements; we didn't think you were sewing. We've been really curious. We've known for about a week," Jamie continued. "We think it's great. Looking forward to hunting together."

A week later the crossbows were finished and the eight of them met in a cleared field to practice. The women were enthusiastic. "Standing here you have three targets. Thirty, forty and fifty yards out. We have pretty much sighted the crossbows in for you. The pins are set for the three ranges. Just use the sights and breathe like we talked about." David said patiently. They fired their first volley at the thirty yard target and all placed their bolts on the target. "That's excellent Sophie! You all did much better than we expected." They continued the practice until the women could no longer pull the string back. Then they added additional volleys with the men drawing the crossbows for their wives.

"We had no idea you four would do so well, I'm impressed. However, shooting at a live target is nothing like this. You are firing at a known range and know what pin to use. In a hunt things get confusing. You will need to practice often so it becomes second nature. The hard part will be being able to correctly and quickly determine the range. That I can't teach you," Roland said.

Rosalind looked at her three friends then volunteered, "We can commit to four days a week. This will be fun. Maybe we can go to fifty pound pull as we get stronger! How much does you crossbow pull Roland?"

"Don't get ahead of yourself, Roz, forty pounds is really enough. You really need to draw the bow evenly for the bolt to go straight. It gets harder to do it evenly as you increase the weight."

They practiced faithfully four times a week with the men. Their consistent accuracy won much praise from their husbands and each other and their confidence grew. Jayne came up with a plan to learn ranging. They made a game of it. Whenever they were out they carried a knotted measuring string. Anyone could call the challenge, "range it," and the rest would have to respond. The range would be measured and a prize or penalty claimed. Their constant challenges to each other and their antics were a source of amusement and curious looks by the community. One day the four were visiting the fish market in Harbor Town when Sophie spotted Phoebe and shouted, "Range her!" Her companions began shouting the range then pulled out the string as shocked shoppers came to a stop and watched their antics. Jamie then let out a whoop and shouted.

"That's two loaves of bread you owe me, Roz!" They all began laughing as Phoebe just stood not quite knowing what had happened. They then settled down and tried to explain to Phoebe what they were doing, but somehow they were unable to communicate their game so Phoebe or any onlooker could understand. Finally, Phoebe just laughed and they hugged in greetings. Jamie then noticed the change in Phoebe's aura. "You're with child aren't you?" Jamie said slowly with a bright smile. Phoebe nodded affirmative as the four sisters embraced her again with loud affirmation, again bringing all activity to a stop at the fish market.

"Let's go someplace where we can talk alone," Phoebe whispered. "You seem to have attracted a lot of attention. Do you always get so many strange looks?"

"Sophie's Mom was always cautioning us, but usually we are quite proper and sedate." Rosalind said piously as her companions snorted. They walked back to the ship and sat with Phoebe and drank tea with jam and bread. They were all so excited for her. "Have you told Captain Ron yet?"

"I was waiting for confirmation and you just gave me that. I'm so very happy! I would love to stay here with you and the colony. My husband is a sailor and I knew that when we married, so I will not ask him to stay. I do hope you three can deliver my baby!"

"I think that's going to work out," Jamie said with a smile after she worked on some calculations counting on her fingers twice. You will have a spring baby."

"Then it's off to sea for me. I love Ron more than anything but sea life is so lonely at times. At least he's mine most nights. Having a baby, that's going to be a challenge. I really enjoy having friends...I mean I like having you four as friends."

Sophie, beaming, hugged Phoebe, "We love you too Phoebe!" They spent the rest of the afternoon talking and never had a chance to discuss 'range it'. Most of their talk about babies and the changes they saw and felt in their bodies and their relationship with their men. Phoebe yearned in her heart to have female friends, interesting, dynamic, female friends, like the four sisters. Leaving and returning to sea would be hard, but she would go without complaint. She loved her husband that much.

Chapter 15 The Hunt

The four women were mutinous. Jamie was livid. The men were leaving in the longboat to hunt up river. They would be left behind. They had practiced the crossbow and were equal to the men in accuracy. So what if their crossbows had only a forty pound draw? Sophie was the most accurate of the eight. "Damn that man!" Jamie growled. "Too pregnant to hunt. Fiddle-sticks!" The men had actually been rather gentle about not taking them along. Jayne, who was furthest along in her pregnancy, could no longer see her feet or tie her shoes. She was carrying twins. "Why did he have to be so nice about it? I was ready for a rip roaring fight!" Jamie continued. So instead they stood smiling and waving as the men set off. Sophie had secreted herself aboard in a sack only to be discovered and returned with a lot of laughter and kissing from David. With the wind astern and the tide coming in they quickly crossed Turnagain Bay and were lost to sight. As they entered the high sided area of the river they took down the sails and unstepped the masts and began to row. The river sat in an area of high cliffs. This ran for fifty miles than opened into a huge lake. They meant to explore the lake, mapping and surveying hunting a little before returning. They expected to be gone three or four weeks. It would be arduous, not at all suitable for their pregnant wives. There had been reported sightings from farmers in Novi of large horned animals in the beech woods. These sightings and other speculation regarding animal life was the reason for the voyage. Two other longboats from the other colonies had joined them and involved a dozen men. They would each survey part of the lake then return. Did the bovine and equine lines exist in the new world? They could only speculate.

The three sisters contented themselves with domestic activities for the next three days. They had all promised not to hunt without the men. Jayne was really not up to that much activity and settled down easily. The others plotted. "We should go to Novi and pick berries. We can get a lot for preserves. Phoebe and Jayne can help with the preserves." Rosalind suggested.

"That's kind of tame, Roz, I was hoping to hunt." Jamie replied.

"We would need to take our crossbows I think. Just in case of wild hungry animals." Rosalind added.

"That's not really hunting," Sophie said with a bright smile,

"We're berry picking. Stub can pull that little wagon David made. If we get enough berries Jayne can sell them in the new general store. No promises would be broken." Their plan set, they notified Jayne, Grandmother Ruth and Phoebe that they would be gathering berries for preserves and enlisted their help in the work. They also arranged for the longboat to take them to Novi on Saturday. Their arrival was most unremarkable as they unloaded Stub and her wagon and their large sacks with their lunches. When they slung their crossbows across their backs, they started to get noticed and some remarks.

"You little ladies picking berries? Most of us use our hands."

"Can any of you draw those things back?" The best remark was from the village chief.

"You be careful of those mean rabbits!"

They easily located large patches of wild berries. The berries were plump and blue to purple in color. The three sisters easily filled their gathering sacks and Stubs wagon. Sophie, just by chance, spotted a wild pig sleeping in the sun and quickly fired a bolt through its heart. The pig squealed loudly but did not have a chance to run before it expired. They gutted the pig, and then unloading Stub's cart, put the pig in the cart and shouldered the heavy berry sacks and returned to Novi. Their reception on the return trip was markedly different. Much of the town turned out and looked shocked as Sophie told that it was she who bagged the pig. The village chief remarked that the pig weighed more than the three sisters together, and how did such a tiny little lady learn to shoot. "Lucky shot!" Sophie responded with a shy smile. They donated the pig for the Sunday feast and were in turn invited to return and feast with the village. They returned to Bountiful and Jayne, Grandmother Ruth and Phoebe assisted in making the preserves. They made better then seventy jars sealing each with bee's wax before the day ended. Sunday they returned to Novi to share the roast pig. The feast was a great success. The three sisters, as well as Jayne, Grandmother Ruth and Phoebe enjoyed the food. "I like the pigs skin the most," Jamie said to her friends. "I've never tasted anything so good." The three sisters received a lot of good natured teasing and Sophie was toasted as the 'Itty-Bitty Red Huntress'. As music was always a big part of feasting, the three sisters performed their songs for the village. Their dancing was slightly more subdued this time. The hour was late when the five women caught the out going tide to return to Bountiful. Phoebe stayed the night with Jamie using the bed in the infirmary.

Over the next two weeks the village of Novi saw the return of the three sisters every Tuesday, Thursday and Saturday. They returned with large loads of wild berries but no game. Soon the coming and going of the three sisters no longer drew interest. The six women had a huge storage of preserved berries and began experimenting with drying some. They had more than enough for their own use and considered gifting or selling the excess. It was again a Saturday, and the three made their last planned trip to Novi. As usual they made it with scant comment to the berry patch. As usual they allowed Stub to roam as they began gathering the berries. They were working close together, singing as they gathered the fruit. They laughed and teased each other, barely watching what they were doing. They never saw the bear.

They were less than forty yards from the bear when it saw them. The bear rose up suddenly on two legs. It was brown and stood about seven feet high. It looked at the three sisters growling, then advanced slowly. The three sisters were frozen with terror. They were unable to move, their voices caught in their throat. Before the bear got no more than ten yards toward them Stub was on the bear. Stub just managed to stay out of the bears reach as it dodged and spun biting the bear from behind, then retreating, then returning to bite again. The bear was furious as it spun and tried to catch Stub with its paws or teeth. The three sisters then acted, almost together they unsung their crossbows and fired, each sending a bolt through the bears chest at point blank range. The animal growled in pain and ran off with Stub in furious pursuit, the three sisters in turn pursuing Stub. The bear ran two hundred yards before bleeding out. They reached Stub, holding the dog and rubbing it with the most sincere gratitude. Stub moaned with pure canine bliss. Stub was covered in bear blood and it got on the three sisters hands, face and dresses. The sight of the three of them bloodied and running into the village with their skirts pulled up above their knees and Stub barking caused a commotion in the village. The entire village turned out as the three sisters breathlessly tried to explain they had killed a bear. The villagers thought a bear had killed one of the women or mauled them.

Eventually it was all sorted out and a large party of men went and retrieved the bear. The bear weighed in at thirteen hundred pounds. The animal had three closely placed entry wounds in its chest and three wider exit wounds in its back. The villagers watched the trio in awe.

The bear contained enough meat for all three colonies Sunday feast, and the other colonies were signaled regarding the bear meat the three sisters donated. The colonies responded by sending longboats to recover the meat. The village chief offered to have the bear skin made into a rug as payment for the generous gifts of meat. The three sisters accepted the offer graciously.

The expedition to the lake region had been a mixed success. They were returning empty handed but had much they wanted badly to share. Most of all they were most eager to be home with those they loved. The four women decided to prepare a special welcome home meal and break the news of their adventures gently. The bear skin rug was hanging from the wall in the clinic, and since the three sisters had asked the people of Novi to keep their little adventure secret, everyone in the three colonies were talking about it. They had tried not to notice the smiles and looks they were receiving as they continued their activities; they hoped there notoriety would eventually die down. They were discussing their plan on breaking the news. "I'll just wait until late tonight and tell him a little when I got him occupied." Rosalind started.

"I plan on a complete denial of everything!" Sophie blurted. "Besides the tale has grown so out of portion I no longer believe it!"

"Let's soften them up with a good meal, and then pour the sweet on before we mention anything. After all they won't have heard a thing about it so soon," Jamie said with conviction.

Wearily the men rowed the last mile to the harbor area and began unloading the boat. "I'm not sure if I want a bath or a hot meal first, but tonight I'm sleeping in a bed with Roz." Roland said. They continued to unload and put on their heavy backpacks when a friend approached.

"Well, David, I see you returned empty handed to your 'Itty-Bitty Red Huntress." David looked confused as they continued to walk toward home. Another friend greeted them with "Your little women had *a bear* of a time when you were gone." As they continued their walk home they were met with a lot of confusing cryptic remarks.

"Sounds like the girls had a hard time of it with us gone!" Derek said. "I hope they're okay now. What sort of trouble do you think they got into?"

"I doubt Jayne got into much," Robert said, "She needs help to get her shoes on."

"Sophie I can believe getting into trouble, you think she accidentally shot her cross bow in town? Why else would they call her a huntress?" David asked. They continued their musings as they continued. "I'm truly looking forward to hearing their explanations. Let's milk it for all its worth!" They laughed in agreement.

"Really doubt they were ever in any real trouble, not my level headed Roz!"

As the men approached they were met by their women. They had dressed for the occasion; their hair neatly fashioned and swept up. They wore their nicest dresses. To the men they were even more beautiful than they remembered; the four of them smiling and glowingly pregnant. They all embraced and kissed, with the men less than discreetly fondling their wives. "We've prepared the hip baths for you so go home and clean up, we will serve dinner in the clinic room as its big enough for all of us." Jamie said.

Derek whispered to his companions "They are really turning the sweet on; this is going to be fun!" The women had taken the small tables from their homes and put them together in a row in the clinic. The meal they had prepared was truly sumptuous. Roast baby pig, lobster, fresh baked bread, mashed potatoes with gravy and corn. The men fell on the food like ravenous wolves. The women ate lightly biding their time. They served bubbly pies for desert, made from their hard won berries. Then appetite sated they served ginger beer and tea as they began to talk. "We heard you girls had a hard time with us gone," Derek started.

"We had a little difficulty, but nothing much." Jamie replied some color showing in her face.

"We did a ton of berry preserves," Jayne added, "Grandmother Ruth and Phoebe helped."

"Grandmother Ruth was in on your berry adventure?" David asked blandly.

"Yes, she was most helpful, and Phoebe too; Jamie, Roz and Sophie gathered the berries. It was quite an adventure," Jayne continued.

Eyes averted David asked, "Is that how you accidentally fired your crossbow Sophie?"

Sophie's face reddened, "I never accidentally shoot, I always hit what I..." Blushing and even redder she stopped. More curious than ever the men looked at the four very prim ladies sitting before them. They were all smiling; three of them had red faces. They still had no idea what the women were up to or what trouble they had gotten into. Sophie continued, "We spent a lot of time in Novi picking berries. It was most productive."

Jamie added, "The people in Novi were most helpful. They gave us a bear skin rug, it's on the wall behind you. They were most gracious."

"Because you picked so many berries?" Derek slowly asked trying to understand the conversation.

"Not entirely. How was your trip? You haven't told us a thing," Rosalind interrupted, "we really want to hear about your adventure. Our berry picking was really very bland."

"Almost boring," Jamie added.

"Yes, almost!" Sophie added with a laugh, then blushing brightly concentrated on sipping her tea, not looking up.

"No changing the subject, Roz, we were discussing your berry picking," Roland said looking intently at his demure wife. "I don't understand how and why you were given a bear skin for picking berries. I didn't even know we had bears!"

"Oh, yes, we do, really big ones!" Sophie exclaimed with wide eyes before returning to sipping her tea, again silent.

Trying very hard to understand Derek asked, "So you saw a bear, and someone bagged it? Why did they give you the skin?"

"Well, we did see the bear!" Jamie said slowly.

"Or actually it saw us!" Sophie said very quietly.

"Actually they gave us the bear skin for all the meat we donated." Rosalind added.

"We made lots of bubbly pies, anyone want seconds?" Jayne asked.

"What meat did you donate?" David asked looking totally confused.

"The bear and the pig of course! Weren't you listening?' Sophie blurted, then turning a very bright shade of red, returned to sipping her tea eyes down cast.

"AH-HA!" Derek responded, "You were hunting."

"Ah-ha nothing. We had promised not to hunt without you so we didn't. We were picking berries." Jamie returned trying to sound indignant but only sounding guilty.

Derek continued "So how did you get a pig? Did it choke on the berries you fed it?"

"Don't be silly, Sophie shot it." Jamie responded. Then she found it necessary to concentrate on sipping her tea.

David looking very fondly and with awe at Sophie, "You shot a pig, Angel Girl?"

"Yes, and we all shot the bear!" Sophie said than gave a gasp and looked apologetically at Jamie and Rosalind.

Later that night Jamie and Derek were alone. Jamie was wearing her night gown and Derek was rubbing her feet. "I really like your ritual bonding foot rubs my love!" Jamie said softly.

"For someone who hardly ever wears shoes you have very clean feet little sister!" Derek said as he kissed the sole of the foot he was rubbing.

"I wash them silly, every night before I go to bed, and the rest of me too!" she replied teasingly and laughing as he continued to kiss her foot.

"Were you barefoot when you hunted the bear?"

"We were picking berries! Yes we were all barefoot," she sounded exasperated. "If we had been truly hunting we would have been totally bare like the ancient huntresses of old Earth."

"Ancient huntresses went hunting naked?"

"Totally, absolutely butt naked!"

"And you have this on good authority?"

"Absolutely! Oh, some might have worn a feather. Just one though."

"What really happened Jamie?"

"We were picking berries when the bear surprised us. We froze. If Stub hadn't attacked the bear we would have been killed. It happened so fast. I'm so glad we had the crossbows!"

"Me too. I didn't know we had bears here. I get sick at heart when I think I could have lost you!"

"Stub was the real hero. He saved us and gave us time to act. We had practiced so much it was second nature. I didn't even think." Jamie sat up then pulled Derek down next to her and rolled on top. "The village chief in Novi said our bolts each entered and crossed the bear's heart tearing it open. The bear bled out in seconds."

"Why did you chase after the bear? When you shoot an animal next time, please wait an hour before chasing so it will bleed out. A wounded animal is dangerous."

"We were so worried about Stub we didn't think. She was covered in blood. It got all over us too. Luckily it was all bear blood...you said next time! Oh, Derek, I love you!" Jamie began kissing Derek with wild abandon.

Over the next few days the men got to tell the story of their adventure. Neither Derek, Robert, Roland nor David had seen even a single animal. The other groups had found evidence of a short cow with long horns and long reddish hair living in the beech and maple forest but none had been captured. The north eastern edge or the lake touched a vast grassland. The exploration team reported seeing large wooly cows and what they thought were horses. Their findings needed further collaboration but this was indeed a land of bounty. A new and better organized exploration was being planned for the late winter. It would involve both of the colonies ships and live trapping would be tried. The four of them would not be involved this time.

The leaves on the hard wood trees began to turn yellow, orange and red. None of the colonists had ever experienced anything like the perfusion of colors. The unexpected beauty was fully appreciated with joy and thanksgiving. As the weather became cooler in the early mornings and late evenings, weather made for hunting, the group of friends began planning. Jayne was close to her delivery so she and Robert declined the invitation. Three blinds were made in a clearing that had been regularly bated for the morning hunt, and tree stands set up along the game trails for the late afternoon hunt. The three sisters were very excited to be included. They spent a lot of time and energy planning a surprise they thought their men would love.

The morning of the first hunt arrived with Derek and Jamie up and preparing before the first rays of the sun. Derek had smoked his and Jamie's clothes to conceal any scent and dressed carefully. "Jamie are you ready? Wear lots of layers, its cold out. We can strip off layers as it gets warmer. Are you ready my wild huntress?"

As if waiting for the cue Jamie stepped out into the candlelit room. Her long hair was brushed out and it cascaded in waves across her shoulders and over her breasts. She had a large white feather in her hair clipped to a thin braid extending down in front of her right ear. She wore nothing else. Derek gasp, "My lovely huntress, I've totally forgot what we had planned for today."

"Thought you'd like my costume!" she whispered as Derek reached for her. They were a little delayed getting out of the house. Later as they prepared to leave, "Don't worry, my love, I'm toasty warm. Got three slips on under my skirt and above the knee stockings. I'm warm enough for both of us!" Jamie said with her most innocent smile.

The three couples walked toward the blinds. The three sisters walked ahead holding hands talking quietly and occasionally looking back smiling. They each had their long hair tied in a knot at the nape or their neck as usual and were wearing a tight fitting short jacket. Roland whispered, "They're plotting something wicked, I feel it in my bones."

"Sophie came out of our room in her 'wild huntress' garb, just a single feather, absolutely nothing else. We almost didn't make it out of the house in time."

"Roz too, they are conspiring something."

"Jamie too. This is really going to be interesting," Derek added. "Jamie was real explicit in what she was wearing."

"Let me guess, three slips and above the knee stockings?" David asked.

"I can wait to see what those little vixens are up to. I'm going to play hard to get!" Roland said firmly. Later they entered the blinds as couples. The blinds were cramped. The front of the blind had a dark netting that they could see through and shoot through. Anyone in the blind would be unseen from the outside. As Jamie and Derek settled for the wait, Derek was aware of the smoky smell of their clothing and the feel of Jamie so close and still. Just having her so close was stimulating. He could not stop thinking about what his little trickster had planned. He knew whatever it was, he would like it. Jamie remained very quiet. Derek could hear her slow even breathing. Jamie stirred a little and unknotted her hair letting it flow down her back. Derek loved the scent of her hair and stroked the soft silky strands. As the day warmed Jamie quietly unbuttoned her tight little jacket. As she was only wearing her chemisette Derek could easily see her excellent cleavage. Jamie was a tiny woman, her curves soft and slight, but in the course of her pregnancy her breasts had become much fuller. Derek relished in the changes as he watched her quietly, especially noting the hard little nubs of her nipples pushing at the fabric and the motion of her breasts as she breathed. Jamie stirred very quietly yet Derek felt every move as he slowly burned.

The sun continued to rise and the blind became even warmer and Jamie whispered she needed help removing one of her slips as she was so cramped and hot. Derek complied shuddering slightly as his hands brushed the soft skin of her bare thighs. Later he helped her with the second slip, determined to see all that his seductive little woman could do he continued to resist. Her next move was to untie her garter and slowly roll down her stocking Derek was riveted by every slow move she made. Derek was having trouble breathing at this point. Jamie fumbled with her second garter then whispered, "It's knotted, could you help, my love?" Derek fumbled with the knot without success then reached for his knife. "Don't cut it! They're my favorite garters. Use your teeth on the knot." Derek began working the knot slowly freeing it. As he worked Jamie ran her fingers through his hair. The closeness of her and the scent of her driving him to madness. Jamie wrapped her bare leg over his shoulder then bent to nibble his ear and Derek lost the last of his self-mastery. As he reached for her Jamie gave a slight chuckle and Derek knew he was lost. A herd of deer could have camped outside the blind and they would not have noticed.

Later that day the three couples were enjoying a picnic lunch. The three sisters looking prim with their clothing neat and hair tied in a knot at the nape or their necks. From their outward appearance no one could guess of what had just transpired between them, except from little smiles they exchanged. When the men were finally alone David said, "Roland you look like the cat that got into the cream!"

"I feel like that cat. She completely undid me with a simple knot in her garter." They laughed and talked about their adventure in the blind. "Those little vixens had it all planned out!" Roland continued. "Roz never fails to amaze. Every time I think I truly comprehend her she...she is just delicious to live with, words fail me."

"I don't think I can ever go hunting without remembering my Sophie and her garter!" David said and his friends agreed. Their afternoon hunt was without success as no game came within range. Derek and Jamie sat quietly in the tree stand and watched. Derek had difficulty staying focused on the hunt with memories of their morning together so strong on his mind. They repeated their hunts four more times each time in the firm discipline of the hunt. That evening Rosalind took a large buck. It was a good long shot and it took them and Stub over an hour of following the blood trail before they found the deer. It took the three men to carry the deer out. They returned home then hung the deer to allow it to bleed out. They would process it tomorrow, much of the meat dried as jerky and some combined with pork as sausages. The hide would be tanned and used for a skirt and shoes. The best cuts they would share for dinner tomorrow.

That night Rosalind came to Roland wrapped in the bear shin, her hair down and a feather in her hair. "My wild huntress has returned!" Roland said quietly his voice gruffer than usual, "What pray tell are you wearing under that bear skin." Rosalind responded by pulling off his night shirt and pushing him down on their bed wrapping them both in the bear skin. They lay together skin to skin wrapped in the coarse hair of the bear.

"This is an ancient ritual of the huntress; we must break in the bear!" Rosalind's smile was sultry, her lips parted and her face flushed. Roland was unable to resist.

"Roz you are so beautiful, I love you so much!" Then he surrendered to her. Later they had time to talk as Rosalind lay curled up against Roland her head on his shoulder her finger twirling the hair on his chest. "Tell me my little minx about this ritual of breaking in the bear. How did you learn about it?"

"Through serious academic study of course. It dates to the primitive Earth culture of the huntress. It involves ritual preparation of the bear skin and of course a successful hunt." The ritual preparation was a lot of laughing and plotting giggles as the three sisters rolled up the hide and secreted to Rosalind's home, the idea of the wild huntress a product of their imagination.

"Will the ritual be repeated?"

"Of course, each time a huntress of the clan of the bear makes a kill."

"I think I really like this ritual, keep up you scholarly studies, Roz. I take it we are the clan of the bear?"

"You are most insightful my dear husband."

"Roz, what were the men like during the age of the ancient huntress?"

"A lot like you actually, handsome, strong and very good in bed."

"Really?"

"And they were very obedient to their huntress lovers."

"Obedient?"

"Why yes, they would gladly accommodate their lovers every whim."

"How do I stock up, Roz?"

"I've already told you. You're impossible."

"Then why do you keep me?"

"I'm rather fond of you. And you amuse me. You are very good at amusing me." Roland found the energy to be again amusing later that night before sleep claimed them.

The couples continued to hunt together with each of the huntresses able to introduce the ritual of breaking in the bear at least once. The men quickly learned the delight of letting the women have the first shot.

Chapter 16 Harvest Festival

The four sisters and their husbands were walking hand in hand. Stub was pulling the wagon containing a rather huge picnic feast. "Roz, we've got enough food for a small army with us. Where are you taking us and what devilish plans have you girls made?"

"There's a very beautiful little lake and waterfall on the west end of our island. We are having a picnic with friends." Rosalind replied. They were making slow progress as Jayne was puffing with exertion, her belly swollen with the twins and Robert was hovering. Rosalind smiling at Jayne continued, "We have arranged for you and Robert to have the longboat pick you up for the return."

"Roz, that was sweet of you, but I really hate to put everyone out and tie up one of the longboats!"

"It's not a problem Jayne the boat is coming from the flagship and is bringing our other guests."

A worried frown on his face Derek asked, "Who are our distinguished guests?"

"Captain Ron, Phoebe, Grandmother Ruth and Lord Grandfather, and I almost forgot the first officer. I don't recall his name… George and his wife, Alexandra."

"Lord Grandfather really intimidates me," Derek whispered to Jamie. She smiled up at him brushing his cheek with the lightest of kisses and whispered, "He's only my Grandfather and he really loves us dearly. You can relax a little." The longboat had already arrived and was beached on a small ark of sand near the tiny waterfall. The newcomers had arranged a large tarp on the ground for the picnic close to the sparkling lake and had set up the large earthen wear jugs with the cider and ginger beer. Alexandra and Phoebe had set a wildflower arrangement in the center of the tarp. There were hugs all around as the group of friends met.

Phoebe's face had a beautiful glow to it, a sign of her pregnancy and joy. She had special hugs for Jamie, Rosalind and Sophie, "Thank you so much!" she whispered. Phoebe looking about said, "This lake is a real gem Jamie, it's crystal clear, and it's so peaceful." Phoebe was a very talented artist with charcoal and paper and had already sketched a picture of the landscape. While she worked on other pictures the four sisters looked through her collection of sketches, pictures of her friends, the ship, a picture of the three sisters dancing and more.

"Phoebe these are beautiful, why didn't you tell us you did such wonderful sketches, I love the one of us dancing!" Sophie exclaimed.

"Phoebe is very shy about her drawings, Sophie. She has never shared them with anyone but me," Captain Ron said placing his hand on Phoebe's back affectionately. "She has been so happy since we came here and since making a friendship with you four. I also need to thank you, especially you Jamie, Roz and Sophie for your gift. Phoebe do you want to tell...or should I?"

"We are staying with the colony, our baby will be born here. We will live here. I'm so happy!" Phoebe blurted, tears in her eyes as she embraced her friends again. Whispering in Jamie's ear, "Can I be the fifth sister; Grandma Ruth has adopted me too!" They all laughed and began addressing each other as sister.

Grandmother Ruth overhearing the conversation added, "I've adopted Alexi too, so its six sisters!" Alexandra appeared very happy to be included as a member of the sisters. They all settled down for the feast. "You four ladies are a constant topic of conversation in all three colonies, especially you three. What was the strange game you were doing, no one could even guess?"

Sophie,, pausing a little surprised said, "I hope they're saying good things."

"Always good. They find your antics funny, but the young girls are most impressed, trying hard to be like you. They all tie their hair like you at the nape of the neck, refuse to wear shoes and are learning to dance and sing. You might get flooded with applications for apprenticeship."

Jamie laughed, "Well Phoebe and Alexi will need to join us in 'Range It' then. Don't want to leave two sisters out of our antics!" Sophie, Rosalind and Jamie would explain the game and its purpose. Later they would explain the clan of the bear and the huntress, but not too soon. No need to overwhelm their newest sisters.

"It's not just your antics; it's the way you carry yourselves, your joy of life, your close friendships and your daring. Most of the young girls dream about hunting bears, being talented and beautiful, having a needed and vital skill and finding dashing husbands. You set a high standard for the colony," Lord

Grandfather added. Derek almost choked on his cider as Lord Grandfather spoke. Derek thought and found he agreed. The women were indeed remarkable in many ways. He, however, was never dashing. He did have Jamie. His wonderful, beautiful Jamie, as he looked into her eyes he saw her face color lightly with his gaze. "And you Phoebe," Lord Grandfather continued, "Your art is a unique gift. I would like to hang your art in the library and university. The colony needs art as much as it needs air, water, and yes, music. Art and music give us a soul and mark us as fully human. I'm truly impressed with your skill." Phoebe first looked shocked at Lord Grandfather then beamed with delight. The meal continued in silence for a while. Lord Grandfather's comments had truly moved them all. They had no idea he loved them so much. He was a remarkable man. Their feelings of intimidation replaced with love and respect.

They passed out cold bubbly pies and the group commented on the sweet delicious treat. "You wrestled these berries from the mouth of a bear!" Grandmother Ruth said laughing. "I hope you make more for the harvest festival next week."

"If we work together we can make a ton. It would be fun. We will need to get more berries, without a bear though!" Rosalind said smiling. Alexandra and Phoebe volunteered their services as did Grandmother Ruth. The women began a cheerful conversation regarding plans for the festival and the food and games they were planning, leaving the men free to their own conversation.

"Captain Ron what will you do now. Why did you resign from the navy?" Derek asked.

"I love the sea, and loved being the captain of a ship. But I love Phoebe much more. She really needs close friends and a community to raise our children and to be happy. She has that here, especially now that she feels like she has a family. She was an orphan you know. I'm really all she had. When I went to Lord Grandfather with my dilemma he offered me a new command. I'm to create a militia for the colony. And try my hand at farming; I grew up on a farm, you know?"

"How do you plan to organize the militia?" David added.

"Every available man to be armed and trained. Each colony independently managed by the existing structure. I will train, organize and develop the defense." Rosalind had been listening.

"Don't you mean every available person?"

"No, Roz."

"Then you are making an error. We women have an equal stake in defending the colony. If your defense is lost we will suffer rape and slavery at the least. We need to be included. I'm a crack shot with the crossbow." Rosalind said hotly.

"I was nearly captured by the Imperial Guard and sold into slavery or possibly raped and killed myself. I have vowed to never ever to be defenseless again," added Jamie also entering into the conversation and adding her fire.

"I haven't considered what you have said," Captain Ron replied. Grandmother Ruth also entered the fray.

"I've been a slave. Yes I admit it Casmir, it's time for truth. Our village didn't even mount a defense. Roz and Jamie are right. If we fight it will need to be fierce and devastating. We cannot afford to lose. I would prefer to die fighting than face slavery again. The women need to have a choice to fight. Not all will, but count me in." In the silence that followed each of the sisters added, "Me too!" Derek, Roland and David seeing the fire in their wives could not help, at least momentarily, to visualize their huntress warriors clad only in a single feather firing bolts to defend their home.

Captain Ron paused for a long time then looking directly into Phoebe's eyes, "Your life is more precious to me than anything. I just don't know."

Lord Grandfather then spoke, "The decision must be yours Captain. But remember Roamy culture has a rich history of fierce women warriors who stood shoulder to shoulder with their men. There are other roles besides standing for battle, but I agree with Ruth.

"Every available person then. I would be proud to have you stand at my shoulder Phoebe; I pray it never comes to that!" Phoebe responded by hugging her husband.

"I too, pray it never happens, but we must be ready. We will need overwhelming force and fire to prevail," Phoebe added. "We must be willing to risk everything to survive. They will come. That is for sure." After a long sobering quiet, the conversation again returned to the festival and their beautiful setting. "This pond is so beautiful we need to set it aside as a park so our generations can enjoy it too," Phoebe said wistfully.

"Yes, a public park, and nearby the university built in stone and a temple," Lord Grandfather added.

"A temple?" Sophie asked.

"We need a place for marriages as we no longer have access to the Crystal Cave. Some day the colony's children will be grown and want to marry. This would be an excellent place."

The festival day had arrived. The six sisters and Grandmother Ruth had made hundreds of bubbly pies. They had picked berries together and spent three days baking the pies. The feast included a large hog a hunter had brought in as well as pickled eels, lobster, shell fish and venison. There was music and dancing in the evening and night. During the day they had archery, log cutting and other contests. There were many musical performances with the six sisters performing a number of songs while dancing. The audience for their songs was large and loud with their approval. The women were breathless as they received standing ovations. Jamie noted that many of the young girls and younger women wore their hair knotted as they did and were barefoot, these girls often greeting them with shy smiles. Jamie would have never noted this if Grandmother Ruth had not pointed it out.

Jamie, Rosalind and Sophie were unbeatable in the archery, beating even the men. Sophie's total lack of humility claiming first prize brought much laughter. "I'm good, yes! And I know it," she exclaimed as she claimed her prize, beating everyone, especially David, she even had the audacity to stick out her tongue at David and wiggle her bottom. Jamie and Rosalind were more subdued claiming second and third prize overall.

In the evening they had a dance. Grandmother Ruth has made dresses for her girls. Jamie's was her favorite color deep rich blue. The bodice of the dresses were heart shaped, dropping just low enough to show a good amount of delicious cleavage. The bottom of the bodice secured by a cameo that partially covered the cleavage. The dresses were high wasted to accommodate their expanding bellies with the dress off the shoulder with puffy little sleeves. Sophie's dress was emerald green and Rosalind's red and Jayne's sky blue. The sisters also wore a little shawl just off their shoulders. As usual they left their shoes home. Like in previous dances the sisters had many dance offers, Lord Grandfather dancing with each of his six grandchildren. Derek and his friends also received requests for dances from a lot of giggling young girls which they accepted. Derek relished the dances he and Jamie shared. The Harvest Festival was a greater success than any of the planners expected. As the group of friends were returning to their homes Jayne's water broke.

Chapter 17 Jayne's Girls

Robert looked frantic as he deposited Jayne in their bed. His face was pale and he was shaking slightly. Derek gently took him to the kitchen and sat him down. David and Roland returned from their home bringing additional chairs, they were planning to keep vigil with Robert. Jayne was apprehensive, but composed. She allowed Derek to shepherd Robert out squeezing his hand firmly and smiling re-assuredly to his face. "I will be fine. I've got my sisters to help. I love you, Robert, our twins will soon be born." Robert sat looking like a condemned man. He had not recovered from the loss of his first wife and their twins; and here he was again, his beloved, Jayne, in labor with twins. David heated some cider and added cinnamon then served each with a cup. Then they waited.

The labor was very long and Robert was encouraged to make frequent visits. As always Jayne appeared composed but now she moved uncomfortably periodically and rubbed her abdomen. Jamie gently encouraged Robert to assist and allowed him in and out of the room. Robert's distress was so apparent and discomforting that Jamie whispered to Derek, "Keep him out and occupied for a while. I will give a signal, bring him back when we shout 'here she comes'," Derek nodded.

Twelve hours of labor passed with each hour taking a toll on all involved. Jayne was exhausted, her hair wet from sweat as she worked through the transition phase. With each loud vocalization she made Robert was on his feet pacing. The men doing their best to comfort him. Then Jamie shouted, "Here she comes!" and Robert was allowed in. Jamie had planned to station Robert at the head of the bed to be close to Jayne's face but instead he went around the long way and stopped at the foot as the first baby's head was emerging, and he fainted. Robert did recover quickly and with help from Rosalind made it to the head of the bed in time for the second baby. "Another girl, Jayne!" Sophie exclaimed. Robert looking into Jayne's eyes with tears in his eyes and was speechless. Jayne reached up putting her arms around his neck pulling him toward her.

"Hold on everyone there's another baby!" Jamie exclaimed. And the third little girl was born.

"When my feet disappeared I knew there had to be more than two!" Jayne whispered.

"Was that the day you cried all day?" Robert asked.

"One of them."

Robert held each of his little girls. His face was still very pale but he looked happy and tired. Jayne was exhausted. Sophie helped Jayne to put two of the babies to breast and Robert was sent back out with his friends.

"Well, dad, we're starting a new tradition. We serve a meal to the new father provided by each of us brothers." The men adjourned to Derek's home where he prepared eggs, pickled kidneys and bacon. David heated more cider and Roland supplied some of Rosalind's excellent bread for toast with berry preserves. Their appetites were hardy and Robert received a lot of good natured teasing.

Later when things settled down they chose names for the three girls. Jamie, Roz and Sophie were their names. "I think little Sophie will have red hair, I hope her eyes will be green!" Jayne told Robert, and they were.

Chapter 18 Edward

It was late fall and the colony continued to grow. Babies conceived during and before the long voyage were rapidly reaching term. The three sisters were very pregnant each had hoped to be the first to give birth in the new world; however, six babies arrived before their due date including Jayne's triplets. One evening the six friends were together at Sophie and David's home. "Jamie your pregnancy is the furthest along. I believe you will be first," Sophie said.

Jamie replied, "I think you're right. Derek has agreed to help with the birth!"

"Derek, that's wonderful!" Rosalind gasps while Sophie gave a very meaningful look at David.

"I didn't volunteer for this," Derek said slowly. "I was coerced."

"You were willing enough to be there for the conception, so you should willing enough to be there for the delivery!" Jamie said with a big grin.

"Well, I was, so I'll be there. Just, well...I don't have any idea what I could do."

"Don't worry, Sophie and I will teach you. You'll be wonderful!" Jamie said with one of her full bore smiles that Derek found totally irresistible.

Several weeks later Jamie awoke in the early night. "Derek, my water broke. Go fetch Sophie." Sophie arrived along with Rosalind. Jamie's labor had begun. Derek was kept busy administering back rubs, applying cold compresses to Jamie's forehead and applying counter pressure to Jamie's back during contractions. Derek also timed the contractions and the intervals and kept Sophie posted. Early in the labor while Jamie was still comfortable she requested a ritual bonding foot rub which had both her and Derek laughing. "Sophie why does my back hurt so much with the contractions? This must be the longest labor on record!"

"It's only been four hours, and you're having back labor. You are doing just fine. Your fifty percent effaced and fifty percent dilated, about half way through." Sophie replied. The labor continued two more hours. "Okay, Jamie, almost there you can start to push with the next contraction. You will need to stop pushing when I tell you to." Jamie had a few good pushing contractions with Derek helping her to sit up. He also administered a gentle message to her tummy as they had practiced earlier.

"Sophie! Why does it hurt? I don't want this baby. Make it go back inside!"

"The baby is facing the wrong way Jamie; give me a minute so I can get it to turn. You're almost done sister, you are doing so well. Okay, Jamie, the baby is crowning. Stop pushing." Jamie continued making a grunting sound so Derek whispered "You're still pushing, little sister, you need to stop." Jamie put her head back and took a couple of gasping breaths.

Then glaring hissed, "This is all your fault, Derek, I'm not the only one who should be hurting!" Jamie then turned her head and bit Derek's shoulder hard. When the contraction was over she sobbed, "Oh, Derek, I'm so sorry!" Derek kissed the top of her hear, her hair now soaked from sweating; he whispered, "I love you so much, you are just wonderful!" In two more pushes the head was delivered and the baby was already crying.

"Sunny side up Jamie, I got the baby to turn. He was breech, that's why the back labor. Here, Derek, hold your son." Derek took his son. He was in total awe with Jamie and the baby.

"Are babies always so red and wrinkled?" he asked.

"Yes, Derek, would you like to cut the cord?"

"Oh...yes I would."

"Derek, gave the baby to Roz and helped Jamie deliver the placenta." Rosalind cleaned the baby and wrapped it in a blanket and gave it to Jamie, "You nurse him Jamie. Derek she needs to rest. I think the boys are waiting for you." Derek looked out the window at the rising sun and went out of the room to his friends.

"You look ghastly Derek" Roland said. Let's go over to David's place; he's making burnt breakfast.

"Burnt nothing I'm a great chef!" David replied serving burnt cheesy bread, burnt deer sausage and cider. Robert brought warmed cider with cinnamon. Roland supplied the bread. Derek described the birth of his son ending the narrative with, "As the sun broke the horizon my son was born!" The friends teased Derek mercilessly over the next few minutes. Then Roland said, "I told Roz I would be there too and she was ecstatic, what about you Dave?"

David was silent a long time, "I'm scared to death of losing my angel. I know I won't faint, but the thought of losing her has me terrified!"

"I was scared too, David! That's why I was there."

"Okay, I'll tell Sophie I'm game too."

"Boy will she be happy!" Roland said clasping David's shoulder.

A month later Rosalind gave birth to a baby girl. She and Roland named her Hope because they had come to the new world filled with hope. Two weeks later Sophie delivered a baby girl. They named her Faith; you can never have enough faith. It was wonderful having babies so close in age. The three sisters continued to support and help each other. David, now a practiced carpenter, made cribs for each of the children. Jamie wanted to name her baby Edward. Edward's crib was placed next to Derek's side of the bed so he could easily pass him to his mother for feedings. Jamie's first big fear was that her milk would not come in. It did. Her next big fear was that she would not be able to adequately nurse Edward, but he suckled well and gained weight appropriately. Derek was totally enthralled with his son. He thought he could never be happier than on the day he and Jamie had been sealed, but now he knew even greater happiness was possible. The first time Edward grabbed his thumb he was so excited. "Look at his tiny hand little sister; it's no bigger than my thumb nail. It's so perfect. Look tiny nails and tiny finger prints too!"

As Edward grew Derek and Jamie noticed how he recognized both of them. With Jamie he wanted to cuddle and would set her up with arm movements and facial gestures. With Derek he wanted to play and set Derek up with different facial gestures and arm and leg movements. He squealed with delight when Derek blew bubbles on his feet or tummy. Although Edward had a crib he mostly slept with Jamie and Derek as they just could not easily part with him. "Is he always so vocal when I'm not home?" Derek asked. They had a routine worked out. Derek managed night time diaper changes so Jamie could sleep and he would put little Edward back in the cradle following night time feedings. They often lay awake at night speculating as to what kind of man little Edward would be. Would he marry Hope or Faith?

When Edward was about five months old Jamie woke up in the early hours of morning as Edward had failed to call for his regular feeding. Derek was suddenly awoke by a shriek and immediately went to his wife who had collapsed to the ground sobbing, "My little Edward, my baby?" Derek looked into the crib and his little son lay so still. He was not breathing. Derek felt like he had received a hammer blow to the chest and could not move or speak. Sophie was the first to rush to their home followed by Rosalind. They rushed to Jamie, and they all embraced each other weeping. Derek stood, staring at the tiny baby, afraid to touch or hold him. Jamie held her dead son weeping and rocking him. He could not speak. They were later joined by David and Roland who carried in their babies.

The funeral was held two days later. Edward's little body was the first of the colonists to be buried in the settlements cemetery. Derek was unable to weep. He appeared cordial and controlled through the funeral and over the next few days. Jamie wept several times a day and through the nights, Sophie and Rosalind often weeping with her. Everyone thought and mentioned that Derek was handing his loss so well. He continued to manage the settlements affairs without difficulties. Jamie saw him as distant and uncaring. She felt bitter and angry and after a short angry exchange left their bedroom and began sleeping in the tiny kitchen. Derek appeared to take this in stride, remaining in control and cordial. Sophie and Rosalind saw their friends drifting apart and felt helpless to intervene so they sought counsel from the Lord Grandfather.

The next day Jamie received a visit. "Please come in Grandmother Ruth! I'm sorry things are so messy but I keep crying so much."

"I heard you had a tea set, dear, so I came with a tin of tea to share." Jamie prepared the tea serving some bread and jam. "This is such a lovely tea set Jamie I understand it was your mothers."

"It was hers and we spent many afternoon together drinking and talking."

"I came to talk to you two. Lord Grandfather sends his love and greetings to you and Derek."

"I'm so angry with Derek, Grandmother Ruth, that I have moved out of his bed."

"Oh, dear, that was so drastic, Jamie and not good for either of you."

"Are you really mad at Derek, Jamie?"

"He doesn't care. He seems to act like nothing has happened. I'm just so mad; why isn't he mad too?"

"Mad at whom?"

"At me!" Jamie sobbed. "A healer and midwife that let her baby die!"

"So you are really mad at yourself aren't you?" Jamie had to think for a while.

"How can you understand the pain I feel?"

"Buried six of my children, Jamie, some a few hours old, most less. I understand anger and guilt. I have suffered both. And it did nothing to bring back my boys. It wasn't my fault they died. I had no power to prevent their deaths. Did you Jamie?"

"No, grandmother, I did not!"

"It is normal to feel grief that hurts so very much that you get mad. Grief is good because it is born out of the love we feel. Edward was born under the covenant?"

"Yes, grandmother."

"Then is yours forever, Jamie."

"I know that grandmother so why do I still hurt so?"

"It's supposed to hurt dear."

"Let's talk about Derek. He is hurting too and not handling it as well as you."

"He looks so composed. I hate him!"

"You hate him?"

"No, I'm afraid he blames *me*!" she sobbed.

"He's a man, Jamie, and men find it hard to talk about feelings. We talk about them endlessly. We cry together and then talk more about our feelings, and cry again. Derek needs you. Derek needs to allow himself to grieve with you to be mad as hell and sad as hell. He must grieve, Jamie, or you will lose each other forever." They talked for a long time, both weeping over lost children and about Edward. When Grandmother Ruth left Jamie had devised a plan to rescue Derek.

That night when Derek retired for the night she returned to his bed. She cuddled up next to him with her head on his chest, "I'm so sorry, my love, but I have been so mad at myself for losing our baby that I have taken it out on you."

"Why are you so mad at yourself, little sister?" Derek put his arm around her taking her hand. "It wasn't your fault. You are a good mother and I wouldn't choose anyone else to be Edward's mother. You are truly gifted as a healer and not at fault at all." He continued slowly "I'm so mad too, my love. The day after my little one died the sun came out! I screamed inside. How dare the sun come out when my little boy had died. It came out again the next day and I was madder still and ashamed of my anger. I decided to never eat but got hungry and ate. I'm angry that the world goes on unchanged and my Edward is not here. A hole has been ripped into my heart that goes clear to my soul. Nothing will fill it because nothing can. I hurt so deeply, my love. All I have that I value is you, but I hurt too much to touch you." Derek's eyes were wet and he shook as he talked. His throat felt so tight and there was not enough air in the world to fill his lungs. Jamie was surprised by the extent of his anger and grief. She was surprised he had not shared this. Surprised that he could hide it so well, no one guessed the extent of his grief. She moved up in the bed and put her forehead against his cheek as he spoke and stroked his hair to comfort him. Then, looking into his eyes, "You loved our little Edward, didn't you?"

"Yes with all my heart and soul!"

"Then it should hurt to lose him. Our pain is equal to the love we felt. We loved him deeply, now we hurt for him deeply. It's normal to feel mad because we hurt." Jamie shared why she felt anger because she could not save Edward. "Let us both put aside our anger and just be sad together. They cuddled together and wept for their lost little boy. Later that night Jamie found other ways to comfort her husband.

Over the next several days Derek appeared sadder but his behavior warmer. His work suffered but the colony prospered just as well as if he had been perfect. Jamie overheard David and Roland planning ways to cheer Derek up. She stopped their plans, "Let him be sad; he lost his son! Be sad with him and you can help lessen the sadness.. Watch us girls, we cry together all the time, believe me, it helps."

The weather continued to be cold and the lakes around the colony began to freeze Roland thought it was a good time to cut the ice and store it in some of the root cellars for summer use. Derek organized work parties to cut and haul the ice. The men spent a couple of weeks cutting and hauling ice to the root cellars and covering the ice with sawdust from the carpenters shed. A large store of ice was made in all three villages. It was hard, dangerous work to be out on the ice because it was possible to break through and drown. Jamie worried about losing Derek, especially now since she still so acutely felt the loss of Edward. On the second to last day of the ice harvest Jamie asked, "Why are we harvesting so much ice?"

Derek replied, "The ice will last all summer and allow us to store milk, eggs and cheese longer. And most of all, little sister, to put ice in your ginger beer."

"Isn't ice cutting risky and all of you men are risking your lives so I can have ice in my ginger beer?"

"It has its dangers; Roland fell in this morning, but..."

Jamie interrupted, "Roland, is he okay? Does Roz know? Derek how could you..."

"He's fine little sister. We fished him out, wrapped him in a blanket and delivered him to Rosie and she set to pampering him so much we left him smiling ear to ear. Must admit, I've thought of falling in myself tomorrow just so I could get you to pamper me a little too."

"Derek if you fall in I personally will throw you back in by myself." Then she laughed as they hugged.

Derek continued smiling "I was beginning to think Roland was just getting a little jealous over the attention Rosie was giving little Hope."

"And this you know from experience my love?" Derek smiled and blushed.

Later that night as they held each other in bed Derek said, "You know my love; grief is like waves out in our bay. In a storm they are huge and strong and fast coming in. They can knock you down and drown you, and then they get smaller and smaller and farther and farther apart. They never go away and sometimes a rock gets thrown in and they are big and fast again for a while. I understand my grief better. It's not Edward I grieve for. He is happy having returned to heavenly parents. He will be my son forever as we have been sealed. I grieve for my loss. Not being able to hold him between us at night. Missing his little laugh when I blew bubbles on his tummy. I miss how he looked at me when I returned home. But most of all I miss watching you and him together. Your loving gentle care for him. The way you both glowed when you comforted and nursed him. You always glow from some inner light but when you held our little boy the light was incandescent," Jamie's heart leaped and she felt warmed by his words.

"I too better understand my grief, dearest brother. When he died my arms felt empty without him. My breasts hurt in my need to feed him. I miss his gentle feeding at my breast. I missed being able to comfort him and fill his needs. I miss the way his little body felt and the way he smelled. I miss watching the joy in your eyes when you played with him and how you looked at me when I fed him. We will always grieve the loss our little boy. I'm so glad we can talk about it. I'm so glad I have you to hold in the night."

Chapter 19 The Militia

Winter was an excellent time to organize the militia as there was little planting or fishing to do. Derek had the iron work for the water wheels completed and David's carpentry shop was having idle time. The first thing Captain Ron had done was to recruit George to the militia. This was quite an accomplishment as George was slated to become captain. His skills with the ballista (large ship crossbow) and engineering background made him essential. He would hold the rank as captain and be in charge of coastal ballista stations. Alexandra was overjoyed with the prospect of staying with the colony and became a regular member of the sister's group and its antics.

Captain George ordered constriction of twelve ballista and hundreds of fired clay balls. These would be filled with oil then lit and flung at enemy ships. He also constructed a log and chain boom to close the south channel at Grand Isle and force all shipping to the narrower north channel where they would subject to his batteries of ballista on both islands. He then ordered twelve more ballista but these were not expected to be completed for a year. David was recruited to create shields. He settled on a design using very thin sheets of wood sandwiched between multiple layers of canvas and leather. He used hide glue and pitch gathered from the plentiful large pine trees and came up with a design that was light and could stop crossbow bolts. It had a rectangular shape and had two spikes on the bottom that allowed it to be firmly stood in the ground. It was curved and offered excellent protection and could be locked together to produce a shield wall. The shield was five foot tall and allowed archers to fire over the top. Women's shields would be shorter, tailored to their size. They could be quickly and cheaply produced.

When the call to recruitment was made every man and woman assembled to join. Unmarried, younger women organized into the nurse core. David's wood shop was tasked with making crossbows as was everyone who could do woodwork. Shields were also made for everyone. Phoebe decorated her shield with a bear and received numerous requests for individual designs. Each recruit would need to have crossbow, shield and long knife as well as at least one hundred bolts and incendiaries. Derek designed a different head for the bolts than those used for hunting. These heads could pierce imperial shields and armor.

The new militia drilled every other day to learn the maneuvers and drum signals. They could be called out in under ten minutes and assemble their shield wall at the landing site. Those with ranging skills would stand in the open or behind the second shield wall on a raised platform and signal the range. At fifty yards they would open up with volleys of bolts in rapid continuous fire.

The game 'Range It' became common as many of the colonists competed to become Rangers.

"We need to avoid hand to hand combat if we can," Captain Ron told the assembly of colony leaders. "With overwhelming volleys of bolts and maneuvering we can avoid it until we cut them down or they withdraw." Captain George then added, "Our shore batteries will set a small number of ships afire, but a large group will have some ships able to make a landing."

"Why avoid hand to hand encounters?" the Novi village chief asked.

"Our women may be fierce, but they are no match against a trained killer. I'd rather not risk them if we can avoid it." Then looking into the eyes of each man, "When we fight we take no prisoners. We offer no mercy, no reprieve. If they run we give chase and burn as many of their boats as we can. We offer the same they would give us. Until the last man is no longer standing!" His talk was chilling, but they knew he was correct.

The six sisters and their husbands all had shields with Phoebe's design of a standing white bear against a red background. This was a popular design and much copied. The work of becoming a fighting force was grim. They all prayed they would be spared from conflict, but everyone knew they would be tested.

As winter progressed an expedition was mounted to the lake region to capture the cows and horses they had seen in the mapping expedition. The Novi colony was the sponsor of this expedition and involved the navy contingent of the colony. While these preparations were under way, Jayne finally had her chance to hunt with Robert. Jamie and Derek volunteered to watch the triplets while the couple used the blinds and tree stands. As they were leaving Robert pulled Derek aside, "I have no idea what Jayne is up to, but she came out of our room this morning dressed only in a feather!"

"You are in for a wonderful experience Robert, Just go along and enjoy your hunt...If you see anything let her have the first shot...it's truly worth it!" Derek slapped Robert's shoulder as they left. Jayne was able to introduce Robert to all the delights of the clan of the bear by their second hunt. George and Ron received their introductions also at the hands of their wives. Ron and George were even happier that they had elected to stay with the colony.

Chapter 20 Alone

Spring had arrived and the fleet had to return to Port Hope. Much had changed in the fleet with Captains Ron and George's resignation other officers were promoted up. The ships were heavily loaded with timber, salted fish, pickled sardines and eels. The colony would show an excellent profit in its initial import. The fleet was excited with the prospect of returning and the colonists apprehensive with the loss of the navy. Eventually they would have their own armed coast guard but for now they would depend on their two luggers. It was decided a feast would celebrate the departure. The entire colony had left their homes and come to Grand Isle for the celebration. The food was extravagant.

It was also a time to renew old acquaintances as the water separating the three colonies was a formidable barrier for some. They had a lot to celebrate. Their second expedition to the lake had yielded five of the red shaggy cows. They were unable to get a bull but the cows were all about to calf so they might get one that way. They had confirmed the existence of horses but had been unable to capture one. They had requested some walkers with the next visit from Port Hope so perhaps they might have better luck. Since the Roamy had so few walkers they did not expect any to be sent. But it did not hurt to ask. Everyone was talking about the plans for a permanent university and temple at the new park on Bell Isle. Both mills were now operational at Novi and two more were under construction. The spring harvest of winter wheat had been a success and the new planting had begun. Hope and optimism ruled the day. The fruit trees were in blossom and most had started a kitchen garden.

The six couples sat on a blanket eating from well filled plates when they were joined by Lord Grandfather and Grandmother Ruth. "Alexi been telling us she has missed her second period Grandma Ruth, bet she's pregnant," Phoebe said.

"Must be something in the water," David said dryly.

"I don't think it's the water silly man!" Sophie chuckled, "I'll just have to explain it to you, and show you all over again tonight." She gave David one of her most devilish smiles and he blushed. The babies were all at the picnic. Phoebe's baby boy, Jamie, was only weeks old. Baby Sophie's hair carrot red and she had emerald green eyes. Derek and Jamie loved seeing all the babies but their hearts ached for their little one. As usual the sisters were asked to perform their songs. Many of the other young girls and women also performed and the influence of their original performance was very evident. The three sisters liked that the people of the colony liked them enough to emulate them. The feeling of being odd and out of place was replaced by acceptance of their truly unique selves.

"This will be the most dangerous time for our colony!" Lord Grandfather said slowly. "Without a navy we are vulnerable to attack from the sea."

"We have the militia," Jamie said confidently.

"Yes, and we have our fierce women warriors too!" Lord Grandfather said smiling at Jamie. "I will feel much better when we have our own navy. Captain George has given me plans for two additional race built luggers and we will start building this winter."

"Do you think we will be attacked by imperial forces?" Sophie asked.

"I'm more concerned of them using unconventional forces against us. I'm glad Ron and George are staying on." They continued discussing the race built luggers and the need to increase their level of self-sufficiency in case the returning ships are delayed. "The more we can do for ourselves the better. Right now we are importing everything. There is so much more we need to do. We have a lot of talent here. Next year we will have even more." Then looking at Rosalind, "I'm so happy you have decided to be a healer, Roz. You have so much more you can give this way."

Rosalind responded by smiling, "Thank you, Lord Grandfather, I'm really happy being a healer."

Ruth joined them looking a little sad, "All my boys are leaving!" her eyes brimming with tears. Sophie, Rosalind and Jamie moved to sit with their arms around her.

"You still got us girls." Jamie said. They continued to hold Grandmother Ruth and were joined by the other sisters while she wept quietly. Ron and George replied softly, not all your boys, Grandmother Ruth, and she looked at them smiling. Grandmother Ruth's sadness was felt by most of the colony as the ships departed in the morning. For better or worse, they were now alone.

Chapter 21 The First Encounter

Jamie, Rosalind and Sophie walked in the early morning darkness to the ballista battery on the north side of Belle Isle. Stub was with them as they walked in silence. Jamie and Derek had argued bitterly because he did not want the women to be at the ballista battery alone. Jamie could be extremely caustic when angry and now deeply regretted what she had said. The women reached the site and relived the previous team and settled for a long boring twenty four hours. They were at the sight barely an hour when Stub began barking an alarm. There was a sharp cry from Stub then silence. Jamie said, "Run now and get help, I will delay whoever it is then run myself. Now, don't argue." Rosalind and Sophie took off. Jamie grabbed one of the stout poles from the ballista's capstan and held her ground. Three of the dirtiest men she had ever seen approached her with leering smiles.

"What a nice little piece of ass! Come here girl, we got something for you." Jamie ran at them holding the pole high in the air bringing it down toward the head of the largest man hoping to split his head. He simply caught the pole in his large meaty hand and pulled it from Jamie's grasp. With his other hand he grabbed Jamie's breast squeezing and twisting as Jamie screamed in pain and he pulled her close, pinning her arms, and holding her feet off the ground. Jamie wiggled and twisted kicking him with her bare feet. Her assailant licked her face and tried to kiss her. His breath had a feted foul odor and Jamie bit his tongue as he tried to force it in her mouth. He simply tossed her to his companion who tore open the bodice of her dress and began touching her where only Derek had ever touched her. She fought with fury and when her feet touched the ground and she was shoved to the third man she was ready. She kicked him in the groin and jabbed her finger into his eye. The man howled in pain, but now her first assailant had grabbed her by her face with his right hand and was pulling her toward him again. She took his fifth finger into her mouth and bit as hard as she could and severed it at the second joint. Then turning she spat his finger into his face her eyes blazing with hatred and anger. He screamed in fury, "You gonna feel real pain for that you little whore." Holding his injured right hand close to his chest and swung his ham sized fist at her face. Jamie dodged the blow but was knocked to the ground with his second punch to her breast. She screamed in pain at the blow. Then he knelt over her hitting her again and again to her head, her face, her breasts, her ribs and stomach. Jamie screamed in pain with each blow until she had no more screams in her, the only sound she uttered was a little keening sound. She could taste the blood streaming into her mouth from her lips and nose. The three men began ripping her clothes off her until she was naked. She rolled into a ball to protect herself but the beating began anew and the other two men simply grabbed her arms pulling her flat as the first assailant pushed her legs apart with his knees. "This is how I like my women, full of passion." Jamie was sure she was about to die from the beating. No one could save her, she wished for death rather than this continued humiliation and horror. At some point she no longer felt the blows. Her face was so swollen that between her tears and the swelling she could barely see. The man pinning her clumsily opened his pants and prepared to push himself into her when the soft sounds of strings slapping was heard. Two bolts entered the chests of the two men standing, ripping through their hearts and exiting their back. They just stood there mouth agape eyes open wide in surprise as a crimson rose blossomed on their filthy shirts. They collapsed. The first brute looked about for the source or the bolts when a hand seized his hair from behind and hyper extended his head. Derek's blade sliced through the soft tissue of his neck and a crimson fountain of blood spurted in waves from his ruined neck. Pushing him aside while he made gurgling sounds Derek rushed to Jamie's side.

"Please, dearest love, don't die!" He took off his shirt and covered her and lifted her into his arms. Derek was weeping now.

"Don't be me mad at me Derek!" she whispered reaching to caress his face as she blacked out. They were met by Rosalind and Sophie as they grimly brought Jamie home and lay her in bed. Sophie and Rosalind gently began cleaning the blood from her and examining the injuries. They were lucky that Derek, David and Roland had already started walking to the ballista battery as Derek had a fearful premonition, otherwise they would have been too late for Jamie. Sophie did a scan. Jamie floated in and out of oblivion but heard Sophie say that her baby was okay if they could save Jamie, *A baby? She had a baby.* She heard other voices, her five sisters, Grandmother Ruth and later Lord Grandfather. She heard Derek's voice and she found comfort in the sound. Her whole body hurt. She found the pain unbearable at times, and then the darkness took her again. Later she felt a warm comforting energy envelope her. She recognized it as Sophie and Rosalind. They were doing a laying on of hands and she felt much of the pain deep inside her lessen. She felt so loved and so much comfort in the light that enveloped her that she just allowed herself to fall deeper and deeper into it. Finally she was free of pain. And she slept in the warm envelope of their energy.

Three other pirates were discovered and captured. They gave up quickly thinking their treatment would be mild. They were put in irons and tethered to a huge rock. They waited until Lord Grandfather was able to come. He had been keeping a vigil with Jamie. As he approached the men he recognized one. "Captain Stouman, I see you forgot the excellent swimming lessons I gave you and have returned to piracy." Lord Grandfather's voice was cool and quiet, his face and calm stance indeterminable. Only his eyes betrayed his cold fury. Captain Stouman had no idea what he was in for.

"Well if it isn't my old bastard buddy Casey. Been a long time. I seem to remember last time I saw you I had a little red headed slut with me. She was all eyes for you. Did she spread her legs for you and the crew?" Lord Grandfather ignored the taunts but the muscle in his jaw twitched.

"You three will die, there is no reprieve. Give me what I want and it will be swift, cross me... (he paused long for effect then), it's up to you." Then he looked at each man and pointed to one. "Why are you here, were you sent and by whom?"

The man sneered, "You won't kill me cause of your shit covenant, you Roamy are weak and we will exterminate you and your babies, and especially your women. They get our special treatment!"

Lord Grandfather said very quietly, "Burn him."

A bucket of warm incendiary oil was dumped on the man's head and he was set on fire. His screams and thrashing had the desired effect. The second prisoner began to talk, "Imperials paid us in gold to find you and destroy you. Our ship is in a small bay on the far side of the middle island. We came ashore to look around, maybe capture someone. That's all I know, don't burn me!" Lord Grandfather nodded and three bolts pierced the man's chest and he fell dead.

"Good day, Captain Stouman, we will talk later." With that he walked away giving Captain Stouman time to think and time to be afraid. His orders, leave the bodies, and do not approach. The Middle Sister Island was searched but the pirates had already left, abandoning their captain and mates to their fate. The longboats the pirates had used for landing on the island were found and their jugs of fermented spirits placed on the ground just out of reach of Stouman. Lord Grandfather waited until late in the afternoon of the second day to approach. Stouman had been bellowing, demanding food, water and to speak to Casey for many hours.

"Hey, Casey don't a condemned man get food and water?"

"Why waste food on a dead man."

"I thought you stinking Roamy were civilized."

"You thought wrong. Do you have anything you'd like to tell me? I'm late for dinner."

"You bastard, always thinking you be better than me. You're just like me. When it comes down to the end. What did you do with that little slut anyway? I was going to give her to the crew!"

"I married her. Is that all you want to tell me?" Then he started to walk away.

"They will be back you bastard; you will never see them when they come. Twelve ships we have. They'll slit your throats while you sleep and take their time with your women. Did you hear me Casey? You're all dead!" Lord Grandfather nodded and the jugs of fermented spirits were moved to within reach and Stouman began to drink. Lord Grandfather continued to wait. By early morning Stouman was very drunk. Although he thought he was alone he was being watched and everything he did and said was noted. Stouman began to sing of his twelve ships and his gold. He sang about the colonies on the east coast he had pillaged and in doing so gave a lot away concerning tactics. In the late morning when Lord Grandfather returned he found Stouman dead. Apparently he had gotten so drunk that he choked on his own vomit. The bodies of the six pirates were placed on a large rocky shoal in the bay. Food for the crows, and a warning to pirates.

Jamie continued to sleep in her warm envelope. She knew to open her eyes was to return to the world of pain. If she could just stay like this her baby would be safe. Her friends kept vigil at her bedside. As the hours and days passed with her not responding they became more alarmed and sad. Then she heard a quiet weeping, the sadness and the weeping so powerful that she needed to give comfort. She recognized the source, it was Derek. Her Derek, his heart was breaking. She slowly forced her eyes to open feeling pain as she left her envelope. She saw Derek he was kneeling at the bed side, his arms folded near her head with his face down on his arms as he wept and prayed. Slowly she reached until her hand touched his gray head. She gently ruffled his hair, "Don't cry, my love."

Derek looked at her and he smiled, "I thought I lost you, little sister! I didn't want to live without you." He gently reached out cupping her severely bruised face and kissed her. Even his very gentle kiss caused her to wince with pain so Derek stopped. Over the next few weeks Jamie was pampered by her friends and Derek. When she was finally allowed out of bed and outside she found Stub. She was so excited at finding her Stub she cried. Stub had not been killed but lost sight in her right eye from the blow she had received. Her dog had three legs and one eye but to Jamie she was beautiful. Later that night Jamie asked Derek to lay with her in the bed and he came very cautiously to her side. He had not touched her since their last kiss fearing he would hurt her.

"Could I have one of your famous ritual bonding foot rubs," she asked coyly. As Derek gently kneaded her feet kissing them, she was able to get him to continue his gentle rubbing to her back, and finally, as she began to touch him, she re-lit the flame between them.

A meeting was held with the colony leaders including Lord Grandfather, Captain Ron and Captain George. Captain Ron was speaking. "We are prepared for a frontal attack against Imperial troops; however, we are facing a stealth attack by pirates. We need to redo our plans and think offense. We still need to train for a defensive battle but we need more. Captain George has a plan."

"We will need to hit the pirates hard before they are fully organized and develop a flexible defense for each colony. I suggest each colony build two of these war canoes." He passed out the plans, "And we hit them with incendiaries while they're still on the boats. We need to catch them and cut them down." Work started on the war canoes. Three, eighty foot cedar logs were spiked together and the bottom of the boat carved with an adz. The bottom had a slight rocker to it so it would beech easily. The bottom was flat with a small built in skeg from which a rudder was hung.

The sides were low and flat sided and the boats had two leeboards. The inside of the log canoe was carved out and two mast steps installed. Twenty five men would man each boat. They would paddle or sail as needed. The boats were light enough for the crew to carry so launching and portage was easily accomplished. The masts would fold down when not in use, and carried two generous sprit sails dyed dark gray. The boats had a very low profile and proved very hard to see on the water. Being log canoes they were unsinkable. They drilled stealth voyages to each of the sister islands every evening, until they could do it in total darkness and quiet. The log canoes were fast to paddle and even faster to sail. They organized races to hone their skill. The boats easily reached fifteen knots in the waters of the bay. Hundreds of brittle clay pots were made and filled with the incendiary oil mixture and the pot closed and sealed with a thick fuse and bees wax. A coast watcher was assigned to each of the sister islands and the colony settled down and waited.

Chapter 22 Clouds of War

It was mid-afternoon and already the sky was darkening. David and Robert were the coast watchers on Middle Sister when they spotted distant sails on the horizon. They counted at least ten ships. Not needing further confirmation, the two men signaled the watchers on Grand Island with the signal mirror. Luckily they still had sufficient light, and the signal was confirmed. The colonies semaphores picked up the message and relayed it through the colonies. The wind was onshore and diminishing rapidly and they sailed across the bay to the little rocky shoal where a faster boat would spirit them to the departure point. When night came they expected little wind and thick fog in the bay, typical spring weather for Bountiful Bay. The slowing wind would make it difficult to determine when the pirate fleet entered the little bay on Middle Sister Island, but as it was the only anchorage site on the rugged coast, that is precisely where they would come. The fog would shield them from the pirates but it would also shield a pirate invasion from them. The only advantage was that they knew the pirates were coming and their survival depended on their willingness to fight.

The colony was well rehearsed and sprang into action. Some of the homes were designated safe houses and the children were gathered to them. The six sisters armed with cross bows would defend the safe houses at Bountiful. Pickets were placed along the coast of both islands and Novi to watch for pirate landings and teams of responders would rally to any reported landing. The six war canoes departed separately from each colony with plans to meet in the lee or North Sister Island to co-ordinate the attack. The fog continued to thicken as it blew in across the bay.

The pirates made their landing in late evening and began the process of unloading. The leaders would meet on Middle Sister Island then send small killer teams to the colonies in the early hours of the day. The fog slowed their plans considerably, as did the constant power struggle caused by the loss of Captain Stouman. They were confident and began in bidding fermented spirits to bolster their courage. They had not launched most of their long boats but had them still in davits.

David, Roland and Derek were in the boat that would attack the shipping with incendiary grenades. Captain Ron and George managed to get the other five boats ashore on the lee side of the island and the men began crawling through the thick brush to the enemy camp. They all were in black clothes and had their faces and hands blackened with a mixture of lamp black and pig fat. Each carried at least a hundred bolts and a long knife. They moved very slowly taking well over an hour to cover the short distance. Then they waited. Just past midnight a lone boat slipped out of the fog and moved quickly into the little harbor. In total silence they moved through the ships tossing the incendiaries on to the ships each ship getting at least ten. They also tossed several through the windows of the stern castles. The result was immediate as the boats began to burn. The sailors were easy to spot in the light of the fires and were picked off by crossbows from the boat. The fires spread rapidly and screams from men trapped inside the burning boats filled the air. The attacking boat had also brought barrels of pig's blood and fish entrails and these had been dumped into the water prior to the incendiary run.

With their entire fleet apparently burning the pirates ran to the beach to look at the fires. At that point the hidden archers opened up on the pirates. They were easy targets silhouetted against the burning boats. In total surprise the pirates waded into the bay to escape the archers. Some of them wounded and bleeding from crossbow fire. Then horrific screams filled the night as sharks began taking an occasional pirate. This drove the pirates ashore where the archers patiently waited. Repeatedly the movement of the pirates between the shore and the shallow bay continued as archers drove them into the water and sharks drove them to land. Those in the boats lucky enough to escape the fire by jumping overboard faced the archers in the boat, sharks and the very real specter of simply drowning.

By morning the ships had burned down to their waterline. The smell of burnt flesh permeated the air. Pirates who had tried to surrender were simply executed on the spot. Not a single pirate was left standing. Teams examined the bodies delivering a fatal blow to the head to any left alive. Six hundred bodies were recovered. Hundreds had perished in the burning ships, never to be counted and only the gods knew how many were taken by sharks. The bodies were simply stacked on the beach and left. The pirates had unloaded considerable supplies on the island but these were left for later pick up by a lugger as the war canoes would not have room. They also left six longboats the others burning on the boats. The archers tarried on the island carefully looking for any hidden survivors. None were found so the war canoes returned to the colonies.

    The returning men were met by their waiting wives. They had suffered no fatalities but several had suffered burns from handling the incendiaries, David had suffered a friendly crossbow bolt to his upper arm, the bolt had simply passed through the soft tissue leaving the bone intact. Sophie managed the wound well. Many of those on the land action had blundered into poison ivy in the dark and needed treatment. Other than that, no one else was injured. The homecoming was joyful as worried families reunited. No pirate landings had been made in the colony. There was no celebration as the brutality of the one sided fight took its toll on the men. They had broken the covenant they had made. It was necessary to survive, yet the horror they committed still appalled them. Some of the men wept openly with shame for what they had needed to do. Still they had survived; there really was no other option.

    Over the next few days Lord Grandfather called for a renewal of the covenant. He visited with groups and any individual needing counseling or just warm support. The day of renewal was planned for Sunday and included the community feast. Each colony held its feast and pledged themselves to the covenant. Those who had participated in the fighting performed ritual washing prior to the feast. Jamie snuggled with Derek at the meal and whispered the pirates got exactly what they deserved, and she for one did not feel at all bad. As she had been the only person to suffer at the hands of the pirates, Derek understood her feelings and agreed. They would need to be always alert. This time they had won. They could never afford any other outcome. Derek returned Jamie's hug.

    Two weeks later the colony's lugger anchored in little bay of Middle Sister Island. The burnt hulks of a dozen ships could be seen on the bottom of the clear bay. The corpses of the dead had been disposed of by birds and land crabs and human bones littered the beach. Most of the thousands of bolts fired had been retrieved but a few hundred more has washed up on shore and these were recovered. The battle sight had a chilling aura to it. They gathered the large chests and supplies left by the now dead pirates and disposed of the multiple jugs of fermented spirits. Then they returned home. In the chests they found the contract for their extermination and the list of eighteen hundred pirates who would join the expedition. All of them had perished. They found a record of the payment promised to each man and recovered the gold. It was a fortune in gold as well as even larger amounts of Imperial sterling coins and copper tenth's. The Imperial Magistrates apparently very eager to ensure their destruction. They were willing to spend five times what the colonies had costs to create to see them destroyed. The treasure would be put to good use. They faced a powerful and determined enemy with a long reach. Such an expenditure of imperial treasure would certainly weaken the enemy, but they needed to remain vigilant. They continued to hold mock drills weekly alternating between offense and defense. Racing the log canoes became a sport that was well liked and followed by everyone. More of the log canoes were built. The race built luggers that had been started were finally launched and fitted out. They had a small very formidable navy.

Chapter 23 Pink Fish, Brown Bears and Bees

No sooner had the war ended when Turnagain Bay was filled with millions of pink fleshed fish. The fish were intent in making it up the rivers and streams and were even seen jumping the dams they had constructed for the mills. The fish were abundant and many just took them with hand spear. Their pink flesh was delicious and was oily. The fish dried well and those not consumed fresh were dried. The fish eggs were also consumed, however, Jamie did not like the fishy tasting, salty eggs. Stub loved them; of course Stub simply liked eating. Drying racks were now a common presence at all the colonies as the fish were caught in abundance.

The fish brought the bears. For the most part the bears were indifferent to the colonists but avoided the settlements. Still, having bears so close was frightening. The bears avoided the islands but Novi had cattle to protect. Two bears had been killed as they approached the settlement to closely, however, no other incident with the bears occurred. The colonist took the abundance of fish as a gift from the gods and evidence of the power of their renewed covenant. The bears simply feasted on the fish.

The sisters organized a fishing trip; they even arranged to have one of the long boats. The colony managed to obtain six additional long boats that had formerly belonged to the pirates. The women insisted on rowing. Usually one man worked a single pair of oars, but as the women were so tiny they sat two to a seat each working their own oar. Jamie and Sophie on the last row, then Rosalind and Alexandra, and then Jayne and Phoebe sat in the first row. David sat at the rudder and each of the men held the babies with Derek assisting with two of the triplets. Stub sat majestically at the bow. They had packed a large lunch and carried their fishing supplies. The initial attempt at rowing provided a comedy show for any onlookers. Sophie repeatedly fell off her seat when she pulled back on the oar. not sufficiently lowering the blade into the water, and was laughing so hard she had everyone laughing. Another problem they encountered was frequently tangling the groups of oars as they often lost their rhythm. Sophie quickly discovered she could easily splash David as she pulled back on the oar and soon had him quite wet. Their strokes with the oars were so uneven that David had to frequently use the rudder to keep them on course. The women were all wearing their flower pattern skirts and white blouse with a deer skin laced vest, they also wore soft deer skin gloves and chipped straw hats. They all were bare foot as usual and had their hair knotted at the nape of their neck. Derek was happy to see Jamie being so silly with her friends. The awful experience with the pirates was now behind her. They all carried their cross bows. Eventually the sisters decided to sing to maintain their rhythm and Sophie lead the group in the bawdiest song she knew. They were after all in a pirate longboat. With their new found rhythm they managed to beat the tide and crossed to Novi. Stub jumping into the water to cross the last fifty yards herself.

They ate their lunch in Novi before walking to the area they intended to fish not knowing how the bears would react to the food they carried. As they approached the section of river they planned to fish in, the bears moved away. "I've learned that when a bear becomes aware of your presence he will either run off or run over to eat you. They seldom ever just keep fishing," Alexandra said.

"I'm grateful these bears decided to leave, I'm sure Stub's presence helped," Sophie added.

"Poor Stub looks fiercer than any pirate with her stub leg and missing eye." Phoebe mused.

"That's why we love Stub; she has an honest beauty you have to look hard to find." David said with a laugh. "You can't but love a dog as brave and loyal as Stub." David rubbed Stub's head and Stub moaned in canine ecstasy.

The men had made double pronged spears for the women. They had decided the sisters would fish and the men would tend to the babies. However, feeding the babies would be left to the women, as Captain Ron explained to Phoebe, "My milk hasn't come in yet!" and she reacted with a kiss, then a gentle bite to his chest. Even though the fish were so abundant in the water spearing them proved very difficult. After literally hundreds of unsuccessful attempts Alexandra finally got a fish. "Alexi's got a fish!" Jamie shouted as they all ran to see her fish. At first none of them wanted to touch the fish, then Rosalind grabbed it to have it wriggle free of her grip and flop around on the ground. The sight of the six of them trying to grasp the slippery fish had the men laughing and the fish in the end managed to escape back in to the water. Eventually they developed better skills and began taking fish, everyone except

Sophie, who still seemed unable to get a fish. Finally, taking a lunge at a fish a little too far off shore Sophie fell into the river and began trying to catch a fish with her bare hands. When she succeeded she threw the fish to David with a loud "Wah-hoo." David wadded into the river to assist Sophie and she managed to pull him in. David then simply lifted her into his arms and carried her out silencing her with a kiss. Sophie laughed and continued to kiss David. This was the second time Sophie had totally soaked David. Gratefully it was a warm sunny day and they all dried out. They returned to Bountiful that evening with a good load of fish. This time the men rowed. Derek cut the fish into fish stakes for grilling and Grandmother Ruth and Lord Grandfather joined them to share in the catch. They spent the evening eating and talking. The women brought their instruments and they ended the evening with singing. Derek loved to hear Jamie sing with her sisters. Sophie repeated the bawdy song she had sung in the boat and Grandmother Ruth taught them several more bawdy songs with each of them laughing in delight.

The next project was organizing the gardens. Jamie, Sophie and Rosalind's homes were in a row on First Street with Jayne's across the road from Rosalind. Phoebe and Alexandra were close by on ribbon farms. The village homes had close to an acre and they planned extensive gardens. Jamie wanted her kitchen garden and herb garden in raised beds next to the house so Derek made the raised beds. The others copied the pattern. The sisters traveled to Novi several times carefully obtaining berry bushes and replanting them in their gardens. They had obtained the blue and purple berries as well as red and black berries. They also found a small native tree that produced a large fruit that tasted like custard pudding so they also transplanted several pudding trees. The rest of the garden was dedicated to root vegetables like tubers and turnips, and with squashes, beans and melons.

In addition to their gardens they planted window boxes full of flowers. Many or the flowers they found growing in the wild. The flowers produced larger blooms under their care and truly made their homes beautiful to behold. Jamie had carried Clemencies seeds from her original home and planted them at her new home. When they began to grow and blossom Jamie did all she could to manage not to cry. Derek held her not quite understanding why she wept.

The night they first plowed their garden Derek convinced Jamie to sleep under the stars in the new garden. Jamie suspected Derek was up to something and was eager to discover what. Jamie was forever the trickster in their relationship; was it now rubbing off on Derek? As they lay on a blanket under the stars and moons they snuggled together. After they had been kissing for a while Derek whispered, "You introduced me to the huntress ritual of the bear for which I'm very grateful. Tonight I'm going to introduce you to the ancient farmer's ritual of the first plowing."

With a devilish twinkle in her eye Jamie replied, "Dearest husband, haven't you worked hard enough plowing. You wish to work at it all night?"

"No, you misunderstand my love. It's not the garden I wish to plow!" Jamie gave her chuckling laugh and put her arms around Derek's neck and they spent the night together in the garden.

Jayne wanted to bathe the triplets so Jamie and Alexandra came over to assist. Jayne had successfully bathed the triplets before just not together. And Jamie and Alexandra really liked helping with the babies. Jayne had a large wooden tub in the kitchen and had already warmed the water. Each of the sisters took a baby and sat them in the water assisting them to sit. The babies were delighted to play in the water and splashed happily. "Which one do I have?" Jamie asked, "Little Sophie is easy to pick out, the other two harder."

"You got Roz, Alexi you got little Jamie." They continued to hold the babies while they played in the water. "They can stay in the water as long as it's warm or until one of them poops," Jayne said, "At least one usually does." They, however, did not and when the babies were removed from the water they cried. "They just love their bath; it's so nice to have help. You were so kind to come at such short notice."

"And miss a chance to see my namesake?" Jamie laughed, "Not a chance. Alexi I heard your husband and Ron were planning a business, could you tell us more?"

"We have combined our farms and added one more. We are keeping pigmy goats. The men are planning to build a cheese house. The both of them are so excited. I've tasted some of their cheeses and they're really good."

"I really miss cheese," Jayne said. "I would like a good white cheese and perhaps a good sharp cheese."

"They're also working on a soft cheese and very strong cheese."

"Eww, I tried stinky cheese and it was awful! But I will have to try yours at least once." Jamie said diplomatically.

"I just happened to bring some samples!" Alexandra said with a shy smile. After the triplets were dried, dressed and fed the three of them sat for tea and cheese. "We really need to thank you Jayne, you're finding that large store of rennet is what gave George the idea. We brought a lot to the new world and only a few farms were using it to make cheese for their consumption."

"I love this white cheese with the yellow rind," Jamie said, "Its mild and has just a hint of saltiness. I even like the stinky cheese, the trick is not to smell it before putting it in your mouth." The women laughed, "It smells like Derek after a hard day at his iron shop." They laughed again.

"I got this white cheese with holes in it, give it a try Jayne." They all sampled the cheeses and continued sipping their tea.

"You know the head women's storehouse is to become a general store in the next week or so. I'm going to be store keeper as Roz has resigned as head woman. I would be glad to carry your cheeses on consignment like I do the berry preserves." Jayne said.

"That would be so kind of you Jayne. Roz seems so very happy as a healer."

"Yes and I'm so grateful to have the help. The three colonies keep me on the go. Did you hear they laid the foundations for the temple and the university? They are to be stone. Been too busy to go and see." The women continued their discussion the temple and their excitement. "I plan to visit it with Derek I really want to see it when it's done," Jamie said.

Derek, Roland and David were speculating in ways to stimulate new products for the colony when David suggested keeping bees. "Many of our farmers kept them, but we didn't bring any
   on the boats."

"I did notice a swarm by the river but didn't think much about it." Derek replied. "We certainly could use the wax, and a little sweet honey can go a long way."

"I know how to build the boxes, maybe we could try it and if it goes well, sell our hives to the farmers," David said.

"It would give your wood shop an additional stream of income to," Roland added. "We could make it a partnership, perhaps Robert too. I have no idea how to get bees."

"I do." Derek continued "I was fascinated with bees as a child. Let's start with the boxes then we can get some bees. We can start small keeping the hives in the garden, then branch out. I'll get the women to sew a bee suit for us." They assembled a number of boxes for bee keeping and melted the bees wax casting them into thin sheets for frames. When they had enough for several hives they began to hunt for wild hives. Derek made a thread lasso with a downy feather tied on. The lasso was about two feet long. They then stationed themselves near a field of wild flowers and waited. Eventually Derek and Robert managed to lasso a bee then they attempted to follow the feather to the hive. Several attempts were made when at last two wild hives were located. At this point progress stopped because none of the men knew how to safely extract the hives. The bee suit was progressing slowly and only the hood was completed. Then word got to them a farmer had located a swarm and wanted to buy a box. The four partners arrived in Novi with one of their bee boxes, smoke pot and hood.

"I'll buy the smoke pot too, not sure I will need the hood yet but I'll take that too, swarms usually don't sting so it will be easy." The four partners then watched the farmer as he gently brushed the swarm with his bare hand until he found the queen. At that point millions of bees began landing on his arm and face. He quickly placed the queen into the box as the bees continued to follow the queen. He brushed the few reaming bees from his arm and face and put the lid on the box.

"Why weren't you stung?" David asked.

"Swarms are usually docile. Approach a hive and they will sting. Keep working the hive and eventually they recognize you. I seldom wear the hood, been stung a gazillion times. I really like this smoke pot. Its copper I think. A new design?"

"I designed it," Derek replied. "You really made handling the bees look easy. We located some wild hives but weren't sure how to approach."

"Tell you what, these are quality boxes, and the smoker too.

You supply me with them and I'm sure other farmers will follow. If you want to keep bees I'm more than willing to teach you." Soon they had numerous orders for their boxes and smoke pots. Most farmers electing to make their own bee suits which pleased the sisters who really did not want to be in the sewing business. The idea of keeping the bees was also put on hold. Sophie and Rosalind, afraid to have hives with small curious children about, and Derek not really having time to handle the bees care. David's wood shop did a brisk business supplying boxes and wax drawers. Derek's smoke pots were on high demand. Roland and Robert designed a hand operated centrifuge to extract honey from the combs leaving them intact and started selling them to farmers. Eventually they brought all their different aspects of construction under one roof. When the partners did finally have their own hives to manage they kept them at farms that allowed them for a share of the raw honey. By the time autumn arrived they had small jugs of honey, squares of honey in the comb and wax for sale on consignment at the general store.

Chapter 24 Summer

The weeks passed and Jamie busied herself with her vegetable and herb garden. The three sisters made frequent field trips finding and collecting plants and materials to make remedies. Sophie and Rosalind continued to drill the remedy cards and rubrics. Both of her apprentices were showing great promise. Best of all, Jamie was pregnant again. This pregnancy filled her with hope. She and Alexandra had become very close as their pregnancies were due about the same time. Derek had been most gentle and caring and was pampering her so much it was driving her nuts. It showed her how much he loved her so she accepted it. Jayne was so busy with her three babies that they would go several days not seeing her. When Sophie and Rosalind were out they most often had little Grace and Hope on the back frame David had made. Jamie was not prone to jealousy but seeing all her friends with babies did make her sad. Her heart still hurt for her lost son. Jamie assisted her sisters with baby care and readily took the triplets when Jayne needed a break. Being a healer still demanded a lot of time and energy but Sophie was now carrying a considerable amount of the load. Still the women found time to keep up their archery skills. Phoebe and Alexandra's homes on the ribbon farms they shared were close enough that they were daily visitors. Little Jamie was the only boy in her sisters families. Jamie was hoping for another boy.

Derek needed to make frequent visits to Novi as the other mills were in construction, but he always took Jamie with him. Derek had great difficulty when they were separated especially after the attempted rape by the pirates. Derek had gotten Captain George to give the sisters lessons in knife fighting and they practiced with wooden knives. The women had become very proficient in using their small stature in getting under opponents and placing their knives in the arm pit or groin. Derek had made the women long thin knives with a double edge. The knife was thin enough to conceal when held like they were instructed yet long enough to do lethal damage. Everyone hoped that these skills would never be called upon. Jamie was fiercely committed to never being defenseless again. She always carried her knife. Baby care was not much of a problem for the sisters as Grandmother Ruth was always willing to take a baby or three for a day or evening.

The best part of summer was the long warm days. No need for shoes, time to just be with friends and the long warm nights with Derek. The pirate battle seemed like part of a distant past; summer was its own reality. Was it just two summers ago when the lived by the pond, just her and Derek? So much had happened in such a short time. Jamie felt happy. The Clemencies were blooming and the windows were bordered by the lavender flowers. The garden was producing a plethora of berries and they had fresh vegetables with their meals. Jamie had obtained some chickens and they ranged freely in the garden and kept them supplied with fresh eggs. Sophie was given a pigmy goat and the three sisters helped with its care and shared the milk. Eventually each would have a goat, compliments of Alexandra and Phoebe and yogurt and cream cheese would be added to their accomplishments.

It was a sunny day under a clear blue sky and Derek and Jamie had a private picnic at Crystal Lake. Jamie was sitting, her back to a tree as she watched the work progressing on the temple. Derek lay on his back in the grass with his head on Jamie's lap. He appeared to be sleeping. Jamie slowly ran her fingers through his gray hair. Other couples were walking around the lake and a red headed toddler chased a frog in the grass. "Derek which of the stones on the temple are yours?"

"Not sure little sister, all of the men are bringing stones for the building. Mine look like the rest. Why do you ask?"

"I grew up in a stone house with a shale roof. I like stone. It's so permanent."

"Would you like a stone home my love?"

"Oh yes, our home is just fine. I'm happy as long as you are there. Pretty soon you won't be able to nap on my lap as my belly expands with our baby."

"Then you will nap on mine then."

"Really? I remember we had problems last time we tried that!" Jamie said laughing.

"That, my love, was your fault, I'm innocent!"

"I would like to name our new baby Casey. It will work for a boy or a girl."

Derek rolled over and kissed Jamie's belly, "A kiss for little Casey."

Then he stood and assisted Jamie to stand. "Let's get a closer look at the temple." Holding hands they walked to the temple site. The foundation was barely completed. Although it was not a large building, it was larger than any seen in the colonies save for warehouse row on Grand Isle. "We are looking for slate or copper for the roof. David has organized survey teams to look for minerals. Lord Grandfather expects to take five years in the building. Since it's all volunteer labor and everyone is so busy that is to be expected."

"I've seen Phoebe's drawings of the temple plans. It's beautiful. I see we are using that white stone for it." Holding hands they walked around the perimeter of the temple. They were not alone as other couples were also walking around the structure. "When will the university be built?"

"We still have the library, little sister. I don't expect to run out of space there to soon. Besides we are still too small for anything bigger."

"With the pirate attack and all we missed the spring festival this year, so...." Jamie paused smiling mischievously at Derek.

"Okay, what are you little vixens planning?"

"You'll like it, I'm sure." Derek knew he would. He also knew his little trickster well enough not to pressure her for an answer. She would reveal all in time. In fact the less he pressured the sooner she would spill the beans.

Festival day arrived. As it was also a feast day it was attended by all. There was several log canoe races in Turnagain Bay, as well as longboat and dory races. The three sisters took part in the women's longboat race with Grandmother Ruth at the tiller. They had a rocky start as Sophie kept falling off her seat and managed to get the steersman wet. Just before the race was to start the triplets started crying which caused Jayne to have a large let down of milk. The race was halted until the babies were fed then resumed. With the sisters singing one of their bawdiest songs they crossed the finish line first, Grandmother Ruth wet from Sophie's accidental splashes and Jayne from her let down.

As usual the three sisters won the archery contest. This contest they introduced moving targets. A large wooden disk was rolled along the ground and the participants shot bolts with hard wood tips at it. Very few archers could hit the target. All six sisters did. Sophie's deportment at the award ceremony had not improved since the last and she was loudly cheered.

The meal was wonderful. There were a lot of vegetable dishes as well as a whole roast pig. Each family brought a dish to pass as well as a dessert. The bubbly pies were the most sought after. Rosalind's no knead bread was much emulated with many variations and versions served. Her latest variation, sourdough, had won a prize at the baking contest. Honey, still in the comb, was also available and the children responded well to this chewing the wax long after the meal.

The singing contest was next. There were many performers and the influence of the three sisters was very obvious. Dancing had now become part of the performance. There was a group of pre and early teens that preformed the pirate song and did a truly excellent job of it. Their dances were a sincere copy of the original. The six sisters were again the last to perform. The audience was expecting a rousing song and dance from the sisters. When the song started they sat demurely on the stage with Jamie partially obscured behind them. Their only instruments two wheeled fiddles, a double reed pipe and Jamie on the flat drum. The song was a popular lament usually told by the male point of view about an unsuccessful seduction and the loss of a cherished woman. They had reworked the song telling it from the female view. They all wore the high waistline dress Grandmother Ruth had made for them when pregnant. It was a truly lovely song and the women's voices harmonized well, the song had power bringing many in the audience to tears. For the final verse telling how she finally got her man Jamie stood for her solo. She had padded her belly so she appeared very pregnant and stood presenting herself sideways to the audience. When the song finished she sat down. For a long pause the audience was still, and then a roar of approval and laughing followed. A second song was requested and still sitting demurely with a very pregnant looking Jamie now up front and centered, they gave a rendition of their bawdiest rowing songs, the incongruity of the quiet demure presentation, the very pregnant Jamie and the words of the song had the desired effect and the audience loved it.

The dance followed and much of the conversation was centered on the musical performances. The sisters were received with warm accolades as well as laughter. The six sister's husbands again got a lot of dance requests by many of the young women. Jamie danced every dance unless she was part of the band or assisting sisters with baby care. Derek managed to get only two with her. Derek danced with Grandmother Ruth, the tremendous love she felt for her six granddaughters apparent in her conversation. The dance went very late into the night. When it ended it took several trips of the longboats and every available dory to return the participants. It was nearly dawn when Derek finally carried a very bubbly and energized Jamie across the threshhold.

"My body's so tired but my brain won't stop!" Jamie said with a giggle.

"Let me help you then." Derek then helped Jamie out of her dress and Jamie lay on the bed in her chemisette. As it only came to her mid-thigh her legs and feet were exposed. "Do you want me to help you into a nightgown?"

"No, you may rub my feet...please?" Derek lay on the bed next to her.

"Okay, but I will need to kiss you first!" so Derek kissed her forehead. Then he kissed her eyes, "I love those eyes, they're the color of summer rain."

"You're so funny Derek." Then he kissed her nose.

"And that little cute nose, it wrinkles when you smile."

"It does not!" Then smiling her nose did wrinkle.

"And those kissable lips!" Derek kissed her and she rose for a second but Derek shook his head, "I have lots of places to visit, those will have to wait their turn." Then he kissed her neck. Jamie chuckled.

"You're whiskers tickle!"

"Every time I see your neck I want to kiss it." Then continuing to move down he kissed her just above her heart, "That heart belongs to me! Now for a special spot just next door."

"That was more bite than kiss!" Jamie said with a little moan as she arched her back toward him.

"I got carried away! But now the other side beckons and it won't do to leave your other nipple bereft of my attention." Jamie again arched her back as he nuzzled her.

"You left wet spots on my chemisette!"

"Shall I remove it?"

"No you are going to rub my feet; you have such a short attention span my love!"

"Feet? Oh, yes, just a few more stops." He then kissed her navel, "A kiss for the very center of you, my love."

"Didn't know that was my center!"

Then kissing her belly again he whispered, "And one for Casey." Then moving lower he kissed her again as she gasped rolling her hips into the kiss.

"You are so bad!"

"I might have to come back here later."

"I would like that!" her voice a little husky. Then Derek kissed her knees.

"When was the last time I admired your lovely knees?"

"Let me think...ah, this morning!"

"So long ago. I need to give your knees more attention."

"My feet need your attention or did you forget again?" Derek then kissed her feet and lightly tickled one. Jamie lightly kicking and laughing said, "You're supposed to be relaxing me, did you forget that too?" Derek picked up a foot and kissing the sole began to gently rub her foot.

"My, do you have dirty little feet, my love."

"Was too tired to wash, but if you warm the water in the morning I will permit you to bathe with me!"

"Will I also be forced to scrub you back?"

"Oh yes...and other parts will also require your attention."

"You are such a harsh taskmaster."

"And I of course will need to scrub you thoroughly."

"Thoroughly?"

"Very thoroughly!"

"I will need to seriously consider your offer."

Jamie then reached up with her other foot and caressed his face. "My other foot also requires your attention!" Derek kissing that foot began to rub it. "When we sang our first song I really thought we went too far when the audience got so quiet."

"It took a minute for what you meant to sink in. They loved it. And your second song, who would have thought such a rowdy song, could sound so beautiful. You, looking like you were going to deliver any moment really added to the song."

"It was Roz's idea. She can be really wicked."

"Are you rubbing off on my little sister, you naughty vixen?"
"Derek?"
"Yes my love."
"Could you come back up here, I require your further ministrations." Derek lay next to Jamie holding her close and kissing her. "You silly man you're still fully dressed." Chuckling quietly she began working his buttons.

Chapter 25 A Second Harvest

Summer was coming to an end, the days slowly becoming shorter. The fruit trees that had blossomed so beautifully in spring produced no fruit. This, however, was expected as it would take three to four seasons before they would produce fruit. The pudding trees however did produce well. The fruits were also gathered from the wild stands of the trees. The fruit bruised easily and did not keep well but it was enjoyed while available. Roland's copper shop had been very busy making barrels of all sizes and Jamie had a large one in her kitchen, in which she layered shredded cabbage with salt. She kept it covered with a loose lid and a heavy rock. She also busied herself pickling eggs and cucumbers and canning green beans. The root vegetables were moved into the root cellar as they were harvested. They would not have the head women's store house to draw supplies and need to be self-sufficient. They had a huge store of dried, smoked fish and sausage as well as cured hams. These were hung from the rafters of the loft. Their flour also was stored there. This was a very busy time as so much needed to be made ready for the coming winter. They now had their own well and obtaining water was much easier. Derek used a yoke and two five gallon bags to bring water to the home every two or three days. Jamie could easily get the water herself but Derek would not even think about it. Most of the colonies women did the water gathering, but the sisters did not. Derek explained it thus, "You, my little shrimp, weigh less than the water bags." It was not true, but they did enjoy their husband's attempts at pampering.

The general store still operated on a system of credits as it had as the head women's store house. Most of the colonists preferred this system. But they also started using coins. Every squared log and barrel of goods exported had a value and this value was listed to its source. These credits were used to pay for the land and for the building supplies. Any additional profit would be credited also. At this point, most of the colonists owned their homes. Some were now taking their credited funds in coins. These coins further traded amongst the colonists for other goods. They had an abundance of silver and copper coinage for this purpose thanks to the pirates. Derek had made a metal dye and counter struck the coins with an "R" over the imperial symbol. They were simply called sterlings and tenths. All the shops continued to pay its laborers in letters of credit, but these too were usually traded for coins. Barter was the preferred method of exchange between the farming families. The general store acted like a bank and could issue letters of credit also. These were all kept recorded and managed by Jayne. Most of the necessaries for survival were still procured by fishing, hunting and gardening. Other comfort items came from the store. Jayne also had a moderate sized kiln and produced clay pots, dinnerware and other items she sold at the store. Phoebe, using colored clays and a glaze was able to decorate the dinnerware with floral patterns or pictures of everyday life; this added greatly to the appeal of the fired clay items. Two of the neighbor's preteen girls enjoyed working at the store and learning to use the turning wheel. Beth and Sue slowly became more like family to the group of sisters. It was the lure of triplet babies that had attracted the girls. They were a tremendous help with the babies and earned money for their help in the store. They were very shy and emulated the six sisters in dress and hair style. They were actually a year apart in age but were often mistaken for twins. They had strawberry blonde hair and hazel eyes. Jayne loved them as much as her own.

 David's explorations to find minerals led to the discovery of several metallic ores and a black rock that burned. These were logged and put into storage until they could analyze the findings or had sufficient labor to exploit the finding. David also located an excellent source of slate and a soft gray rock with rose colored swirls that could be easily cut into blocks. These findings too were cataloged for future use. It seemed that the more they searched the more bounty they found. This was truly a blessed land. The tiny colony continued to prosper. Next summer would bring the return of the fleet with new colonists and new opportunities.

 Payment for healing skills was usually in goods. That is how the chickens and much of the hams were obtained. The healers never gave a price but accepted whatever payment the families could manage. The pigmy goats were seen as gifts as they felt no need for compensation from a sister. With three healers they were able to manage their time better and rotated a day off schedule. Two healers manned the clinic at any given time. Rosalind's skill and proficiency were increasing rapidly.

 Robert, assisted by his brothers, added a dormer to his home. The dormer was divided into three rooms, each with a window facing the garden. These would be for their children. The dormer extended over the addition added last winter when Derek built his. No furniture would be needed for the rooms for some time. One of the rooms was used for food storage. David had also added an addition to his home too, as did Roland. All the families in the colony were growing. And the homes stretched to accommodate the growing families. Most of the additions were squared log walls rather than the construction originally used.

The harvest festival was held late and lasted five days, each of the colonies having their own events and vying for attendance. Novi had a large corn maize about three acres in size. It was the corn maize that garnered the greatest attention. David and Sophie managed to set the record for the longest time lost in the maize but Sophie's bright smile and disheveled look made her friends wonder if they were, after all, really lost. Each colony had its own version or an archery contest, most with moving targets. Sophie, Jamie and Rosalind getting the first three places in all contests. The rowing contest was also held but the six sister's boat was disqualified for excessive splashing, of overtaking boats, and they stopped mid-race thinking Jamie had started labor, but her contractions stopped when she stood to exit the boat.

The log canoe races where held several times with the six brothers crewing two different boats. The competition in the boats was fierce at times. The boats were very well matched and extremely fast. They carried way too much sail and used long hiking out poles with the crew crawling out on the poles to keep the boat upright. The dories also raced and the sisters crewed in the dory races. The dories seemed sedate after the log canoes. The log canoes also made moonlight excursions for couples and the six couples took advantage of the offer. Jamie loved snuggling under a blanket with Derek as the boat ghosted along under darkened skies.

Much of the fair centered on the colonies products, including exhibitions of the short hairy red cows. They had all calved and they had obtained a bull. There were also exhibitions of cooking and baking. The bee keeping equipment was displayed and an active hive was present at the fair. Phoebe's art exhibit was also a great success and other arts and crafts were featured. Jayne's and Phoebe's decorated flatware also had rave reviews. The cheese exhibit was also a great success. Ron and George also contracted with the farms with the cows to purchase their milk adding additional flavors to their cheeses. The fairs ended in the usual feast with music, singing contests and a dance. Jamie was having difficulty with frequent episodes of contractions and fatigue. Her feet were usually swollen by evenings so they retired early.

Jamie and Derek often lay together in the bed as Derek would place his hands on her belly to feel the baby kicking. Many times the kicking would stop when he placed his hand on the spot. Jamie preferred sleeping on her left side with her belly against Derek's back. That way Derek could also feel the nightly barrage of kicking. "This pregnancy is so different. I'm feeling little Casey so much sooner. I feel like I've been pregnant forever!" Jamie whispered after they were snuggled close together. Casey, a boy, arrived a week later just before the first snow. Lord Grandfather had tears in his eyes as he held his little namesake.

Alexandra's little boy, David, arrived two weeks later. Beth and Sue now veterans of baby care were overjoyed to have additional babies to visit. When the sisters visited each other there seemed to be wall to wall babies. Little Faith and Hope were walking and talking, however only the mothers understood them. Little Jamie, (Phoebe's Jamie), was crawling and putting everything he could find in his mouth. The triplets were growing at their own individual pace. Little Sophie was walking at nine months and teasing her sisters terribly. Little Roz could crawl, but little Jamie insisted on being carried everywhere, and so Robert did. The harvest that year had been truly bountiful.

Chapter 26 Beth and Sue

Beth and Sue spent a lot of their time with Jamie holding Casey and asking endless questions about babies, pregnancy and healing. They also spent even more time with Jayne. They loved the triplets and also liked working in the store. They had become adept at using the clay wheel and enjoyed making bowls and cups. Many a night they simply slept over at Jamie's or Jayne's homes. They were given one of the new upstairs rooms as their unofficial room. The girls had been so quiet and shy when they first started coming over, but were now very vocal and happy. When out in the village they had a reputation of being very shy, never looking up and some suspected they were mute. They were always poorly dressed and their hygiene deplorable. Their mother was rather reclusive and not well known to many of the village members. Their father was seen as a jovial man who worked at David's wood shop. He worked well but had frequent episodes of absences claiming his wife was ill. The change in the girls since becoming so attached to Jayne and Jamie was seen as miraculous. Jayne and Jamie had made them skirts from doeskins and had given them shirts and vests. Jayne had noticed severe bruises in the girl's backs and ribs and mentioned it to her sisters but Beth and Sue begged Jayne not to tell anyone. The two girl's hygiene was the first noticeable improvement. Then it was noticed they were even walking like Jayne and Jamie and tying their hair in a knot at the nape of their neck or allowing Sophie and Rosalind to braid flowers into their hair. Their appetites were ravenous and Beth was beginning to blossom and develop breasts as her hips rounded. This had her terrified when Jamie noticed it, especially when she had to return home. The sisters always dressed in their baggiest dirtiest clothes when their presence at home was requested and Beth would bind her chest. It almost seemed that the girls could be gone several days before their absence was noticed and they were requested back home. They often had tears and needed extra hugs when they had to return home. Jayne and Jamie were feeling very suspicious and helpless regarding the girls. So they developed a plan.

With Beth and Sue occupied at the store Jamie, Rosalind and Sophie made a visit to their mother bringing fresh bread and berry preserves. When the woman came to the door it was evident they were not welcome. She partially hid behind the door but it was obvious her face was severely bruised and she had slurred speech and poor balance. Jamie explained she was a healer only to have the door shut in their face. They then went to Grandmother Ruth not knowing what to do.

"I'm not sure how much I can tell you but Casmir is aware of problems in their family. They had an older sister who died when she was fifteen. It happened before the voyage. They could not determine if it was accidental or purposeful but she fell to her death." Grandmother Ruth said, looking sad.

"They have bruises all over their back and ribs," Jamie said. "And Beth became terrified when I mentioned she was developing breasts. She binds them when returning home."

"David has also come to see Casmir, he thinks their father is having trouble with alcohol and was asking how he could help," Grandmother Ruth added.

"I may be really out of line," Jamie continued, "But I think their father is beating them and his wife. She was really bruised herself and refused us at the door. How do we protect the girls? Beth is truly terrified…I suspect she is terrified of other abuse now that she is beginning to develop into a young woman."

"Those girls have just blossomed since attaching themselves to you. Casmir has commented on that. Are you willing to openly confront the parents with me and Casmir?"

"Yes, we love those girls." Jamie replied.

Rosalind added, "We will keep them with one of us until we can resolve this."

"Then we must act tomorrow as we cannot just hold the girls. Casey and I will visit the home early in the morning. We can collect you on the way. For now I will accompany you to Jayne's. I'll bring supper and we will talk to the girls, we must go very gently."

That night was declared girl's night and they met at Jayne's home. They planned for Robert and Lord Grandfather to arrive for dessert. Sue and Beth were excited to have dinner as one of the sisters. They were also delighted to receive attention from Grandmother Ruth. Dinner went well as they talked about the babies and the general store. Then Jamie added, "We stopped by to visit your mom with fresh bread and berry preserves." Beth and Sue looked pale. "We noticed she had a lot of bruises and her speech was slurred and her balance poor."

"Mom drinks too much sometimes and falls a lot," Beth said in almost a whisper.

"Those weren't falling bruises Beth, those were hitting bruises." Jamie added slowly.

"Like the ones on both of you," added Jayne as she gently touched Beth. The two sisters sat frozen in place. Jamie put an arm around Sue and Grandmother Ruth continued.

"We know about Marie too."

"Pa didn't mean to hurt Marie, he don't mean to hurt Ma either. When he's drinking he gets so mean. When Marie started to turn into a woman he... he never meant to hurt her. Pa loves us!" Beth said crying. "Ma tries to protect us... she drinks too, then..." At that point she was crying so hard that Jayne and Grandmother Ruth were holding her and her speech no longer understandable. Sue was also crying and clung to Jamie with Sophie and Rosalind adding to the hug. Beth continued, "I was so afraid, Pa hadn't seemed to really notice me. He never noticed Marie either until she started to change. I need to protect Sue. I don't want to go home...ever!"

Grandmother Ruth asked in a whisper, "How did your father hurt Marie?"

"I don't know but he was drunk and was calling her a whore and dragged her by her hair into his room. She cried so much after that, told us she was going to run away. She said I had to protect Sue, we should run too, and it was too late for her. When she did run weeks later Pa went after her...she died that night. Pa said he was sorry, he said he loved Marie, he said she was bad. She never ever had a boyfriend, none of us had friends. Marie wasn't bad!" The two girls continued to sob. Jayne and Jamie had no idea of the extent of abuse the girls had been subjected to. They waited for the girls until they could regain their composure before signaling Lord Grandfather and Robert to come.

When Lord Grandfather arrived with Robert the girls appeared startled, but Grandmother Ruth and Jayne were able to comfort the girls. "We want to help you and your parents," Lord Grandfather said softly. "What would you like to see happen?"

"Could we stay with Jayne and Jamie?" Sue asked looking hopeful.

"Oh, yes!" Jayne replied, "You know I love you both."

"And me too!" Jamie added.

"Then you are welcome here forever," Robert added.

The next morning Lord Grandfather, Grandmother Ruth, Jayne, Sophie and Jamie arrived at Beth and Sue's parent's home. When their father came to the door Lord Grandfather simply pushed his way in. "We are here to talk about you daughters."

"So what have those little liars been telling you?"

"They have said a lot, but all of it we have previously suspected. We are taking the girls. Neither of you may contact them without my and Ruth's supervision. Is that clear?"

"Fine...that Beth was starting to turn into a whore like her sister anyway."

"Your daughters are beautiful and innocent young women, they deserve better," Jamie said hotly.

The girl's father looked at Jamie. He appeared very angry and was having trouble with balance and speech, "You're that whore healer, and I know you. You and that group of sluts you hang out with. You just wait."

"We are also here to offer you help." Lord Grandfather continued. "Your daughters love the both of you. We have resources to help you. But we also mean to protect the girls."

"You can have them, but you won't keep them... I'll see to that."

"Where is your wife?" Grandmother Ruth asked, "I would like to speak to her too."

"Sleeping somewhere, how should I know? Get out of my house." Then glaring at Jamie, Sophie and Jayne, "You meddling bitches better watch you backs!"

The next morning a very sober pair of parents showed up at lord Grandfather's home to apologize and ask for help. The girl's father appeared totally charming, the wife very quiet. Lord Grandfather sat with them frequently over several weeks listening and encouraging them in their attempt to stop drinking. They appeared to be doing well and a date was set for a supervised visit with their daughters. Beth and Sue were apprehensive but hopeful the visit would go well. They loved their parents and wanted them to return the love they felt. The day of the visit they wore their deer skin skirts with flowered shirts and deer skin vests. They had new shoes that Robert had gotten them and allowed Phoebe and Alexandra to braid their hair in a stylish coil on the top of their head. They had two long curls that hung by their ears and all six sisters accompanied them to Lord Grandfather's home for the visit. Beth looked so beautiful as a young woman just beginning to show her gentle curves. They arrived early and began to wait. They continued to wait, after two hours the girls were very quietly weeping. The six sisters taking time for lots of hugs returned to Jayne's home. Two more visits were planned with the girls parents again not showing up. On the third aborted visit the girls looked sad but did not cry. Their appetite was affected and both were losing weight. The girls responded to the continued attention of the six sisters and Grandmother Ruth. After the third visit Lord Grandfather refused to make visit dates with the girls' parents. Weeks passed and the girls seemed happier. They were kept busy and spent a lot of time working the clay wheel and having music and singing lessons. At breakfast one winter morning Beth spoke.

"Are you planning to adopt us, Jayne?"

"I would absolutely love to adopt both of you. I love you both. I was planning to ask you if you preferred being my daughters or sisters."

"We love you too Jayne!" Sue added, "Sister would be good too. Then Jamie, Sophie, Roz, Alexi and Phoebe would be our sister's too."

"They would all love that too, but I'm sure they would also love being aunts."

"I don't think Ma and Pa are going to try to get us back. I don't know if they even love us." Beth said sounding very sad.

"I can't speak for them, but I can assure you that Rob and I do love you. I know my sisters do too." Jayne continued, "Grandmother Ruth already thinks you're her granddaughters." Beth and Sue laughed at that.

"Yes, she has said as much," Sue said.

"You have time to think, either choice is fine with me. I love having you in my home and in my family."

Days later Grandmother Ruth met with the six sisters. "Casmir has told me to let you know the girl's parents are drinking again and he is concerned for your safety. He specifically told me to tell you to keep two buckets of water on hand every night."

"The girl's father has threatened us, but he was quite drunk." Then Jamie added, "We will keep water on hand, thank Lord Grandfather for me." Several days passed then Derek awoke to the smell of smoke in the house. Acting quickly he roused Jamie and grabbed little Casey and they exited the home. The home was ablaze with the roof too far gone for the water to save and they watched helplessly as their home burned to the ground. Jamie's books and the bear skin were currently loaned out to Rosalind or they would have lost everything. Sophie and David took them in. The next day as they went through the ruined home they did recover Jamie's tea set. Nothing else made it through the fire excerpt for the stone hearth. Derek thanked the gods he was able to save his beloved Jamie and Casey. The blaze was suspicious but they had no proof of foul play. There had been reported lightning that night. Jamie was quite shaken by the fire and had difficulty sleeping for weeks.

"Well, little sister, it looks like you will have to let me build a stone house after all!"

"Oh, Derek we could have died, what woke you up my love?"

"Stub was scratching the door and then I smelt the smoke."

"That dog keeps saving us!" Jamie rubbed Stub's head and the dog moaned.

Sophie's home was cramped with three additional residents but they all got along well. Derek was able to build a frame for a new home and he and his five brothers assembled it in one day. Then Derek began the slow task of gathering stones. Huge numbers of stones appeared at the home site each morning as anonymous friends contributed stones. Derek also began harvesting shale for the shingles and started with the roof. The home slowly was built. They were able to use the original hearths. The walls were white pine on the inside with the window trim of hard wood. Derek had sufficient credits to purchase windows for each room including one for each of three dormer rooms. The large kitchen had a water pump next to the sink so water was always available. The clinic had its own door at the side of the home and they had a large sitting room with the kitchen behind it. Their bedroom was behind the kitchen. There was a small circular staircase in the kitchen leading to the dormer with rooms on either side of the stairs and one down a narrow hall. The dormer over the clinic also had a small circular staircase in the remedy preparation and storage room behind the counseling room The dormer could be accessed from either side of the house. The stones from the hearth would warm the dormer rooms well in cold weather. The third room would be warmed from the small clinic hearth. They had a small fireplace in their room. They planned to keep Casey with them for now. Jamie was delighted with the home and arranged it a lot like the home she grew up in. David even made her a rocking chair for the hearth area. Phoebe's art in frames adorned the walls. Jamie's tea set had its own place of honor. Jamie loved the house and decorated it beautifully. As all their flatware had been destroyed they purchased floral pattern dinnerware from the store and cups and mugs Beth and Sue had made. The home had cost Derek most of his earned credits but he would recover quickly because iron work orders were still coming in and his copper products were also in demand. Their biggest problem was their loss of food storage. The sisters pledged to assist with any food needed.

The day they moved in they were entertaining all six of their friend's families as well as Lord Grandfather and Grandmother Ruth. Sue and Beth now included as family. The wall between the clinic and sitting room slid in a track and disappeared making a very large room for entertaining. They had everyone's tables and chairs and were eating a quiet dinner together. Babies and toddlers were everywhere. Alexandra and Phoebe brought cheeses, Sophie bubbly pies, Rosalind sourdough bread, Grandmother Ruth a vegetable dish with fruit and a spicy sweet sauce and Jayne a meat dish. Fires burnt in both hearths and the home was cozy. "I really like my stone cottage!" Jamie said, "I was expecting something small like my parents had."

"We are planning on at least ten children," Derek said with a grin, "And we did need an extra room for Sue and Beth when they stay over." Sue and Beth beamed at Derek then blushed and smiled at Jamie. The conversation continued until Stub's barking brought it to a stop.

"Sophie! Your house is burning!" Alexandra shouted. The men rushed out and started throwing water on the fire but the water simply spread the fire. They watched helplessly as Sophie's home burnt to the ground. Sophie clung to David and their little girl and wept. Sophie and family then moved into Jamie's home taking the room above the clinic and little Faith the middle room. Sue and Beth appeared in shock. They looked at each other with wide eyes and pale faces. Beth held Sue while they wept quietly. Work started on rebuilding as soon as the embers cooled with David and Sophie electing to build in stone also. Later the sisters were talking, "That fire looked like it was caused by an incendiary grenade, water would have doused any other fire," Rosalind said grimly.

"Who do you suspect?" Beth asked in barley a whisper.

"It wouldn't be right to accuse anyone with out evidence, so I won't. But we all must be vigilant, this was no accident." Over the next few days no one slept easily. The men made nightly patrols of their homes. Buckets of water replaced with buckets of sand. Later Jayne was working at the general store and Beth and Sue were in the back room tending the triplets when they overheard a conversation in the store. Three women were talking about the fires.

"They took those girls in and look their houses are burning!"

"My husband works with those girls father and he said they have a history of starting fires."

"You don't say!"

"He said he tried to warn them but they took the girls in anyway. Bad blood, you know like their older sister. She was trouble too. Got her self killed, you know?" Beth held tight to her younger sister as they wept bitterly into each other's arms. They had been so happy and truly believed they had found a loving family to belong to but now they needed to run. Run before they were formally accused and before any more pain could be directed toward the sisters they loved. That night they were unusually quiet at home and during dinner. Jayne had also heard the conversation and hoped the girls had not. But their quietness alerted her and she spotted them as they ran. Leaving the triplets with Robert she got Jamie and sent Sophie for the other sisters and headed to the dock area.

Jayne and Jamie casually walked to the longboat Beth and Sue were preparing. "Why hello girls, Jamie and I were just coming for a quiet boat ride under the moons. Could we join you?" Before either girl could find their voice they were joined by Sophie, then the rest each just happening to arrive seeking a boat ride under the glowing moons. They asked the girls if they wanted to row then allowed everyone to pick seats. Sophie was at the tiller so they could avoid splashing. The tide was at its lowest as they started out rowing. The bay was flat calm with no wind and they rowed about for a long time. Finally Beth said in almost a whisper, "We were running away."

"We know, we all came so we could say good bye, we all love you so much," Jayne said choking back a tear.

"We would love you to stay for at least a while longer, maybe till spring," Jamie added in a whisper.

"We can't stay; we have to leave so the fires stop!" Sue added.

"We all know you didn't start those fires, anyone with an ounce of sense will know that!" Jayne added, "The fires won't stop because you leave. They will stop when we catch the arson."

"It's my Da, he done it before and me and Marie got blamed," Beth said weeping as she reached for Jayne. Jayne held her and Jamie held Sue as they sat in the boat as it drifted. "We really liked being sisters! But we have no blood relation with any of you. Otherwise..."

Jayne held Beth tighter, "We're only sisters because we love each other. Rob and I are third cousins, Rob and Roland brothers with Sophie their little sister. Jamie is their third cousin, I think, and Alexi and Phoebe friends. Roz is Derek's sister. You would fit in well as our little sisters."

The girls laughed at the description of the family, "But Derek is so much older than you Jamie!"

"He just turned twenty one, his hair went gray after an illness, I'll be nineteen soon," Jamie added with a laugh. "Could you please return home with us for a while, it's so much fun having younger sisters?"

"Do you have a clan name, My Pa is the north river clan, I don't want to be that," Sue said firmly.

"We are the bear clan!" Rosalind said quickly, and Jamie laughing affirmed the name.

As they returned to the shore they noticed a home blazing in distance and they were nearly panicked. Alexandra and Phoebe said they would take care of the boat and the rest ran up the hill from the beach toward Jayne's and Rosalind's homes. Arriving at the scene, they found neither house burning. Some distance off

Beth and Sue's home was a burning inferno. David and Derek were having burnt hands bandaged by Sophie. A burnt scar was apparent on Jayne's home but the fire had been put out by the sand buckets. Beth and Sue looked in horror as their home collapsed in the fire. They clung together kneeling and weeping. Jayne and Jamie knelt beside them holding them. Later, they sat in Jamie's home as Derek and David told them what had happened. "We were patrolling the homes as usual when we spotted your Dad throwing an incendiary grenade at Jayne's home. We shouted and luckily his throw was off with the grenade hitting the side of the house," Derek began.

"I threw sand on the fire, then Rob started to fight the fire so we gave chase to the arsonist, we chased him back to his home and ran inside, he was carrying two or three additional grenades. We don't know if he accidentally dropped them or what but the house exploded in fire," David added.

"We tried to get into the house to save your parents, but we couldn't. We burned our hands trying but it was just too hot, we are very sorry," Derek said looking into Beth and Sue's eyes. Beth and Sue let go of Jamie and Jayne and hugged Derek and David. They continued to weep, unable to speak.

Days later the bodies of their parents were laid to rest in the little cemetery. Beth and Sue stood with the sisters each holding Grandmother Ruth's hand. Sue looked at Grandmother Ruth and asked, "Is it possible to love someone very much and still hate them?"

"Yes, you can love them for who they were and still hate them for the pain they caused." With that, the sisters returned to their homes. Now the youngest sisters, they would stay with Jayne and Jamie. They also promised their other sisters to spend time with them too. With so many sisters to love they would never be alone.

Chapter 27 Blossoms of Spring

Plants were again greening everywhere, the marsh marigolds and skunk cabbage fully blossoming. Jamie and her sisters finding daffodils in abundance transplanted hundreds to their window boxes. Derek and Roland helped David install the new windows in his home as the other brothers helped with the interior and David and Sophie moved into their new stone home. Beth and Sue were the first guests to sleep over.

One afternoon, Derek, returning home, found Jamie on the roof. She was straddling the crown. She had rolled up her shirt at the waist shortening the skirt to just above the knees to allow her to work on the roof. Sophie was holding the ladder while Rosalind watched the babies. Sitting on the roof exposed Jamie's entire legs. "Are you trying to display your beautiful legs to the entire village?" Derek asked not quite sure he wanted his wife on display.

"I had contemplated nude sunbathing up here," she teased, "but all the men were gone from home working, so I was planting flowering sedums." She then swung her leg over the roof crown and moved slowly to the ladder when her bare feet slipped sending her flying off the roof. Derek easily caught her, her shirt now totally in disarray. Lifting her higher he planted a kiss on her inner thigh. Jamie laughed, "Such scandalous behavior, what will the neighbors think?"

"Well, what do you think neighbors?" he asked Sophie and Rosalind.

"We are traumatically scandalized," Rosalind said laughing

"Can I borrow the roof when David comes home?" Sophie replied.

"Why are you planting flowering what-you-call-its on the roof?"

"My parents had them. They will flower all through the season and still be green for the winter. When they're established the house will look ancient. I'm planting some between the stones too, as well as my vines." Jamie was really delighted to find several varieties of sedums as well as a trumpet vine. "Our home will be so beautiful."

"Please let me do the roof work."

"Ok, I got more sedums for Sophie's roof." Derek found himself planting the flowers as Sophie directed, changing her mind several times. "Our houses will be so beautiful, thank you, Derek!"

Sophie kissed his cheek smiling.

Not only were the plants blossoming that spring. Sue had a growth spurt and had caught up to Beth and had started to bud breasts and her hips were rounding. They had, in the past, convinced most everyone they were twins, now they were able to continue their tale of twin ship. No longer in fear of their developing bodies they enjoyed dressing better, allowing their sisters to style their hair and make clothes for them. They felt pretty, and loved in their very large family. Jamie was shocked to discover that neither girl could read. She had given them a book her mother had given her that explained the physical changes happening in a young woman's body and about menses when the girls admitted they did not read. Jamie then gave the girls oral explanations and was regularly barraged with their questions, boys also being a frequent line of questioning. As Jamie and Jayne were so busy they recruited Alexandra and Phoebe to take on the task of getting the girls to read. Later, they learned that reading skills were not well established in Roamy culture. With the blessings of Lord Grandfather Alexandra and Phoebe were formally called to the office of school teacher, granted a stipend and set up day school at the library. Beth and Sue were their first pupils. The girls were eager to learn, their minds as hungry as their bodies had been when they joined the sisters. In no time they had nearly a dozen students in their school from all three colonies. Music was added early to the curriculum, as well as math. Beth and Sue had sweet singing voices and now sang regularly with their sisters. Both learning the wheeled fiddle and flat drums.

Derek had work to do at the new mill and Jamie and Casey were to come along. Beth and Sue had spent another night in their room above the clinic and Jamie was preparing breakfast. Derek was sitting in the rocking chair next to the hearth. Sue was sitting in his lap reading out loud from a book while Beth helped in the kitchen and fussed over Casey. Jamie, smiling at Beth asked, "Would you like to go with us to Novi today, we are visiting the mills."

"I've never been to Novi." Beth replied, "I'd hate to miss school."

"We would make the trip a learning experience for you, and you could help with Casey."

"Could I carry him on the back pack?" Sue exclaimed looking up from her book with a bright smile.

"I'm sure you both will have enough carrying time to be thoroughly tired," Jamie responded with a laugh. The girls were excited to be going to Novi. "We will have lunch in Novi at the general store. They have a little kitchen that serves meat pies." They did not need to carry lunch as Casey would be nursing and they would eat in the village. The girls dressed very similar to Jamie all in their doe skin skirt and vest. They all wore similar pastel colored shirts. They all had their hair in a long thick braid and were barefoot as usual. Jamie wore her heart shaped pendant. Beth took the back pack with Casey in it and they left for Novi.

Then feeling a little apprehensive, Sue asked, "Who should we say we are? Just in case someone asks," both girls looking shy and frightened.

"We tell the truth of course, you're my youngest sisters." The girls beamed with the statement, both hugging Jamie.

"Can we tell everyone we are twins?"

"I'll leave that one to you. Everyone knows I have a plethora of sisters. I've always had at least two with me when we visit, a duo of twin sisters will be accepted, no problem." The longboat ride was accomplished without difficulty they simply rode across in one of the boats making a regular run.

"I want to check the lumber mill first; I fitted an improved pulley system to run the band saws."

"You seem really excited about your band saws, my love, what have you done?"

"I have several of the band saws tethered together and run off an overhead pulley. I'm using leather belts and steel pulleys. I think we can cut a log into uniform planks with a single pass. It will be tried for the first time today. I get a royalty for product enhancement. As it is I'm part owner in the mills and get a quarter of a percent on production. This will really boost production."

"Do you also get a royalty from the flower mill?" Beth asked.

"I do now, but the town plans to buy out my shares next year. They will still come to me for iron work."

"How do royalties work on the flower mill?" Beth asked continuing her questioning.

"The farmers have their grains milled at no upfront costs. The mill takes ten percent of the grain by weight. That grain pays the labor costs and mill upkeep. It also pays the royalties for the original developers, I being the principle."

"So then the village will get the royalties when they buy you out."

"Beth, you really have a good head for business!" Jamie laughed.

"Jayne is teaching business skills to go along with Alexi and Phoebe's math," Sue added.

"Ok, mill first, then lunch!" Jamie added.

The mill was powered by a large water wheel and had large spinning shafts overhead that had been made from trees. Derek's band saw blades were powered from the overhead shaft with thick leather belts geared to the standing band saw blades. The whole system was huge. With a nod from Derek a squared log was positioned then two workers began moving the log through the blades. It was towed through held on a sliding platform. The log easily sliced into uniform lumber.

"How did they used to do it?" Sue asked.

"Two men, one on a platform with the one above and one below to handle the other end of the huge long saw, they simply sawed through each plank one at a time."

"The poor guy on the bottom must have been covered in saw dust!" Sue exclaimed.

"He wore a special felt hat with a very large brim, but it was a dirty job. With this wood planks will be much cheaper to produce. The type of structures in the colony will change and our export value will change." They also viewed Derek's huge powered circular saw and the plank drying area. Then they went in search of lunch. The general store had a small back room with tables and chairs next to a small open hearth. It was quite cozy

"I can't wait to tell Jayne about this," Beth said.

At that point the lady who ran the general store entered and Jamie could feel the sudden panic in Beth and Sue. Jamie quickly took their hands and whispered, "Just take a deep breath and smile, follow my lead!" The girls looked into Jamie's eyes, nodded and put on their best smile.

"Jamie, it's so good to see you again. Are these two more of your sisters? Hello, Derek it's good to see you too."

"Claire, this is Beth and Sue, my youngest sisters."

"I can see the family resemblance; you are both such pretty young women. Your strawberry hair is so pretty." Clair smiled at the girls as they returned the smile their faces taking on a pleasant redness. They ordered meat pies and ginger beer than Clair left.

"Claire is in my Pa's clan, thought for sure she would recognize us!" Beth whispered.

"That would be awful, everybody hated us!" Sue added in a whisper.

"I don't think you have anything to fear. People seeing you will see only two very pretty young women. People judge you more on how you look now rather than any images they recall of you as a child," Jamie added still holding their hands. "You both have really blossomed so much. You are indeed my little sisters," Jamie added firmly.

"Not to mention my young sister-in-laws," Derek added with a smile. When the meat pies were served the brilliant smiles on the girls were real. They engaged in pleasant conversation with Clair asking a myriad of questions about the operation of the kitchen. As they left, Clair addressed Jamie.

"I really like your younger sisters. All of your sisters are so nice. These two are smart, I've never enjoyed answering so many thoughtful questions, I hope you all visit again soon." Beth and Sue were literally skipping as the finished their tour of the other mills which would begin operation in a few days.

"This will be a lumber mill too. The other a grist mill but it will also make cider in the fall."

"Who were the other investors in your mills?" Beth asked.

"David, Robert and Roland in the first two, with these Ron and George too. They let me use their credits to purchase the labor and materials. The first two mills were a real stretch. Our investments are really starting to pay," Derek said.

"Are you rich Derek?" Sue asked. Derek laughed.

"I have Jamie, who brings me much joy. I have seven sisters and five brothers who I love dearly. With those riches I am a wealthy man. As for money, I have little and need little."

"I've always said you were a hopeless romantic, big brother!" Jamie said, laughing. She hugged him tightly standing on tip toes to kiss him and laughed again. They returned to Bountiful in time for supper, Beth helping with the meal and Sue playing with Casey. The girls spent another night with Jamie then returned to Jayne's home for several days. Within a few days the girls were operating their own kitchen, selling meat pies, ginger beer and tea in Jayne's back room. They had regular customers, mainly workers from the mills and dock areas, everyone accepting them as just another two of the sisters.

Chapter 28 Return of the Fleet

The fleet returned weeks earlier than anticipated. The colonists were shocked to learn that no additional colonist came with the fleet. The supplies they had ordered had come and additionally a handsome profit from their imports. They had been counting on more colonists to assist in the development of their abundant resources. When the naval officers came ashore it was to a hastily convened meeting with the community leaders. They met at Derek and Jamie's little stone house as it had a room large enough to accommodate everyone.

The captain of the lead ship began, "Lord Grandfather, Roamy council of elders has requested you to resume your calling as Admiral of the Fleet as well as you remain Lord Grandfather."

"That is an unprecedented request, but yes, I accept."

"We learned of the pirate attack plans and we're unsure we would find any of you still alive!"

"We defeated the pirates and intensified our defensive capacities." Captain Ron replied.

"Well it's far from over. The entire Imperial Navy is on its way along with an elite guard contingency. We weren't sure we could beat them here. We have come to offer naval support or evacuation, the choice is yours."

"Such a decision needs to be taken up by the entire community," Lord Grandfather said. "We will visit each colony and deliver word on what we face and let them decide, it's their homes." Word spread quickly regarding the current peril and each colony would be heard and their decision honored. The questions being asked in each home as the colony faced possible total destruction for a second time.

The six families of sisters met in Jamie's home for dinner and discussion, Sue and Beth also (being now full sisters). They ate a simple meal of pink fish steaks, fresh warm bread and pickled cabbage.

"This is my home, and I will not simply give up without a fight!" Jamie said starting the discussion.

"They have offered to move the colony further north to a more hidden site." Ron said trying to play devil's advocate. Phoebe looked at him aghast.

"And leave my home we've worked so hard for? Never!"

"Running will only by us a short time," Sophie whispered.

"They will continue to search until we are found. I say let's make our stand here. Even if we are killed." Beth and Sue gasped at Sophie's statement but nodded their agreement.

Alexandra slowly, but in a firm voice, added, "I've had a wonderful life, I have a loving husband and a child, I would rather die in battle with my sisters than become a slave or see my children become one." At that point, one of the babies started to cry and Alexandra seeing it was hers got up to nurse her baby; she was weeping quietly. Little Sophie had grabbed a toy from little Roz and by simply standing and holding it up denied it to Roz who began to cry. Jayne distracted little Sophie and returned the toy to Roz and held little Sophie in her lap. She had tears in her eyes as she started to talk.

"I say let's fight, but if I fall you promise to raise my children and tell them about their mother so they can remember me."

"That really is the dilemma we face. When we fight some or all of us could die. If we run we only by time and eventually we face the same dilemma. If we return, we still face the same threat. If we win, we win our freedom for the generations. We win a home and a future for our children. I say fight!" Rosalind said her voice shaking but strong. The men watched in silent awe as their gentle women showed such a fierce desire to defend their home. Could they expect anything less of them? Eventually the colonist voted to stay and fight. Ten families elected to evacuate and return to Port Hope so they were given passage in one of the luggers which left for home. The colonies had built two race built luggers but turned them over to the navy as they were more experienced sailors. They had built enough war canoes that every man held a position on the canoes. The colony would throw everything it had into the naval battle and the women would defend the land. Pregnant women would be exempt from battle but they would hold the safe houses. Children old enough to handle a crossbow would also defend the safe house. The colonists grimly began their preparations for war.

Chapter 29 A Furious Garrison of Women

The colonists knew the enemy was coming. They had little time to plan. The fleet would deploy in a line along the North Channel of Grand Isle and draw the Imperial navy into a battle in Bountiful bay. The race built luggers would harass the ships as they came into the river. The log boom was still in place blocking the south channel and it was hoped it would stop any troop ships long enough for the ballista batteries to set them afire. As all the men would be engaged in the naval battle the islands would be defended by the women and their shield walls. They would need to hold long enough for reinforcements from the war canoes and the other colonies to respond. More than a single landing site could mean disaster. The war canoes would be deployed close to the north shore and hidden until they would dash out between the opposing lines of ships and use their incendiary grenades. Hopefully no landings would be made.

Bountiful had a slowly rising sandy beach that ended with a low steep dune that led to the village. The shield wall would hold the ridge of the dune. A trap was dug ten yards out from the face of the dune. It was a deep pit filled with spikes then carefully covered with saplings, then mats and sand, a narrow path across at the center. Warehouses and overturned dories created a funnel that hopefully would cause any troops to directly assault the shield wall. Two ballista batteries were each hidden in two warehouses and these would fire canisters of incendiary grenades into the troops at the prescribed signal. The children would again be in safe houses along with pregnant women and those unable to fight. Bountiful had forty-eight women that would make the shield wall. Sue and Beth under protest would guard the safe houses with their crossbows. Nothing left to do but wait. The navy had an additional surprise, it was a long shot.

The enemy fleet was spotted by coast watchers on Middle Sister Island and the Roamy fleet was deployed long before the Imperial Navy entered the bay. The winds were heavy and from the south west giving neither fleet a clear advantage. The two fleets approached in long lines preparing to rake each other with ballista fire, the incendiary grenades giving Roamy an advantage. Then a commotion on the two lead imperial frigates as men were thrown overboard and the Roamy flag rose. The ships were turning to catch the imperial fleet in crossfire. As the ships closed the distance the war canoes deployed running between the ships tossing incendiary grenades into the rigging and decks.

The three troop ships along with four luggers ran into the south channel of Grand Isle and were stopped and trapped by the log boom. The ships began taking fire from the shore batteries. One troop ship immediately went up in flames. The luggers worked as a shield for the two remaining troop ship sending longboats to cut through the log boom. By the time they managed to cut through the covering, luggers were lost to fire as well as a second troop ship but the one troop ship sailed in. As the tide was incoming the landing would most likely be Belle Isle.

The six sisters met at Jamie's home to prepare for battle. "We only have forty-eight warriors. We must make them attack us directly for this to work, if they flank us we will be cut down in short order." Alexandra said eyes wide as they contemplated battle.

"We need to make them really want to hit our shield wall real bad for them to miss our trap!" Sophie added.

"I have it!" Jamie shouted. "The six of us wearing only a feather standing in front of the shield wall. We say nothing, just stand, we are the best rangers any way. They will come straight at us!"

Rosalind blushing with embarrassment added. "That just may work." The six sisters undressed, brushing out their hair and making a thin braid in front of their right ear for a long white feather. They strapped on their knife belt and shouldered their crossbows and bolts adding their sacks of incendiaries, while Beth and Sue watched wide eyed in silence.

Jayne and Jamie held the girls as Beth and Sue silently wept. "No matter what happens to us," Jamie said, "Remember we love you, we will win, we must." Then holding their heads high they took up their shields and walked to the site of the coming battle, each pausing to leave a hug and kiss to the girls. Their presence and deportment at the battle sight had a riveting effect on the women gathered there. The women gawked wide eyed and some blushing, but the sisters stood regally, backs straight chin up and naked. Jamie explained the plan and their need to make the troops come straight at them. Over half the women also began undressing and since Jamie brought extra feathers they all donned a feather. In the end all of the women warriors would face the enemy only in a feather.

The troop ship pulled into the bay and began unloading its army. From the color of the flags they knew they were facing Praetorian Guard. The ship carried two hundred and fifty troops. They exited the ship in close order. Their movements slow and deliberate to maximize the fear factor. They also brought out hundreds of impalement shafts and put these along the beach at a forty-five degree angle. The women set their shield wall and hid the crossbows and incendiaries behind the shields and stood silently in front of the shield wall. The wind blowing their hair and feathers they stood their ground, erect, proud and waiting. The guard seeing only forty-eight naked women standing to defend the colony thought this would be an easy battle some of the men speculating on which of the women they would have. The drums called them to order and they moved in to close order assault, twenty-five men long, ten men deep. They had never faced a village that put up a defense, but less than fifty naked women, this would be sport. The commander moved forward and read the list of imperial charges against them calling for immediate surrender with promises of clemency. Among the charges treason, wanton savagery against imperial agents and theft of imperial property. The women continued to stand mute, in silence they waited. Then the drums sounded no quarter and the guard began to beat their spears against their shields. Between the drums and pounding of the shields the noise was terrifying. The women stood, holding their ground, in total silence. Their silence was more frightening than all the drumming. The drumming continued for what seemed forever. The guard than gave a shout brought their spears forward and began a slow march forward.

The other colonies seeing that Bountiful was the target organized its longboats and each sent forty of its warriors to points along the coast to fortify the shield line. They needed to be stealthy to avoid ballista fire from the troop ship. With the speed of the developing battle they feared they would be too late for the shield wall. They were also shocked to see in their field glasses their sister warriors standing naked in front of the shield wall. The sailors on the troop ship were so interested in watching the women warriors at the shield wall that they did not see the longboats cross.

The troops advanced slowly and the women stood their ground, not moving or speaking. At one hundred yards the bulk of the women moved behind the shield wall as the six sisters continued to stand boldly in the open signaling the range with whistles. At fifty yards they also moved behind the shield wall and at thirty yards the crossbows fired their first volley. The first line of attack dropped as well as some in the second and third rows. Then stepping over their wounded the next row fell into the pit. As the men screamed the women flung incendiary grenades into the pit and into the massed troops. Then on signal the ballista fired canisters of incendiary grenades. The troops in full route fell back to the beach. The women continuing to fire at the retreating troops. Nearly half were dead or wounded. The women stood in front of the shield wall and screamed in a loud high pitched wail. Moments later they were joined by eighty warriors from the other colonies. The new arrivals a little shocked by their sister's lack of dress. The guard obviously would regroup for a second assault.

Jamie simply took charge. She ordered the women to circle back and gather at the hidden ballista sites. The six sisters would continue to stand alone at the shield wall and draw the enemy. Then the archers could cut them down in a crossfire and ballista canisters. With all the fire and confusion the guard seemed still unaware of the ballista. "Don't expect a slow march, they will hit us hard."

"What if any make it through to you?" one of the women asked.

"We will do our best, that's all any of us can do, go swiftly, may the gods favor us." Jamie then looked to her five sisters, "If any of you survive give my love to Derek and the girls." Each pledging themselves to the same message, they stood mute holding hands for a long moment, then standing alone before the shield wall as the guard prepared their second assault. They willingly were offering themselves to assure victory.

The sea battle went as planned. The changing of sides of the first two frigates totally catching the Imperial Navy by surprise. The war canoes attacked so swiftly that half the fleet was ablaze before the main body of the fleet even engaged. The enemy had four first raters but three were already blazing infernos. The race built luggers had drawn off the frigates and were heavily damaged but with the incendiary grenade canisters had set most of them on fire. Facing the total destruction of the fleet the Imperial Admiral dropped his colors and the battle swiftly ended. The war canoes continued their attack taking out three more ships before they too discovered the battle was won. The Imperial Fleet Admiral surrendered all sea born activities, Lord Grandfather demanding total unconditional surrender. As naval hostilities ceased they got word of the ongoing land attack. Derek's heart nearly stopped and immediately the war canoes raced to the harbor at Bountiful. The six brothers terrified for their women.

Beth and Sue became increasingly restless as the faint sounds of battle were heard. Then Sue said, "Aren't we sisters too?" Simultaneously and in complete silence the girls shed their garments, brushed out their hair and braided a feather into it. Then, taking their crossbows and bolts, slipped out the clinic door and raced to the harbor. In the commotion of the arriving reinforcements they went unnoticed and joined the fighters on the right flank as they crept into position.

The imperial guard reformed their ranks and prepared for a quick assault on the shield wall. With all the smoke and confusion the arrival of the additional warriors and the flanking move went unnoticed. Imperial officers having all they could do to stop the panicked retreat and getting the troops to regroup. Several men had been killed by the officer core to restore a semblance of discipline. In this attack the officers would follow the men with swords drawn to 'encourage' slackers.

The second assault started similar to the fist with the beating of the drum sounding no quarter. The formation now much smaller and very tight began at a slow march to the shield wall. The six sisters simply stood in front of the shield wall, not moving or making a sound. At thirty yards the troops broke into a run and the crossfire started along with incendiary canister. The officers and most of the ranks wiped out in seconds. The sisters had sprinted behind the shield wall and seized their crossbows when four survivors of the charge crested the top of the dune. Alexandra and Phoebe fired their crossbows instantly killing one. Sophie's bolt hit one in the chest but unstopped he simply struck Sophie with his shield sending her flying through the air. She landed hard striking her head on a rock. She rose to her feet slowly seeing stars then blood streaming from her head wound covered her face effectively blinding her. She fell again feeling dizzy, her assailant finally succumbed to his wound. Rosalind was unable to get off her bolt when another assailant knocked her off her feet then shoved his spear tip deep into her thigh. She screamed in pain as the assailant raised his spear for a second thrust but Rosalind rolled on the ground avoiding each subsequent jab. Phoebe, Jayne and Alexandra attacked a huge man but he simply brushed Jayne and Phoebe away with his shield like bees against a bear. Jayne and Phoebe went flying through the air, landing hard. Phoebe unconscious and bleeding from a scalp wound. Alexandra then took a glancing spear cut to her shoulder and again to her ribs as she danced to avoid the spear, trying to get close enough for her knife. Jayne seized one of the spears and coming up from behind drove it into his back, piercing his heart, she too spattered with blood. Jamie, seeing Rosalind, rolling to avoid the continued jabs of the spear ran to her, then slipping under the mans guard as she had drilled and drove her knife into his groin severing the femoral artery then into his belly aiming for the liver. She was splattered with hot blood as the man bled out falling on and trapping Jamie with his body.

 The war canoes started their assault to the ship moments after the troops fell in their second attack. As their approach went totally unnoticed the ship was instantly ablaze. The captain struck his colors and began abandoning the ship under a white flag. As the men walked on to the dock to surrender the captain asked to meet with the garrison commander. The garrison of furious naked women, standing, facing the surrendering sailors with the eighty reinforcements behind them. The women warriors stood mute then parted as the six sisters approached. All were covered in blood. Rosalind was being assisted to walk by Phoebe and Jayne, the bleeding of her thigh held in check by an improvised bandage. Sophie, face and chest bloody and too dizzy to stand alone was held up by Jamie and Alexandra. Jamie then walked slowly to accept the proffered sword of surrender. At that point Beth and Sue rushed up hugging first Jamie as she was literally covered in blood. They hugged her screaming her name. They were wide eyed with fear and shock seeing their sisters so battered and bloody. The girls, now too, covered with blood. They then rushed to each of their sisters with tears of relief and hugs. "You are the commander?" the captain asked incredulously, "Praetorian Guard defeated by naked women and little girls?" As Jamie accepted the sword of surrender.

"Roamy women and girls." Jamie replied.

Chapter 30 Peace

Beaching the war canoes the men raced to the now finished battle as Jamie accepted the sword of surrender. Derek was shocked at the sight of Jamie naked, only for a feather and literally covered in blood. He wanted to rush to her and hold her so tight against his body but he knew this was her hour. The now fifty warriors of the garrison walked slowly back to the shield wall in close order, their backs straight and heads held high, their movements elegant and regal. Sophie had stopped David from simply picking her up and asked, "Please, give us thirty minutes behind the shield wall, then come for us." Once behind the wall and blocked from view, the women in tears of relief from the terrible fears and danger they had faced together, held each other, each of them needed to at least touch the six sisters as they stood together. Beth and Sue were unable to relinquish their hold on Jayne and Jamie. The women dressed in silence, then leaving the shield wall, standing, left one by one for their homes. The sisters exhausted and shaking just sat.

Then on the beach the men began examining the fallen Praetorian Guards administering a death blow to any not dead. The sailors watch in mounting horror as not a single member of the guard was left alive. The bodies were simply stacked for disposal. The surviving ships were just beginning to enter the harbors of the colonies as Derek and his brothers went first to the general store for blankets then to the shield wall. The women were waiting for them, Derek and Robert, also bringing blankets for the girls. Derek gently wrapped Jamie in a blanket and pressed her close holding her as she continued to shake and then weep into his shoulder. "You are such an amazing woman, a true queen among queens." Derek whispered, his voice hoarse. David and Roland simply picked their woman up into their arms holding them and weeping themselves. All of the men relieved to have their wives back in their arms, Beth and Sue also receiving hugs from their brothers as they were wrapped trembling into blankets and held by Derek and Robert as they lifted them to carry them home.

"We need to take everyone to the clinic," Jamie said, "I have wounded to tend." And with that they returned to the little stone house.

The captured sailors were given the task of taking the dead bodies of the Praetorian Guard to the rocky shoal, now named

Pirates Rock, for disposal. The causalities in both navies were heavy and the healers working with Grandmother Ruth treated Imperial as well as Roamy. Ruth was well known and loved by the men of both navies, they addressed her as Mother Ruth. Her love and caring nature were balm to the men on both sides. Stories of the land battle went through the ships companies like wild fire. It named Jamie as the leader who led fifty fierce, naked women and girls to defeat the eight hundred man Praetorian Guard. According to the stories, Jamie and her daughters, as well as a red headed leader bathed in the blood of the fallen men. In the stories she was portrayed as a huge dark haired firebrand with cold eyes the color of ice. The wounded men were invariably shocked to learn their gentle, beautiful soft spoken healers were the leaders of the naked garrison that defeated the Praetorian. Most of the injuries were burns and lacerations. The officers thrown overboard by the mutiny of the frigates were rescued. As the hostilities had ended, old friendships between the officers and men of both navies were renewed. The leaders of the communities planned to meet at the home of Derek and Jamie to write the Peace Accords, the Admiral of the Imperial Navy having the authority to make binding treaties.

With the clinic wall opened and numerous borrowed tables in place, the leaders met. The Imperial Fleet Admiral and all fleet commanders and ship captains of both fleets were present. The colonies leaders, including the six brothers and the leaders from Novi and Harbor Town and the eight sisters, as the garrison leaders were also there, Beth and Sue as special guests of the sisters. Lord Grandfather and Grandmother Ruth were presiding. The demands were simple. All moneys carried on the ships were forfeit; this alone more than doubled the existing treasury of the colony. Roamy ships were allowed free excess to the sea lanes without harassment and free trade was allowed between Imperial and Roamy merchants. All harassment and enslavement of Roamy would cease and their property could not be seized. The treaty was duly signed and multiple copies made, and the Imperial navy was allowed to leave. They had entered the harbor with over one hundred ships, two thirds were lost. The Praetorian no longer existed. The price for their folly was very heavy. They had defeated their enemy twice and now hoped for a lasting peace.

"Lord Grandfather," Sue asked, "Does this mean the Imperial

Magisterium will stop persecuting our people?" They were taking a quiet meal at the little stone house enjoying the company of family.

"No, it simply means the navy will leave us alone. The Magisterium will always be there to try and hurt us, they will use other surrogates. We must always be vigilant." Then switching subjects Lord Grandfather continued, "I'm so proud of all of you, giving your healing and nursing skills so completely to the Imperial Navy. They were most grateful and impressed."

"When they found out I was one of the leaders of the garrison they would get really quiet, several times I was asked if Jamie, Sophie and their daughters really bathed in the blood of their victims," Alexandra said blushing.

"The blood on me was all mine!" Sophie replied.

Then Jamie bent face down on the table burying her face in her arms shaking with emotion. Derek went to her thinking she was crying but Rosalind snorted a laugh, "She's laughing Derek!" Jamie shook her head, yes, laughing so hard she started to hiccup.

"What did you do my wicked little vixen?" Derek asked his land lovingly caressing her back.

"I was working with a group of about twenty men that Roz and I were treating for burns. Roz mentioned my name as we were speaking. Then this very young sailor, less than sixteen asked if I really bathed in blood with my daughters." Jamie and Rosalind were both laughing so hard they were unable to speak for a long time, with Jamie continuing to hiccup.

"And you told them what?" Derek asked not knowing how to respond.

"It was a ritual from the old earth culture of the warrior huntress. You could have heard a pin drop. I just said it calmly with a stone face."

"And that wicked little smile of yours!" Rosalind added. At

that, the entire group at the table laughed. Jamie continued to hiccup.

Chapter 31 A Covenant People

The days immediately after the battle the colony felt elation over the victory. The relief they felt and their gratitude to the gods for their delivery readily apparent as each family celebrated. As the days passed Derek noticed subtle changes in Jamie's behavior, she was less spontaneous in her interactions with her sisters and seemed quiet and sad, the brothers also noting a similar pattern in their women. In their intimate relationship she was less playful, but still appeared to respond well. Something was missing. She shied away from hugs and was losing weight. Usually talkative and funny, she seemed just a little too quiet. One day Derek came home early hoping to have some time with Jamie. Beth and Sue were watching Casey and were glad to see Derek. "Jamie really looks awful, I think she has been crying a lot," Beth said. "Did you know she has been vomiting after meals and scrubbing herself several times a day?"

"We're really worried about her Derek," Sue added. "She's not here, we don't know where she went."

"I have an idea." Derek left feeling he knew where she was. Derek walked to the little lake and saw Jamie sitting on the ground near the temple construction site. Derek could feel the sadness that emanated from her. She was crying quietly and alone. Derek approached very slow and quietly. Jamie could feel his presence and loving concern long before he sat next to her. Derek slowly reached out his hand and Jamie took it, squeezing it. Her face was red from crying. Her hair in a single thick braid was becoming undone with gossamer strands of hair blowing gently in the light breeze. Slowly she leaned into Derek until she was across his lap holding as tight as she could. She buried her face in his shoulder. Derek just sat, holding her while she wept. They just sat for a long time.

"I love the temple site," Jamie whispered. "I'm so sad, I've murdered men, Derek. I'm a healer, I thought I save lives. I can't get the blood off my skin or his face out of my mind. I've broken my covenant and lost all the promises from the gods!" Derek held her closer, cupping her face in her hands and brushing the gossamer strands of hair from her face.

"Yes, you have killed men, as have I."

"I scrub and scrub my body but I can't feel clean. I can't keep food down. I want the pain I feel to stop! Do you feel that too?"

"Not as strongly as you, but yes. Taking another man's life is always hard. We value our own life so much; it hurts to take another's. I can see how you, a gifted healer, would be so strongly affected."

"You do?"

"Yes, you are such a gentle loving woman, Jamie. I think you would rather die than inflict pain."

"Derek?"

"Yes, little sister."

"Could you love a murderess?"

"With all my heart and soul forever, for eternity. You mean so much to me!" Derek continued to hold her kissing her on the forehead and stroking her hair.

"In my mind I know I had to kill. They would have butchered all of us. But my heart just hurts so much."

"My gentle love, you hurt so much because you care so much. You are a healer. You have a good heart. Let's walk around the temple site." Derek stood then, taking Jamie's hand helped her up. They then walked arm in arm around the temple. "You're not the only one having trouble, all of your sisters, to name a few."

"I didn't know!"

"You've been a bit of a recluse, talking to your sisters always seems to help." Derek said and Jamie laughed.

"Talking to you helps the most." Later that day the sisters got together to talk. All of them were struggling with feelings of quilt and shame. Those who had participated in hand to hand combat having the strongest feelings.

"It wasn't murder, David explained it, murder is different...can't explain why though," Sophie said quietly. "Lord Grandfather has declared this Sunday as Covenant Day. We will all fast then break bread and renew our covenants like last time."

"I still feel the blood on my skin," Jamie said with a shiver, "I want so much to renew my life!" Saturday came and after supper the entire colony began its fast. They spent time in prayer, then Sunday they performed ritual cleansing in their homes. Beth and

Sue stayed with Jamie that weekend. Then they assembled for their shared Sunday feast. Prior to the dinner, they took loaves of bread and broke them and passed them, renewing their covenants. Then they enjoyed the feast together. Then, true to Roamy custom they had dancing and music.

"I love music!" Jamie told Derek as they danced. She was looking into his eyes and smiling. "It reaches into my soul and touches my heart!"

"That song you and the sisters sang was so beautiful and so fitting for tonight, where did you find it?"

"Grandmother Ruth. It was composed four hundred years ago and sang when the Hundred Years War ended. We thought it summed up well what we have experienced. Oh, Derek, it was such a beautiful song, especially when the warrior women approach the gods for forgiveness, I almost cried when I sang it."

"I could tell, you have such beautiful eyes, like a summer rain." Jamie laughed, brushed him a kiss on the cheek. she had to break step and stand on her toes. "You always say that!"

"Well it's true, and your nose..."

Jamie, laughing, smiled interrupting. "It does not wrinkle!" And it did.

Chapter 32 Of Kitchens and Horses

Beth and Sue's little kitchen continued to do well. Every night they would make ten meat pies. They would slice up potatoes, onion, carrots, rutabaga, turnips and a sausage. They would blend in some herbs from the garden and a bit of clotted cream then fold it all into a pie shell and crimp it closed. They would bake it in the still warm oven after dinner and let them cool. On their way to school they would stop by Jayne's store and put their pies to warm by the hearth. Then when school ended mid-day they would return to run their kitchen in time for lunch. Jayne and the sisters encouraged them and they kept books of their expenses and profits. At first they managed to break even but later as their clientele increased they were doing better. They had regular customers who came in for lunch and others as they had from business in Bountiful. Eventually they subcontracted with Phoebe and Alexander who also made meat pies for their kitchen. They also sold Phoebe's and Alexandra's cheeses and Jayne's tea. They were very excited with their success, and the kitchen brought more clients into the store which Jayne liked. Jayne was talking to Jamie as they had lunch in the little kitchen. "They seem so happy with their little business. Did you notice they've started calling themselves Elisabeth and Susan and they act so mature?"

"Yes, I still call them Beth and Sue. Beth is sixteen now and Sue fifteen, can't believe they're almost adults!" Jamie whispered.

"See those two young men?"

"The twins?"

"They eat here every day the kitchen is open, I think they're sweet on the girls."

"Beth does blush a lot when that one is near."

Rosalind and Sophie came into the kitchen and sat with Jamie and Jayne ordering meat pies. "I see those boys are back," Sophie whispered. "I think Beth is too young for a boyfriend!"

"Look who's talking, how old were you when you married David." Jamie laughed.

"That was different; I was so much more mature!" Sophie said loftily. Rosalind just snorted covering the laugh with a cough.

"You were just four months younger then Beth when you sat in my trailer and bemoaned that you were still single. Sue is ten months younger than Beth."

"I don't recall the conversation!" With that response both Jamie and Rosalind laughed, Sophie blushing. Sue and Beth came to sit with their sisters.

"The boys are back!" Beth (now Elisabeth) said giddily, blushing bright red.

"Tell us about the boys." Jayne said in a low voice.

"They're from a farm on Novi. Jeff the oldest by two minutes is so cute!" Beth was smiling brightly. "He's so shy; I think his brother Will is sweet on Susan."

"Jamie, how did you know Derek was right for you?" Sue (now Susan) asked.

"I'm not sure, I think I liked him the first time I saw him but didn't realize it for a long time." Jamie responded thoughtfully. They continued their conversation in low voices. It was obvious to all that their youngest sisters were quite taken by the boys. "You know there is a dance this Saturday, why don't you tell the boys?" With that their faces colored even more.

Later, when the girls were busy cleaning up, Jamie approached the boys and just happened to drop in the conversation the Saturday dance. The boys responded with shy smiles. Later, when the kitchen was much quieter, Will and Jeff asked the girls if they would like to meet at the dance.

Jamie was sitting with Derek as they shared dinner with their group of friends. Elisabeth and Susan were also there. "I saw you both dancing with boys at the dance last night, wasn't that the third or fourth dance they have come to?" Derek asked.

"Yes, the fifth, it was Will and Jeff. They are both so sweet!" Susan opined.

"We have been talking together about betrothal. It's such a big decision," Elisabeth said with a sigh. Jamie kicked Derek hard under the table before he could reply.

"Yes, it is, it's the most important decision you will ever make, I hope you do as well as I," Jamie said smiling at her youngest sisters and looking meaningful at Derek.

"I wish you much happiness with you decisions," Derek said. The girls just beamed at him and Jamie gave him a nod that no one else saw.

"Why did you invite us over? You had something about a

business venture I understand." David asked.

"Novi is planning an expedition to the lake region. They are hoping to capture some horses and are looking for capital to fund the trip." Derek said. "George has developed a kind of a fish trap to get the horses. I'm suggesting we fund the expedition. It is a risk as previous expeditions failed to capture horses."

"A fish trap for horses?" Roland asked.

"We have hundreds of those poles the Praetorian were planning to impale us on lying about, I just came up with a practical use for them," George said. "We build a corral well hidden buy brush then use the poles and ropes and nets to build a wide funnel. Then we gently drive a herd into the corral by way of the funnel."

"Won't they just jump over?" David asked.

"Some will, I don't think a pregnant mare will. It's worth a try," George then outlined the expected costs of the expedition and the cost per share. "I'm basing the cost on a one hundred share total. I thought we would take the bulk of the shares but leave it open to others in the colony. The cost includes the labor costs by the way."

"How will we be paid for our investment?" Susan asked.

"We make money on the sale of horses. The more horses they capture, the more we could make."

"We will each take three shares," Elisabeth said after talking in a whisper to Susan.

"You have that much?" Derek asked.

"More actually, but we don't want to risk it all. Our kitchen is doing well, we have been thinking of other ways to invest," Susan said.

"You two have always impressed me with your business sense!" Jamie laughed. The conversation continued and between the friends sixty-four shares were sold. The other shares were bought by others in the community. Derek also decided he would accompany the expedition to oversee the work and that meant Jamie and Casey would also go. Sophie talked long and hard to Jamie but finally convinced her to leave Casey with her. Sophie loved having babies in her home. With all preparations made the expedition left, taking both luggers and camped at the opening of a vast grassland. They made two corrals, a smaller one to contain their camp and a larger one to trap the horses. The first night Jamie and Derek settled down in their tent.

"This seems so familiar," Jamie said as she snuggled next to Derek.

"It should, it's our tent from when Roland rescued us!"

"How did you...we don't have are divider up," Jamie said with her most wicked smile.

"I thought we could dispense with the divider this time...you know...in case of thunderstorms or something." Jamie put her arms around Derek pushing herself tight against him and whispered, her voice husky.

"Let's finish what we started on the last thunderstorm!"

The capture corral was built more than two miles from the encampment. It was located in a little grove of aspen enclosing a popular watering hole and well hidden. The funnel extended out in a wide arc over a half a mile. Their plan was to hide in blinds until a herd of horses approached the watering hole, then gently drive them into the funnel, and then into the corral. The plan worked and they had twenty-five horses within a week. They simply followed each other into the corral. Separating and bringing the horses onto some manageable arrangement was another problem, but by the end of another week the first shipment of horses were placed on the luggers and returned to Bountiful and Novi, Derek and Jamie returning with the first horses. The horses quickly sold returning the initial investment. The trap continued to bring results; over the next month groups of horses were brought in. On the third trip Elisabeth, Susan and Jamie were looking at the horses that had come in when they were joined by Sophie and Rosalind. They were all quite taken by a group of smaller chestnut colored horses with blonde manes. They had been recently castrated and appeared to be calm, gentle animals.

"I really would like to have one of those horses!" Sophie said in a whisper. Elisabeth and Susan just nodded their agreement. "None of the farms have bought them; they say they're to puny for real work."

Susan suddenly smiled, "Aren't we principle investors. Let's take our shares in horses!" By the days end the village was treated to see five young women traveling all over Bell Isle on horseback laughing merrily as they rode. They rode all bareback their long skirts hiked up to above the knee and barefoot as usual, their long hair flowing behind. The scene anywhere else would have been a scandal, but the colony was used to its eccentric group of sisters.

Chapter 33 Fiona and Lisa

Derek was busy working in his metal shop. A fifth mill was planned and he had much metal work to do. He knew the fleet would be returning as three of the faster frigates had arrived two days ago, they had stopped in Harbor Town. After taking a lunch break with Jamie, in Elisabeth and Susan's kitchen, he returned to work. He had heard that six more ships had arrived but thought nothing about it. While working quietly at the forge he felt a hand on his shoulder and turning he could not believe his eyes, "Father." Derek grasped his father in a strong embrace, "I thought I'd never see you again." Olaf had tears of joy in his eyes as he held his son.

"Your mother and sisters are here too! We haven't told your sisters you are alive yet. I would love to have them meet you and your wife. Is Rosie here too?"

"I have so much to tell you, bring everyone to my home tonight. We'll have dinner. I want you to meet my Jamie and your grandchild, actually grandchildren." Derek too excited to work left the shop chief in charge and went home. Jamie was very happy for Derek and went to Rosalind's home to tell her and get help for the meal. Sophie also rushed over followed by Elisabeth and Susan.

"I'm so scared, Roz! What if they don't like me?"

"Jamie they will love you, believe me. I've never met my youngest sisters. I'm scared too!" The sisters borrowed tables and chairs and opened the sliding wall. Then they began food preparations. They planned a simple meal of venison sausage, tubers, fresh vegetables and sourdough bread. They had bubbly pies for desert. Sophie would watch the children then bring them over after dinner. Phoebe and Alexandra arrived to clean the house a bit and Jayne brought over a flower arrangement for the table. The sisters all hugged Jamie and Rosalind wishing them good luck and left just before Derek's family arrived.

Derek had opened the door before his parents were even close to it. Carol smiled as Derek hugged her and kissed her cheek, "It's so good to see you, mother!" Fiona and Lisa, when they first saw Derek, let out a scream and literally jumped on him with hugs. They were both crying and Derek was trying to fight back tears himself with little success. "Please come in, all of you." As they entered the home they saw two young women standing close together. Both had long dark auburn hair and gray eyes. One was slightly taller, both in long pretty dresses. Olaf looked at the women, "Such beautiful women, you must be Jamie, and you are my Rosie." With that Rosalind broke into tears and fell into her father's arms weeping. Then she turned to Carol holding her firmly as she continued to weep. "Lisa, Fiona, this is your sister Rosalind, you've never met." After a brief hesitation the girls put their arms around their sister and they hugged. Olaf and Carol took Jamie's hand, "Derek has done well!" Then they hugged Jamie followed by the girls.

Jamie, smiling and feeling quite dizzy as she held on to Derek said, "We have prepared dinner, please come." They sat at the table not quite sure want to say. "I thought the colony was new but your home looks like it's been here for a century," Carol began.

"It's quite new, I planted sedums on the roof and with my vines that makes it look ancient," Jamie said quietly.

"Your home is so beautiful on the inside too; I understand you are a healer?" Jamie smiled and nodded.

"How is it that you are here father?" Derek asked.

"I was recruited by a Lord, somebody's grandfather I think, those ore samples you sent were high grade iron. They brought a lot of mining families over too."

"That was Lord Grandfather, it's a title." Derek laughed.

"We had to agree to keep a covenant, that was easy; it's just good sense. I never thought I would have a chance to start over. I'm so glad to have the girls out from under the Imperial thumb."

"How are things back home?"

"Very bad, the Magisterium has spent so much money that they are taxing the life out of everyone, things are really bad now. Everyone fears food shortages, the guard has been brutal. I heard the Praetorian are no more."

"Jamie and her band of women warriors destroyed them."

"I heard about a warrior group headed by a Jamie that destroyed the guard, you can't be that Jamie, you're a tiny little woman!" Carol said looking at Jamie with wide eyes.

"Afraid so, we had a lot of help, it was down to fight or die, so we fought."

"I've heard rumors regarding your fighting apparel."

"Most likely you heard the truth." Jamie blushed; she had hoped to avoid this but thought the honest story would be best. She didn't want lies to come between her and Derek's parents. The girls just stared at Jamie, eyes wide as saucers, mouths agape. Jamie guessed they too had heard the story and braced for questions regarding her bathing practices. Feeling Jamie's discomfort, Derek changed the conversation. "So you and miners have come so we will independently produce our own iron?"

"Copper too, and stone masons too. They did a lot of recruiting. Remember old Jimmy?"

"Yes he was an excellent black metal smith but never cared to advance to master."

"Well he was Roamy, he came too, and he introduced me to the Lord."

"I'm glad you came, I can work iron but not refine it."

"Of course not, you're only a journey man." During the dinner Lisa and Fiona continued to stare at Jamie. They were obviously burning with questions. Finally the dinner ended and Sophie arrived with the children. Sophie stayed for moral support with Susan and Elisabeth. Jamie introduced everyone to her sisters, and then Phoebe, Jayne and Alexandra arrived.

"You have quite a large family, Jamie!" Carol said.

"Yes, I do." Lisa and Fiona looked out the back window and spotted Jamie's horse and became so excited. Jamie suggested they visit the yard while Derek and his mother talked and visited with the grandchildren. As they walked into the yard Stub approached and the girls froze in obvious fear. "That's just Stub. Don't be deceived by her looks. She is a brave, gentle dog." The girls approached slowly and rubbed Stub's head. Stub moaned with delight then rolled over offering her belly. The girls sat next to Stub continuing to rub with Stub moaning in doggy ecstasy. Jamie laughing, "You have made a friend for life."

The girls walked through the garden looking at the raised beds and the espaliered fruit trees. They had never seen so many varieties of plums. They had questions about the pudding tree so Jamie cut a fruit for them and they ate as they slowly approached the horse. "I know you're curious, so let me set the record straight, I don't bathe in blood!'

The girls looked shyly at Jamie blushing, "We did want to ask. Were your sisters in the group of six at the shield wall?"

Rosalind laughed, "Yes, we were and naked as a jay, I'm a sister too. Everyone calls us the sisters."

"Then we are sisters too!"

"Yes, you are, ten of us strong!" Jamie said smiling, "Do you know what that is?"

"Oh, yes, it's a horse!" Fiona whispered slowly moving forward and extending her hand. Phoebe had grabbed two apples and explained how to give the apple to the horse. The girls fed the horse, their joy visible on their faces.

"Would you like to ride?" the answer was instant approval and Jamie led the girls around the corral sitting on her horse. "His name is Thunder."

"If your mom approves we can take you ridding with us in the morning!" Sophie said.

"We're still staying on the boat." Lisa replied sadly.

"Let me talk to our mother, I'm sure you can stay with me, I really want to get to know my youngest sisters, besides you can tell me all about Derek!" Rosalind said.

"We'd love that Rosie!"

"You can call me Roz, all my sisters do."

Derek's parents stayed in the room over the clinic, Lisa and Fiona stayed with Rosalind. The next morning and nearly every morning after the little community was treated to the site of ten pretty sisters riding about in scandalous attire.

Epilogue

Seven years had passed and the colony had prospered. It was the annual Landings Day festival, and Derek and Jamie were eating a picnic in the park by the little lake. Casey was walking his younger sister as they held hands looking for frogs in the grass. "Don't let Stephanie go near the water, Casey!" Jamie called. She was nursing her newest baby, another little girl named Rebecca while Derek held little Roland who loved crawling. Fiona and Lisa were sitting nearby as they sang together using the wheeled fiddle, a group a very smitten young men hovering near. "The temple is so beautiful now that it is just finished, and I really like the rose colored stone for the university," Jamie said as Derek held her close. "Do you think the girls will be betrothed soon?"

Derek laughed, "No doubt they have quite a gathering of admirers. They are pretty busy working in Elisabeth and Susan's former kitchen, and it is also doing well. They will be quite a catch for some lucky young men." David, Sophie, Rosalind and Roland joined them sitting on the blanket, their children running to join Casey, the young women carrying babies.

"Well, hello, Governor General Derek!" David said with a smile.

"I still have no idea why I was appointed Governor General." Derek said with a rueful smile.

"The other brothers and I have been discussing that very question." Roland said with a smile.

"And your conclusion?"

"It's all that gray hair!" David added, everyone laughing.

All the sisters sat together sharing the baby care and child care needs. Sophie now had three children, Rosalind two. Jayne was expecting, but only one this time. Alexandra and Phoebe both had two with Phoebe due again in a few weeks. Elisabeth and Susan lived on farms with their twin husbands in Novi and both were pregnant. They would be there too for the dance. They never missed a dance. That night they held a dance and as Jamie held Derek close, while dancing she had time to think. So much had happened since that spring she had run from her home to escape slavery. She had been so afraid and unsure of herself, so doubting of her skills and abilities, her future so threatened, her loneliness so complete. Now she had so much. She had a group of close friends, brothers and sisters in the truest sense. She had a valuable skill for her community and the means to pass it on. Most of all she had her Derek, her best friend, her lover and her husband for time and eternity.

For Time and Eternity

Made in the USA
Charleston, SC
26 February 2014